W9-BXM-704

Over the Sea to Die

Also by Richard Grindal:

Death Stalk

OVER THE SEA TO DIE

Richard Grindal

St. Martin's Press
New York

OVER THE SEA TO DIE. Copyright © 1989 by Richard Grindal. All rights reserved.
Printed in the United States of America. No part of this book may be used
or reproduced in any manner whatsoever without written permission except in
the case of brief quotations embodied in critical articles or reviews. For
information, address St. Martin's Press, 175 Fifth Avenue, New York, N.Y. 10010.

Library of Congress Cataloging-in-Publication Data

Grindal, Richard.
    Over the sea to die / Richard Grindal.
        p.   cm.
    ISBN 0-312-04573-5
    I. Title.
  PR6057.R55094   1990
  823'.914—dc20   90-37293
                                                               CIP

First published in Great Britain by Macmillan London Limited

First U.S. Edition: December 1990
10 9 8 7 6 5 4 3 2 1

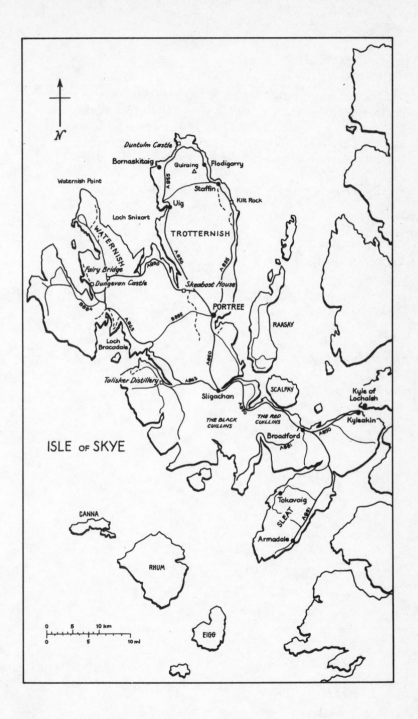

Speed, bonnie boat, like a bird on the wing,
Onward, the sailors cry:
Carry the lad that's born to be king,
Over the sea to Skye.

Skye Boat Song

1

The day was grey. Across the narrow stretch of sullen sea Skye waited, grey too, its peaks hidden by low clouds or mist, Mackinnon was not sure which. As he had driven through Glen Shiel and past the Five Sisters of Kintail a fine drizzle had spotted the windscreen of his car, but only briefly and the rain had held off. The ferry had left Kyleakin and he watched it approaching, crabbing its way through the currents of the straits. He could count no more than half a dozen vehicles aboard.

The stretch of tarmac opposite the Lochalsh hotel where he was waiting had been neatly marked out in parallel lanes for the cars and coaches that would be queuing for the ferry when summer brought the tourists. Today there was only a fishmonger's van, white once but now edged with rust and stained with the mud of a long winter, and a Volvo estate car driven by a man wearing a shooting jersey and with two black Labradors asleep in the back, their heads between their paws. He had stopped his car behind them to form an incongruous file of three.

His first sight of Skye had not disappointed him. Knowing its reputation and its average rainfall, he had never been tempted to believe the brilliant colours of the picture postcards and the photographs in the Scottish Tourist Board's brochures. The Cuillin mountains and the barren hills would, he supposed, be hidden in mist more often than not.

Island of mists and barren fruitlessness, he thought,

7

paraphrasing a poem he must have learnt at school.

He had bought, with a twinge of shame, a guide book on Skye from Hatchards in Piccadilly, feeling that since his roots were in the island he should not have needed one. But he had been born in Aberdeen and had spent his boyhood in England, and when he was studying medicine in Edinburgh had never somehow found the time between examinations and a frenetic social life to visit the island where his father had been born. Even now his visit had come about more by chance then by intention; if his plans had not gone agley he would be embarking not on the ferry but on a plane for Corfu with Judy.

The quarrel that had led them to cancel their holiday had seemed to be no more than one of the squalls that from time to time had upset the calm of their relationship, but unlike previous rows it had not blown itself out. Instead it had been prolonged into almost two weeks of acrimony and reproaches which had become progressively more bitter, until they had agreed that neither of them could face the prospect of spending two weeks together abroad. Only afterwards had he learned that Judy had been given a better offer, a drive through the Loire in the Lotus of a Sloane Ranger friend to the Côte d'Azur where they would stay in the villa of his parents behind St Tropez.

Mackinnon had been resigned to having no holiday that year, for it was too late to make other arrangements and in any case the money he had paid for the package holiday in Corfu would not be refunded. Then the head of the medical department had approached him. An old friend, a GP in Scotland who had himself been at Guy's, needed a locum urgently for four weeks. When he learned that Scotland meant Skye, Mackinnon had made up his mind unquestioningly. He had never believed in fate or predestination or whatever one might call it, but this seemed like some sort of signal and the opportunity was not likely to recur. Extending his holiday from two weeks to four was easily arranged by the head of the medical department and all he had needed to do was to pack a suitcase and set out in his little Toyota on the 600-mile drive to Lochalsh.

Now, when he had driven aboard and the ferry had begun its short journey across the sound, he left the car and stood watching the island as they approached it. Over the sea to Skye, he thought, and smiled. No flight of fancy could compare the ferry to a bird. An ungainly metal box, it juddered uneasily on top of the choppy water, missing the weight of its full load. Besides the fishmonger's van and the two cars, a dozen foot passengers were making the journey. Judging by their dress and their manner they were not holidaymakers and Mackinnon wondered what reason they might have for travelling to Skye. Were they mainlanders who had found work on the island? He thought it unlikely. The member of the ferry's crew who came to collect the fare had time to talk.

'You'll not be on holiday, I suppose,' he said to Mackinnon.

'No, to work, but only for a month. I'm a doctor.'

'Then you'll be here to take Dr Tait's place.'

'That's right. Do you know him?'

'He was on the ferry first thing today. His wife was driving him to the hospital in Edinburgh.'

'Already?' Mackinnon knew that Dr Tait's reason for needing a locum was that he had to undergo open-heart surgery, but he had assumed that Tait would not be going into hospital until after he had arrived, allowing at least a little time to hand over the practice.

'The doctor will be all right,' the crew man said. 'He's a strong fellow.'

The driver of the van had also left his vehicle and was lighting a small cigar. He was not Mackinnon's idea of a fishmonger, not much more than a lad with curly black hair that hung to his shoulders and wearing jeans and a tee-shirt and a wristwatch that looked like a gold Rolex Oyster. The crew man was meanwhile having a long conversation with the driver of the Volvo, who had wound down his window. Mackinnon thought that they glanced briefly at him with the curiosity of islanders wondering about a stranger.

Kyleakin was no more than a village but it had the look

of a dilapidated English seaside town with faded paintwork and signs hanging outside every shop and house offering bed and breakfast, souvenirs, petrol and bar lunches, but half-heartedly, without any real expectation that they would tempt holidaymakers to stop there before moving on into the island.

Mackinnon did not stop either, driving through the village quickly and shrugging off a slight sense of disillusionment. Scenic beauty and a romantic history were what Skye offered visitors, and the islanders had a right to flaunt and exploit its attractions.

As he drove towards Broadford he turned his attention to practical matters. He had spoken to Dr Tait twice on the telephone, the first time simply to find out what doing the locum would involve. Then, the following day, he had called him to confirm that he would do it and when he could start. Tait had suggested that he should arrive at his home in north Skye early in the evening in time for dinner. The journey from Edinburgh, where Mackinnon had spent the previous night with friends, had taken a much shorter time than he had anticipated, for the roads to the north had been greatly improved. Now if he drove directly to Tait's house he would be there in not much more than an hour, between one and two o'clock, in all probability well before Mrs Tait returned from driving her husband to Edinburgh. So, not wishing to be an embarrassment, he decided it would be best if he were to spend the afternoon exploring Skye.

Broadford, the second largest town on the island, was far smaller than he had expected and as he drove through it he had time to make only two mental notes which might later prove useful: the police station was on the left of the main street and further on he saw a road off to the right which led apparently to the Doctor Mackinnon Memorial Hospital. He knew that the Mackinnon whose memorial the hospital was could not be a relative, for his father had told him that they had none left on Skye.

As the road wound round Loch Ainort, one of the many sea lochs that cut into the islands like fiords, the clouds seemed to lift until he believed he could almost see the summits of the mountains to his left. Then the weather closed in, abruptly as though regretting its moment of clemency, and rain came, soft and fine but dense enough to obliterate everything, so that when he reached Sligachan he could not even make out the outlines of the Cuillins.

A hundred years ago, his guide book had told him, the inn at Sligachan had been one of the most famous climbing centres in Europe, each year drawing scores of climbers who wished to tackle the finest and most awe-inspiring mountain range in Britain. Artists used to come as well, to sketch and paint and try to capture the ever-changing pattern of light and shade over the peaks and lochs. Today there was no more than a handful of people around, couples mainly, hoping for good weather on an early holiday. As he ate his bar lunch at the inn, Mackinnon watched them staring dejectedly through the steamed-up windows and wondering when the rain would stop. Skye was putting on its dreariest face to receive him, as though telling him that he must love the home of his ancestors, warts and all.

A man sitting next to him at the bar was inclined to talk. He told Mackinnon that he was a shopkeeper in Broadford and had left his wife to run the business while he escaped for a couple of pints of beer. They chatted about the weather and Mackinnon was not surprised to be told that the previous three days had been warm and sunny, the best weather that the man could remember for that time of the year.

'Will it clear up this afternoon, do you think?' Mackinnon asked.

'Now it might. As you'll have heard, the weather here changes from one hour to another.'

'If it does I was thinking of taking a walk up into the Cuillins. I've the afternoon to fill.'

The man looked to see what he was wearing. 'You'll have other clothes with you?'

'I've an anorak in the car.'

'I was thinking of footwear mainly. You'll be needing

11

boots if you go hill walking. The paths will be boggy and treacherous.'

Mackinnon smiled. 'All I had in mind was a leisurely stroll. I'm no rock climber.'

'Even so. Anyway, I'd advise you not to go alone. In this weather you could easily find yourself lost.' Mackinnon must have looked incredulous for he added, 'It's easily done in the mist. You'd be astonished how many times the rescue team has to go out in a year just to find people who have got themselves lost in the mountains.'

He began talking about the Mountain Rescue team, an organisation of volunteers who were called out when there was a climbing accident or when people were lost. Not infrequently a helicopter would be sent out from the mainland to help the rescuers. He could recall three fatal accidents within the past twelve months on the mountains and at least twice that number of people who had been lost.

'Some idiots go up into the Cuillins wearing no more than jeans and a tee-shirt and with training shoes on their feet. Training shoes! I've seen them.'

Although he was inclined to believe that the man was exaggerating, Mackinnon decided to take his advice. By the time he had finished his lunch the rain had stopped, but instead of taking a walk he set out to explore Skye by car. Turning inland from Sligachan, he drove past Loch Harport to Loch Bracadale, more of a bay than a sea loch with a fine natural harbour. The loch was a breeding ground for young seals, but he could not expect to see any in that day's weather.

When he reached the ruins of a chapel he stopped, left the car by the road and was glad to breathe the soft island air after so many hours of driving in a closed car. Ahead of him was the peninsula of Harlosh, which jutted into the loch and where there were several ruined duns or ancient forts, but Mackinnon was more interested in the land around the mouth of a small river which ran into the loch at that point, for it was there, by the River Caroy, his guide book told him, that the Clan MacLeod had gathered armed for the last time.

They had come there in 1745 expecting to be told that they were going to fight for Prince Charles Edward, only to hear from their chief that he had declared his loyalty to King George II. Disillusioned by what they felt was a betrayal, most of the 1800 clansmen drifted away, many of them to go and die on their own for the Young Pretender.

As he gazed at the scene of that poignant moment in history, Mackinnon experienced an emotion stronger than the one he had felt when he had first sighted Skye that morning. His own names were Charles Edward. Ian, his father, although he had spent no more than his boyhood on Skye and had lived and worked abroad for most of his life, had been an ardent Jacobite. Like the majority of exiled Scots he had clung tenaciously to his Scottish origins and had encouraged his son to do the same. Mackinnon could still recall the hilarious laughter of the other small boys when he had arrived wearing a kilt for his first term at a preparatory school in the south of England. He had survived the hilarity and the teasing and in time his pride in his Scottishness had won the good-natured respect of the other boys. Skye was full of memories of Prince Charles and of Flora Macdonald who had helped him to escape capture after his disastrous defeat at Culloden. Mackinnon would have time to savour them all while he was on the island but this was his first experience of one and for that reason oddly moving.

He set out on foot towards Harlosh Point, wishing for exercise, but the rain cut short his walk and he returned to the car and drove on towards Dunvegan, the home of the MacLeod family for seven hundred years. He could catch no more than a glimpse of the castle down the drive which led to it, but he knew that in any case the best view of it was from the sea. From Dunvegan the road turned inland, past Fairy Bridge to Edinbane and then by Loch Snizort to Skeabost Bridge.

He had intended to fork left beyond Skeabost and drive up the Trotternish peninsula, which he knew was the real Prince Charles country, but the tedium of driving and the monotony of the windscreen wipers was beginning to chafe, so he drove on instead to Portree and found a place to park in Somerled Square in the very centre of the town. Since he would be living and working about fifteen miles to the north of Portree, he was likely to be visiting it frequently, so it would be useful to know his way around. The police station and the magistrates' court, he noted, were both in Somerled Square which, he knew, took its name from Somerled, the legendary Lord of the Isles from whom the Macdonalds, the other great family in Skye, could claim descent. In the half dozen streets around it he found a post office and a chemist's shop and then walked up to the hospital where he learned there was a health centre with a group practice of four doctors.

When he started walking round the pretty harbour, the rain became more than a drizzle, bouncing off the ground and slanting on a westerly wind that had sprung up so that the golf umbrella he had brought with him from London was no longer keeping him dry. So, taking shelter in the Royal Hotel, he ordered afternoon tea. Here was another link with Prince Charles, for it was at the hotel, then MacNab's Inn, that the prince had taken his farewell of Flora Macdonald.

As he was taking his tea he thought not of the prince but of what life on Skye would be like. A history going back to the early Celts and Norse invaders and beyond that to heroic gods and goddesses still gave the island a veneer of romance, but there was a different history as well, of bloodthirsty slaughter in senseless clan wars, of evictions and forced emigration, of a struggle for survival by crofters living on land that was too meagre and too poor to support them. All that must have left its mark on the islanders, some of whom were going to be in his care for the next four weeks.

After tea he drove north towards Staffin, slowly, for he was conscious that he might still be too early. As he was passing the Storr with its cliff face of black rock and the pinnacle of the Old Man of Storr beneath, the fickle rain stopped and for the first time that day there was a break in the clouds. By the time he reached Loch Mealt he could see away to his left a small sunlit patch on the hills. Not much bigger than a man's hand, he thought, but surely a good omen, as though Skye was at last welcoming him with a promise of peace and contentment.

To his right between the loch and the sea a small car-parking area had been asphalted for those who might wish to stop and admire the view. Feeling that he still had time to waste, he pulled off the road, left the car and walked to the cliff's edge. From where he stood he could see to his right the water spilling over from the loch falling in a spectacular cascade to the sea below. To his left, towering above him, was the black basalt cliff face of Kilt Rock, almost three hundred feet high, he supposed, grooved with vertical folds that resembled the pleats in a kilt.

As he stood admiring its grandeur he saw two figures walking along by the cliff's edge at the top of the rock. Seen from that distance they were no larger than dolls. Both were wearing cords or jeans; one a man, tall and burly, but the other much shorter, slight in build and wearing a pinkish sweater; must be a woman, he decided. He wondered who they were. It was not a day to be walking the cliffs.

Suddenly, as he watched, the figures stopped walking. The man turned and picked up the woman as easily as though he were picking up a small child. The woman seemed to struggle and for a long moment Mackinnon could see them against the sky. Then the man swung the woman, in much the same way as a parent playfully swings a child in its arms, and threw her, easily, even casually it seemed, over the edge of the cliff. Horrified, Mackinnon saw the figure falling, its arms whirling as though clutching for anything that would check its fall. He heard no scream, no sound of a body striking the rocks below or splashing into the water, nothing except the plaintive cries of gulls circling out at sea.

2

As he drove back to Portree, Mackinnon tried to convince himself that what he had seen was not an illusion, a trick of the evening light. After the momentary paralysis of horror he had remembered the binoculars in his car. Fetching them, he had gone as close to the cliff's edge as he could and scanned the base of Kilt Rock. There had been no body that he could see, either on the rocks below or floating in the water. Nor, when he swung the glasses upwards, was there anyone at the top where he had seen the two figures walking and the brief struggle before one had flung the other over the edge. He found himself wondering whether anyone would believe him.

In the police station at Portree a sergeant who had been working in the office at the back came out to the counter. Mackinnon could hear voices crackling over a radio telephone somewhere.

'Good evening, sir. What can I do for you?'

'I have to report a murder.' The words that Mackinnon had rehearsed on the drive back to Portree sounded forced and unreal.

The sergeant looked at him steadily. 'May I ask who you are, sir?'

'My name is Mackinnon. Dr Mackinnon. I've just arrived on Skye to do a locum for Dr Tait at Staffin.'

'You would be from London, then?' Evidently the sergeant knew that Dr Tait had arranged for a locum while he would be in hospital. Many people on Skye probably did.

16

'Yes. I drove up by car and crossed over by the ferry before lunch.' Mackinnon wondered why he felt obliged to give the police an account of his movements, as though he were under suspicion of committing some offence.

'And this murder, sir. Where are you saying that it happened?'

'At Kilt Rock. I saw a woman thrown over the cliff.'

'Thrown? Or pushed?'

Mackinnon described what he had seen. The picture of the woman being hurled over the cliff was sharp and clear, a gruesome pantomime made all the more horrifying by its soundlessness. The sergeant's face, stiffened by a disbelief he had been trained to conceal, might have been carved in the local stone.

'Where were you when this happened, did you say?'

'On that viewing point below the rock at the Falls of Mealt.'

'And you could see all this even from that range in this weather?' The sergeant nodded towards the rain which was beating on the windows of the station.

'The weather had cleared while I was there. I even saw the sun for a short time. And I am longsighted.'

After a moment's hesitation the sergeant appeared to decide what he must do. 'Would you mind waiting here, please, sir?'

He disappeared into the office at the back of the station and Mackinnon heard the sound of a telephone number being dialled. He could not make out what was being said in the conversation that followed and concluded that the sergeant must have deliberately lowered his voice.

When he returned to the counter the sergeant said, 'I've phoned my inspector. He'll be here directly. Meantime, if you would repeat what you told me, sir, I'll write it down.'

They went into a room at the back of the station and Mackinnon described once more what he had seen at Kilt Rock while the sergeant wrote it down laboriously in long-hand. By the time they had finished Inspector Maclean had arrived. He was an older man, probably not far from

17

retirement, with the figure and the face of a man who had led an undemanding life.

After he had read what the sergeant had written he began questioning Mackinnon. Could he give any description of the two figures he had seen? Could he make out what they were wearing? What made him believe one was a man and one a woman? How had the woman been thrown out to sea? Would Mackinnon demonstrate as best he could the action of the throw? Had he looked to see whether the woman had fallen on to rocks below Kilt Rock? Or into the sea? At approximately what time had he seen the incident? The sergeant wrote down the answers that Mackinnon gave to the questions.

When the inspector had finished Mackinnon asked him, 'Why don't we drive out there and I'll show you exactly where and how it happened?'

'We'd not see anything in this weather. Besides, it will soon be dark.'

'Then what will you do?'

'We'll go out there first thing tomorrow and also send a boat round to the foot of the cliffs. If it's needed we'll have a helicopter flown out from the mainland.'

Mackinnon looked at his watch. 'Would it be possible for me to telephone Mrs Tait from here and explain that I've been delayed? She's expecting me for dinner.'

'Mrs Tait knows where you are, sir,' Inspector Maclean replied, and then seeing Mackinnon's surprise, he added, 'I had to confirm that you were who you said you were, you understand.'

Mackinnon choked back his irritation. He did not care for his word to be doubted, but on the drive from Portree to Staffin he realised that the police could not be blamed for their reluctance to believe his story. He was inclined to disbelieve it himself. Could it have been a hallucination, the cumulative effect of fatigue after a long drive and nervous excitement? As he approached Kilt Rock he forced himself to keep his eyes on the road in front of him and not glance at the cliff top.

The Taits lived on the edge of Staffin, a village of a few scattered houses and an ugly new community centre which looked oddly out of place. Their house was a square, solid nineteenth-century building with whitewashed walls and a slate roof. A garage had been built on to the house and there were two cars standing in the drive outside. In the garden at the back of the house a few rose bushes struggled to survive around a rough lawn, but the view over Staffin Bay was strikingly beautiful.

Before he had time to knock, Mrs Tait opened the door to him. She was a small, compact woman, plainly but comfortably dressed and with her grey hair cut short, who gave an immediate impression of kindness and competence. One felt that no creature would be too small or too mean to arouse her compassion, no crisis too great for her to handle.

'Dr Mackinnon, you must be exhausted, you poor thing!' She shook his hand, holding it for a second or two longer than custom would expect as though to underline her welcome. When Mackinnon began to apologise for his lateness she brushed his apologies aside. 'Bring your case upstairs and I'll show you your room. You'll be wanting a wash before dinner.'

'And to change.' Mackinnon had worn trousers and a sweater for the long drive from Edinburgh.

'No need to bother yourself with changing.' Mrs Tait smiled. 'Maybe we should have dressed up to welcome you but we haven't.'

After showing him the bathroom and the towels she had put out for him, she led him to his bedroom. He saw at once that it had once been the bedroom of a young girl. The material used for the curtains and bedspread was what one would choose for a child and on one wall hung a large poster, cleverly made from a montage of record sleeves and photographs of the pop stars of the late sixties and early seventies. A collection of tiny glass animals was ranged along the mantelpiece above the fireplace and an old rag doll, missing one leg, was perched on a laundry basket in a corner. On the dressing table a china mug commemorating the marriage of Prince Charles had been filled with pencils, paintbrushes and ballpoint pens, from one of which a blue domino paper mask hung by its elastic. A framed photograph of a group of girls in school uniform, the sixth form perhaps, on the chest of drawers was matched by another taken on a mountain, in which a small girl in climbing clothes and helmet stood proudly on the edge of a precipice. The wardrobe and drawers were all empty and he sensed that whoever had prepared the room for him had been reluctant to remove the sentimental reminders of a happy child.

After he had unpacked and washed he went downstairs and found two people waiting with Mrs Tait in the drawing-room: a young woman who, she told him, was her daughter Kirsten and a middle-aged man whom he recognised at once as the man who had been waiting in a Volvo for the ferry at Lochalsh. Mrs Tait introduced the man as Carl Short.

'You'll take a whisky before dinner?' she asked Mackinnon.

'Have I time?'

'Surely. The dinner'll not spoil.' She poured him a glass of whisky from a decanter and let him add water for himself. 'Talisker. The local malt whisky.'

'It's a fine dram,' Short told him. 'One of the great single malts.'

'At one time they used to send my husband a case every year from the distillery. Not any more, unfortunately.'

They moved into the dining-room where a woman from the village who had cooked the meal waited on them. Hilda, Mrs Tait told Mackinnon, had cooked for the family for almost twenty years as her mother had before her. The lentil soup and poached salmon she had prepared that evening were excellent.

'With your name you must be Scottish,' Short said to Mackinnon, 'but you've lost most of your accent.'

'It comes and goes. When I was at school in the south of England I learned to speak like the other boys, but when I studied medicine in Edinburgh the accent came back. Since then I've been working in London for several years.' Mackinnon laughed. 'I suppose I must be a linguistic chameleon.'

'Then start speaking like a Scot again,' Kirsten Tait advised him. 'The patients will distrust an Englishman.'

'Even as a Scot you'll start with the disadvantage of being an incomer,' Short told him. 'I've lived on Skye for five years and I still haven't overcome the handicap.'

'It's a shame,' Mrs Tait remarked, 'and after all you have done for the island.'

Over dinner Mackinnon learned that five years previously Short had bought an estate in the south of Skye, completely renovated its dilapidated house, planted trees and a fine garden, restocked its loch and made enormous improvements to its three farms at no expense to the tenants. On top of that he had rebuilt the community hall in a nearby village, adding many modern amenities, and allowed the village children to play on his all-weather tennis court and to ride his ponies whenever they chose. He lived on the estate with his wife for most of the year, entertaining friends to fishing and stalking, only leaving to spend two months in London during June and July and one month in Switzerland in February.

'Were you born on Skye?' Mackinnon asked Mrs Tait.

'Yes. I'm a MacLeod. But my husband wasn't. He only came here— '

'My father has been here so long and is so loved by his patients,' Kirsten interrupted her, 'that people have forgotten he is not a Skyeman.'

'My father was born on Skye,' Mackinnon said.

'Really? Then perhaps his family came from Strath. That's Mackinnon country.'

'Many years ago the Mackinnons were hereditary pipers to the Macdonalds,' Mrs Tait said.

'I hope that doesn't make you and me enemies,' Mackinnon said, smiling. He knew that for centuries the MacLeods and the Macdonalds had fought each other on Skye.

'No, you Mackinnons were clever. You contrived to cling on to your fertile little valley while we and the Macdonalds fought savagely over the rest of the island.'

21

After dinner, as they drank their coffee in the dining-room, they talked of Skye, not of its history but of the concerns of the day. Would the coming summer be as bad as the previous one, keeping tourists away and putting some of the small hoteliers at risk of bankruptcy? What could be done to stop more of the island's schools being closed against the wishes of the parents? Was it right that the Crown Estate Commissioners should lease more of the sea lochs for yet another fish farm?

After a time Kirsten said, 'I must be going. Mairi's alone at home and we've lots of work to do tomorrow.'

'What is your work?' Mackinnon asked.

Kirsten smiled. 'I'm a refugee.'

'A refugee?'

'From medicine. Both of my sisters are doctors.'

'You used to be a nurse and a very good one,' her mother said, and then she added to Mackinnon, 'Kirsten has a craft centre on Loch Snizort. You must visit it when you have time.'

'My mother is my best salesman,' Kirsten laughed as she kissed her mother goodbye on the cheek. 'She badgers every visitor to the island until they come to the centre.'

'She won't have to badger me. I shall look forward to coming.'

Kirsten left to drive home and Carl Short left soon afterwards. He invited Mackinnon to visit him in Sleat as soon as his wife returned from Cheltenham where she was spending a few days with her mother. As Mrs Tait and Mackinnon stood outside the house watching him drive away in his Volvo she explained that it was Gloria, Short's second wife, who was in Cheltenham. His first wife had divorced him and was still living in Switzerland.

'Still? Is she Swiss, then?'

'Yes, and so is Carl. His name was Schott originally. He came and settled in this country only about ten years ago and has been incredibly successful.'

'One would never have guessed it from his accent.'

Or from his manner, Mackinnon might have added. He

22

realised now what it was about Carl Short that had been nagging at him all evening. The man was just a little too British to be British. He was polite without being obsequious or gushing, the tweed suit he had been wearing well tailored but conventional, the choice of colours for shirt, tie and socks subdued. No Englishman could have achieved such perfect self-restraint and lack of ostentation, no Scot would have attempted to.

Back in the house Mrs Tait suggested that they should have a nightcap. As she filled his glass she said over her shoulder. 'The police from Portree phoned earlier this evening to say you were with them. No trouble, I hope?'

'Not trouble for me, but what took me there was unpleasant.'

'What was it?'

'I went to the station to tell them I believed I had just seen a woman murdered.'

Mrs Tait was handing him his glass of whisky as he replied. She looked at him squarely but showed no surprise. Mackinnon went on, 'I didn't mention it earlier because I didn't wish to upset your guests. And even now I am not sure I wasn't mistaken.'

'What happened?'

He recounted the story as unemotionally as he could, trying to keep any hint of melodrama out of his voice, with difficulty for the horror picture of the incident had kept flashing back into his mind all evening. By this time he could quite easily have been persuaded that it had been a hallucination. When he had finished, Mrs Tait asked the same question as the inspector had.

'What made you think it was a woman who was thrown over the edge?'

'She was much smaller and slighter than the other figure and she was wearing something pink, a jumper, I should think.'

'What did the police say?'

'They're going to send a boat round to the foot of Kilt Rock in the morning. I've a feeling they didn't believe me.'

23

'One can understand that. We've had only one murder on the island in the last hundred years.'

To change the conversation she began telling him about her husband's practice: the surgery hours, the number of patients he might expect to arrive and the range of their complaints or conditions. She told him of the facilities that the two hospitals on the island offered. The one at Broadford was the main one and it had a surgical unit and a geriatric unit.

'I thought I might sit in with you at surgery tomorrow morning. It will make the patients more comfortable. That is if you don't mind.'

'Of course not,' Mackinnon replied, though he wondered whether it might not be a breach of medical ethics. Still, the relationship between doctor and patient would probably not be bound by any formal rules on Skye. 'What will I do if there are any calls tonight?'

'There won't be. Before he left this morning Donald arranged with the telephone operators to put any calls through to the hospital in Portree. One of the doctors from the health centre there will deal with them.'

When they had finished their drinks Mrs Tait took the empty glasses through to the kitchen. Mackinnon was in the hall on his way to the stairs when she returned and she said to him, 'Tell me, would you recognise those people you saw on Kilt Rock if you met them again?'

'No way! At that distance they were tiny. If I were not longsighted I probably would not have spotted them in the first place.'

Upstairs, as he began undressing, Mackinnon wondered whose this bedroom had been, which of the three Tait daughters had made the poster, climbed the mountain and played with the rag doll. He looked more closely at the school group photograph and recognised Kirsten. She had been a pretty girl, inclined to plumpness, and in the years that had passed she had lost a little weight and some of her prettiness. She looked out at him seriously from the school photograph, not at all self-conscious as one could see that some of the other girls were.

Once in bed he fell asleep almost immediately, weary after so much driving but pleased with the decision he had made to come at last to Skye. He could not have slept deeply, for a noise woke him and he saw from the alarm clock by his bed that he had been asleep for not even one hour. A second noise followed the one that had woken him and he recognised it as the sound of footsteps coming from in front of the house. Without switching on the light he got out of bed and parted the curtains of the nearest window. The night was clear now and the last clouds were hurrying westwards before an impatient wind, leaving enough moonlight for him to make out the figure of a woman outside the front of the house. It could only be Mrs Tait, for the cook, Hilda, had left for home immediately after dinner.

His first thought was that she must have left something in her car in the garage and was going to retrieve it; his second that there had after all been a call from a patient and that she intended to deal with it herself. But she did not go to the garage and Mackinnon watched her as she walked down the drive, hurrying, he thought, and turned into the road that led to Staffin.

3

Surgery next morning was not the ordeal that Mackinnon had feared it might be. He had supposed that the patients would be suspicious of this doctor from London, if not actually hostile and reluctant to tell him about their complaints. As it was, most of them talked freely, describing their symptoms in detail, as though pleased to have found a new audience more receptive than their regular doctor who, they might feel, as patients often do, did not give them enough of his time and enough attention. The only exceptions were two children, one of thirteen and the other younger, who were painfully inarticulate and needed his questions repeated before they understood them.

Relatively few patients came that morning and they did not tax his medical skill. Mostly their complaints were those for which no effective treatment exists: rheumatism and sciatica among the elderly, sore throats and coughs among the children. Two pregnant women, both young, had come for routine check-ups and a clerk from the council offices in Portree complained of nausea and dyspepsia. Mackinnon saw from his medical record that he had complained more than once before but X-rays had revealed nothing and he wondered whether the man might be malingering. Another man came to have a bad gash on his leg dressed. The wound, caused by an accident with a tractor, had been neglected and had become infected but Dr Tait had treated it in time to avoid his losing the limb and now it was healing nicely.

Mrs Tait who had obviously lectured the man before on his carelessness, did so again and he accepted her reproaches smilingly. She did not spend the whole time in the surgery but introduced each patient to Mackinnon, only staying during the consultation when she thought that the patient might need her support. Mackinnon realised that she was genuinely fond of her husband's patients.

After surgery he did the day's calls. Mrs Tait insisted on driving him in her husband's Rover because, as she pointed out, were he to go by himself he would waste so much time trying to find the houses he had to visit. Only two of the houses were in Staffin, some in neighbouring townships, Stenscholl, Brogaig, Glashvin and Digg and the remaining scattered around Trotternish, the peninsula north of Portree. Townships in Skye, Charles had learned, were neither towns nor villages, but areas of land owned by crofters, who shared common grazing rights.

One of the patients he saw in Staffin was an old woman named Jean Kennedy. Mrs Kennedy was small and dark, with a skin weathered to the colour of stained wood, and quick, intelligent eyes. She would be ninety-nine later that year, Mrs Tait told Mackinnon. He examined her carefully but could find nothing to account for the dizziness and noises in her head of which she had been complaining.

'You'll be fine, Mrs Kennedy,' he told her. 'We'll warn the Queen that she must be ready to send you that telegram next year.'

'I'll no accept a telegram from herself,' Mrs Kennedy replied stiffly. 'No from an Englishwoman.'

'There'll be great celebrations when you reach a hundred, I can tell you,' Mrs Tait said. 'I wouldn't be surprised if we were to drink the distillery dry.'

'Maybe, but we'll no be short of a dram even if we do.'

Mackinnon smoothed over what he realised had been a gaffe by chatting as he finished his examination. Mrs Kennedy answered his questions readily enough, but he had the feeling that all the time she was scrutinising him.

'You'll be from the island, then?' she asked him. 'With the name Mackinnon.'

'My father was born on Skye.'

'In what part?'

'He never told me. My grandfather was a crofter who started a small shop and sent my father to study in Edinburgh.'

'Then he's no still alive?'

'My grandfather? No, nor my father.'

After they had made the calls in the townships around Staffin they drove north and Mrs Tait told Mackinnon about the country through which they passed. To the right, out at sea, was Staffin Island and then Eilean Flodigarry, to the left the strange rock formation of the Quiraing, the result of some primeval upheaval of basalt rocks.

'That's the only part of the island where I never like walking,' Mrs Tait remarked. 'You'll think it absurd, but I can feel evil out there, as though it is haunted not by fairies but by some long-forgotten terror too horrible to describe. Other people get the same sensation.'

'Then there are fairies on Skye?' Mackinnon asked, smiling.

'Everywhere. They're not like the fairies in English children's stories. One might be better calling them "little people". That's what they are; little people who have fairy cattle, spin and weave fairy clothes, sing and make fairy music. You'll have heard of the Fairy Flag of the MacLeods, of course?'

'No, I have not.'

She told him that the flag was a banner of yellow silk which, according to legend, had been given by fairies to the MacLeods of Skye. If it were raised in battle when the clan was in danger of defeat, it immediately multiplied their numbers with a fairy host of MacLeods, thus assuring victory. Waved in times of famine it would bring herrings miraculously into the loch, and spread on the marriage bed it would guarantee fertility.

'You'll have had your fill of fairies before you leave Skye.' Mrs Tait glanced at Mackinnon as she was driving. 'Not to mention water horses and the giants who live here, the Fiennes, and earlier than them the gods and goddesses.'

'Do the people here believe in these legends?'

'Certainly, the older people, anyway. When I was a girl, in the days before television, they would tell stories and sing songs about these old folktales at every ceilidh.

They called on a patient in Flodigarry and then drove on past the ruins of Duntulm Castle and on to Kilmuir, with its monument to Flora Macdonald in the graveyard on top of the hill. They had rounded the top of the peninsula and were heading for Uig, where they would visit the last patient of the morning.

When they passed a signpost pointing to Bornaskitaig, Mrs Tait remarked, 'We have a rather grisly legend about that place.'

The legend was that the Macdonalds and the MacLeods both claimed a promontory of land at Bornaskitaig and, deciding for once not to fight over it, they agreed that each clan should race for it in their best war galleys, the winner being he whose hand first touched the land. The MacLeod ship was winning when young Macdonald struck off his left hand with a dagger and flung it ashore. Then Macdonald pointed out that a Macdonald hand, that of his son, had been the first to touch the land and claimed it. Tradition had it that this was the origin of the Macdonald crest, a hand holding a dagger.

'Many of the legends of Skye seem to spring from a love of violence,' Mackinnon said.

'Yes, that's true, I'm afraid. Peaceful and law-abiding are two adjectives you could never use to describe our ancestors. They fought, plundered, slaughtered, smuggled and lived by their own laws.'

'Smuggled?'

'Yes. Along here.' Mrs Tait pointed in the direction of the sea to their left. 'This coast is ideal for smuggling: lonely beaches, little bays, cliffs.'

As they approached Uig she told him about the patient they would be visiting there, a retired man named Hector

Monro. Monro, she said, had once owned a hotel in Sleat at the south end of Skye. Then when his wife had died two or three years previously he had sold the hotel and built himself a house in Uig.

'Hector was clever,' she said. 'His hotel was nothing spectacular, no better than any other on Skye and not as good as some. Then he hired a young Italian chef. In no time at all the hotel restaurant gained a reputation and was awarded rosettes in the good food guides. So when Hector came to sell he was able to ask for an astonishingly good price and now he'll be able to live a comfortable bachelor's existence for the rest of his days.'

'But his health is bad?'

'Not at all! He pampers himself, which is probably why he asked you to call this morning. The chances are that he has had a bilious attack, nothing more.'

When they reached Monro's house he was not in bed but reading the newspapers in a room with huge picture windows that overlooked the sea loch. He was complaining not of his liver but of pains in his chest. Mackinnon examined him in his bedroom and came to the conclusion that he was not an energetic man, for he was overweight and the condition of his hands did not suggest that he had ever done rough work. Charles doubted that it was angina but wondered whether it might be prudent for Monro to have an ECG and other tests at the hospital. When they rejoined Mrs Tait in the drawing-room he found that the woman who worked for Monro had brought in a bottle of champagne and three glasses.

'You'll both join me in a glass?' Monro asked.

'Hector, what an extravagance! And aren't you supposed to be ill?'

'It's just to welcome our young friend to Skye,' Monro replied. 'Besides, a glass of champagne relieves my pain.'

'I told you he pampers himself,' Mrs Tait said to Mackinnon. 'He has installed every luxury in this house of his. Automatic garage doors, three televisions, the latest stereo equipment, cordless telephones, even a jacuzzi.'

30

'Comfort is all I have left to enjoy in life.'

'Do you never miss working? Don't you sometimes regret selling your hotel?'

'When Phyllis died I lost heart. If I could have found someone to take her place I might have kept going, but there was only ever one other girl I wished to marry.' Monro looked at Mrs Tait, smiling as he added, 'And she was no longer free.'

'What rubbish!' Mrs Tait laughed and Mackinnon thought her laugh was to cover her embarrassment.

Monro may also have sensed an embarrassment, for he said no more about his wife or the hotel. Instead he asked Mackinnon, 'Tell me, how was the ferry from Kyle running yesterday?'

'It wasn't very full.'

'But was it running to time?'

'I would say so, yes. I only had to wait a short time and when the ferry arrived they turned it round quickly.'

'The crew have been trying some sort of go-slow, to back up a wage claim. Bloody fools! They don't realise that their behaviour will only hasten the bridge and do them out of a job.'

The proposal that a bridge should be built connecting Skye to the mainland was a controversial issue which divided the island, some saying that a bridge would bring more tourists and more prosperity, others maintaining that it would destroy the appeal of the island. Monro was against a bridge, which, he believed, would enable visitors to 'do' Skye in a day, seeing all that they felt the island had to offer and cross back to the mainland before nightfall to continue their tour of Scotland. In that case the hotels and shops would suffer.

'The whole charm of Skye is that it is an island, cut off from the mainland. Build a bridge and you'd destroy that.'

'Don't worry yourself, Hector,' Mrs Tait said. 'They've been arguing about building a bridge longer than I can remember. We'll both be in our graves before it becomes a reality.'

31

'Let's hope you're right.'

Looking out over the sea, Mackinnon could see what he realised must be the peninsula of Waternish; it seemed barren and bare, except for a row of small white patches that were the cottages of crofters, ranged along the headland. Having read in many books of the centuries of deprivation that Skye had endured and the cruelty of the clearances, he was surprised to find signs of prosperity, not always evident in other parts of Scotland. All the cottages he saw seemed to be in good repair and freshly painted.

'I understand you saw someone falling off Kilt Rock yesterday evening,' Monro said to Mackinnon suddenly.

'Yes. How did you know?'

'We have our own telegraph here on Skye which is much speedier than anything Marconi invented. The postman told me.'

'I sensed that the police didn't believe me when I told them what I saw.'

'Well they do now, laddie. Did you know they sent a boat round to the rocks below the cliff first thing this morning?'

'I'm glad to hear it.'

'The boat was seen on its way back to Portree only a while ago. They say there was a body in it.'

'Whose was it?' Mrs Tait asked quickly.

'We don't know yet. The body was covered with a blanket.'

When they left Monro's house Mrs Tait and Mackinnon did not return to Staffin but drove south from Uig and then took the Dunvegan road past Skeabost and Bernisdale towards where Kirsten lived. Kirsten had made her craft centre out of an old Tigh Dubh or black house, which had been partly rebuilt but retained much of its original structure. Black houses had once been a feature of the Hebridean islands. Developed to withstand the high winds one found on the islands, they had double dry-stone walls, each some four feet thick, with a space between which was filled with rubble or peat. Their thatched roofs were lashed down to the inner of the two walls and anchored with boulders, so that the outer wall acted as a baffle and prevented the roof from being blown away. Kirsten's black house had a thatched roof and a chimney added to replace the hole in the thatch through which the smoke from the peat fire would normally have been vented, and a concrete floor had been substituted for the traditional sloping earth floor; sloping because in winter the one room in the house would shelter man and beast through the night, family at one end, cattle at the other. In the Tigh Dubh itself the products of Kirsten's craft centre were displayed: hand-woven cloth, pottery, Celtic jewellery and a few pieces of sculpture. Built on at the back of it was a workshop with a hand loom, a potter's wheel and a small forge. As he and Mrs Tait went in, Mackinnon noticed between the Tigh Dubh and the edge of the loch a small whitewashed cottage.

Kirsten was wearing a workman's boiler suit and her red hair was tied in a bunch at the back of her neck. She came to meet them, wiping paint from her fingers with a rag soaked in spirits.

'Have you had any news?' she asked her mother anxiously.

'Not as yet.'

'Would you like to phone the hospital from here?'

'It's too soon yet, dear. He wasn't due in theatre until ten.'

Mackinnon realised that they must be speaking of the coronary bypass operation that Dr Tait was to undergo in Edinburgh. He had not known that the operation was to be done that day and was appalled.

'For Heaven's sake, why aren't you in Edinburgh with your husband?' he asked Mrs Tait. 'I could have managed.'

'Donald did not wish me to be there. He would only have worried,' Mrs Tait replied and then as though to dismiss the suggestion she said to Kirsten, 'We've just come from calling on Hector Monro.'

'What is the matter with him?'

'He complains of chest pains.'

'I'll bet it was just an excuse to get you round there,

now that Daddy's away,' Kirsten said and then added to Mackinnon, 'Hector fancies Mum you know.'

'Don't be absurd! Come on, now. Show Charles some of your work,' Mrs Tait said and Mackinnon was pleased that she had slipped easily into the informality of Christian names.

Kirsten took them round the display in the craft centre. Much of what was on show did not differ much from what one might find in roadside craft shops all over Scotland that sell tweeds, tartans and knitwear to tourists, but there were no souvenirs, nothing blatantly commercial or mass produced. Two pieces of sculpture caught Mackinnon's eye, one the head of a young man in bronze, the other an abstract shape in green marble in which, using a little imagination, one could see the lines of a woman's naked body.

While they were looking at the display a young girl came into the centre from the direction of the cottage by the loch. She could not have been more than eighteen and had a pretty face but her head was slightly larger than one would have expected and she walked with her shoulders rounded, looking up from a fringe of dark hair in a way that reminded Mackinnon of an anxious sheepdog.

'This is Mairi,' Kirsten said. 'Shake hands with Doctor Charles, Mairi.'

Mairi seemed about to refuse, then, reluctantly, she thrust out her hand, turning her face away as she did so. Her hand, Mackinnon noticed, was rough and snatching it back she moved closer to Kirsten, clutching her arm.

'Show the doctor that brooch you've just made,' Kirsten said to her.

Shyly, Mairi took a brooch from the pocket of the overalls she was wearing and held it out to Mackinnon. It was made from polished steel, an intricate design of curls and whirls and set with semi-precious stones which, Kirsten explained, Mairi and she had found on one of the island's beaches. They continued their tour of the craft display and from time to time Mairi would point out an item, saying nothing, but proudly so that one guessed it was her work.

34

'You'll both stay and have some lunch?' Kirsten asked her mother when the tour was almost over.

'Dear, we dare not. Hilda will have cooked for us by now.'

'You'll let me know as soon as you have any news from Edinburgh?'

'At once.'

When Mairi took Mrs Tait into the workshop to show her what she was working on, Kirsten drew Mackinnon on one side. 'Charles, may I bring Mairi to see you?' she asked and then added, 'Professionally, I mean.'

'Of course.'

'I'd prefer not to bring her to surgery, if that's all right with you.'

'I'll gladly see her whenever you wish.'

'Then we'll come up to the house this evening and I'll bring her to you after the last patient has left.'

As they drove towards Portree on the way to Staffin Mrs Tait hardly spoke. Mackinnon guessed that she must be thinking of her husband on the operating table and wondering how the surgery was progressing. She was not a woman who would show her feelings readily and if sorrow or suffering came she would bear it silently and without complaining. Self-restraint, pride, a stubborn determination to hide behind a mask of unfeeling stoicism were part of the Scottish character, moulded in that pattern by centuries of hard life in a country that gave little and grudgingly. Although he had been exposed to the softness of the south, he recognised his own Scottishness, showing itself in a reluctance to commit his emotions or to admit others to his private world. On an island that independence and self-isolation would be so much stronger. The idea triggered off another thought.

'Is there much in-breeding on Skye?' he asked Mrs Tait.

'So you've noticed it already?' she replied sadly. 'Poor Mairi. She's not mentally handicapped, you know, just a little simple.'

'It was not Mairi who put the notion in my mind so much as those children I saw in surgery this morning. They showed signs of in-breeding.'

35

'You're right, of course, Charles. It is true, especially around Staffin, but that doesn't mean that the people are vicious or depraved.'

'Does Mairi live with your daughter?'

Mrs Tait explained that Mairi's mother had died when she was thirteen and since then her father had been living with another woman. They had not wanted the child and had treated her shamefully, neglecting her for most of the time and beating her when the whim took them. Kirsten had taken Mairi into her cottage, ostensibly as a servant but really to rescue the child. She had learned that although she was simple she was skilful with her hands, and artistic. So now she had trained her to help in the craft centre.

'Kirsten has looked after that girl like a mother would,' Mrs Tait added. 'She taught her hygiene and manners and how to dress.'

Mackinnon would have liked to ask why it was that Kirsten had not married and had children of her own. She was an attractive girl who, if she cared to take a little extra care over her appearance, would be thought by many men as lovely. On top of that she was gifted and self-assured, but must be almost thirty and still unmarried. Although he did not ask the question, Mrs Tait may have guessed it was in his mind and she answered it, though indirectly.

'Although she would never admit it,' she said, 'the real reason why Kirsten gave up nursing was so that she could be here on Skye, close to her father and me. She knows how much we miss our other two daughters.'

'Do you never see them?'

'One is a surgeon in East Africa and the other an anaesthetist in California.'

'Kirsten must be devoted to you.'

'She is, especially to Donald. She worries about his health, too. Scarcely a day passes without her looking in on us, if only for a few minutes.'

'Well, she will be looking in on you this evening and bringing Mairi. She has asked me to examine her.'

'I know. She's afraid the child may be pregnant.'

By this time they were approaching Portree and Mrs Tait said no more about Mairi. Instead she suggested that before driving on to Staffin they should call in at the police station. If a body had been recovered from the sea the police might well want Mackinnon to confirm that it was one of the figures he had seen on Kilt Rock. Mackinnon agreed with her suggestion, although he knew that the figures had been too far away for him to be able to recognise or identify either of them.

The constable at the desk in the police station told them that the inspector did wish to speak to Dr Mackinnon and had left a message for him at Dr Tait's home. They would find the inspector at the hospital in Portree, where the body found below Kilt Rock had been taken until it could be sent to Inverness for a post-mortem.

'Who was it?' Mrs Tait asked the constable.

'Jamie Gillespie.'

'Oh, the poor soul!'

Leaving the car outside the police station, they walked to the hospital. On the way, Mackinnon asked Mrs Tait, 'You knew this Jamie Gillespie, then?'

'Surely. All his life. Donald delivered him, and his brother Willie, too.'

Gillespie's mother, she told him, was a widow who lived on a croft in Staffin with her elder son, Willie. Jamie had left Skye about three years previously to work as a barman in Edinburgh and had only recently returned home.

'I may as well tell you,' she added; 'Jamie was taking drugs.'

'Drugs are quite a problem in Edinburgh.'

'I can't imagine why he came home. He would find it difficult to get supplies on the island.'

At the hospital Inspector Maclean took them to see the body which had been recovered from the rocks at the edge of the sea. Jamie Gillespie, in the jeans and pink-and-white sweater he had been wearing, could at a distance have easily been mistaken for a woman, especially as he had worn his hair long. His back and his neck had been broken by the fall and he had suffered multiple contusions. His face was gaunt and emaciated and Mackinnon noticed hard, purple blotches on the backs of his hands and around his mouth and eyelids, the signs of Karposi's Sarcoma, signs he had been seeing at the hospital in London with disturbing frequency over the last few months.

He said nothing to Mrs Tait or the inspector but he was certain that the post-mortem would show that Jamie Gillespie had been suffering from AIDS.

4

'Would you mind very much if we made another call before going home?' Mrs Tait asked Mackinnon.

'On a patient? Of course not.'

'She is actually a patient but has not asked for you to visit her. It's Jamie Gillespie's mother, Morag, whom I'm thinking of.'

They were driving back towards Staffin from the hospital, where Inspector Maclean had told them that Jamie's mother and brother had come to identify his body and had then returned home. Willie Gillespie, Mackinnon learned, had once worked at the island's distillery but was now unemployed and helped his mother run their croft which was no more than a couple of fields on which sheep grazed, and a vegetable patch.

'I'm worried about Morag,' Mrs Tait explained. 'Poor soul, she's had more than her share of misfortune; first her husband dying unexpectedly, then Jamie going on drugs and finally Willie's trouble with the police.'

'What trouble did he have?'

'He and some friends were caught distilling whisky and given heavy fines. The Gillespies have always been poor and Morag got into debt raising the money to pay Willie's fines.'

'What kind of woman is she?'

'Not as strong as most of the women in these parts. She was a sickly girl and her husband did not treat her well. I think you should take a look at her.'

'I'll be glad to.'

Mrs Gillespie's house was a square, featureless box which contrived to look far more unprepossessing than the primitive Tigh Dubh which, no doubt, it had replaced some years ago. At Mrs Tait's suggestion Mackinnon waited outside in the car when she went into the house, so that she could prepare Mrs Gillespie for his call. That would give her time to talk to the bereaved woman alone; 'women's talk' as she described it.

As he waited, Mackinnon reflected that Skye was proving to be very different from the picture he had formed of the island, a picture composed of his father's memories, of the legends of history, of fragments of poems and songs. That morning before breakfast, thinking that it might help him to get a feel for the practice, he had spent half an hour in Dr Tait's surgery, looking through the medical records of the patients. Many of the complaints and illnesses for which they had been treated were what one would expect to find among people living in a damp climate and no doubt on an inadequate diet, but there were others that were disturbing, too many associated with a disregard of elementary hygiene. The prevalence of in-breeding also made him uneasy, for he knew how it could undermine the health of a whole community. He had been naïve, he supposed, in not expecting to find the blemishes of a primitive society in a sleepy, romantic island.

Mrs Tait came out to call him and he found Morag Gillespie in the living-room of her cottage. She was a small, dark woman whose facial structure showed the same signs of in-breeding that he had noticed in Mairi's, though less pronounced. Her face wore the listless, submissive look of an animal that has been bullied into obedience, but no signs of tears. Mackinnon sensed that a lifetime of hardship and hopelessness may have atrophied her capacity for weeping.

'How are you, Mrs Gillespie?' he asked her.

'A bit low, you ken, Doctor, but nae so bad.'

'I'm so sorry about your son.'

'Aye. He was a good lad, though there's plenty will tell you he wasn't.'

'Is there anything I can do for you?'

'Dinna fash yourself, Doctor. I'll be all right.'

'Perhaps you should give Morag something to help her sleep, Charles.'

'Certainly I will, if she would like that.'

'I'll no take any of those sleeping pills,' Mrs Gillespie said stubbornly. 'A good dram before I'm away to my bed will see me fine.'

'Do you have any whisky in the house?' Mrs Tait asked her. 'I'll gladly bring a bottle round.'

'We're no short of whisky, not at a time like this when people will be coming to the house at all hours. And what am I thinking of? I haven't poured one for you and you here all this time.'

'Don't worry about that, Morag.'

'And yourself, Doctor? You'll take a dram with me, will you not?'

Mackinnon knew that to refuse would give offence. In the Highlands and islands a bereavement was no reason for failing to offer the traditional Scottish hospitality, rather the opposite. Mrs Tait insisted on going to fetch the whisky and obviously she knew her way around the house. While she was away Mrs Gillespie allowed Mackinnon, reluctantly, to give her a superficial examination and he could find nothing amiss with her heart or lungs. He suspected that she might be stronger than she appeared. Mrs Tait came back with a bottle of blended whisky which Mackinnon knew was one of the more expensive brands, and when Mrs Gillespie had poured a dram for each of them the women began talking about Jamie.

'I remember him when he was just a baby,' Mrs Tait said. 'He was such a sweet, affectionate bairn.'

'Aye, and he loved it when I took him to see the doctor.'

'Yes. He was devoted to Donald and Donald thought the world of him.'

'There was no harm in the lad until he fell in with those gypsies.'

'Some hippies came to the island and set up a commune near Tarskavaig,' Mrs Tait told Mackinnon. 'Jamie gave up his job and lived with them.'

'It was themselves put him on to smoking that stuff. The lad was never the same after that.'

Mackinnon sensed that talking about her son was providing Mrs Gillespie with a release for the emotions that she was unable to express. A drink and a chat might be a substitute for a wake. Funerals were great occasions in the Highlands and islands of Scotland but he supposed that the Gillespies might not be able to afford one, even though he had noticed what looked like a large, new colour television set in the living-room.

'Where's Willie?' Mrs Tait asked.

'He's away to have a drink. Seeing poor Jamie down at the hospital really upset him.'

'Has he taken Jamie's car?' Mrs Tait asked.

'No. As I told you last night, Jamie left here in his car at the back of twelve yesterday. I never saw him after that, nor the car either.' Mrs Gillespie faltered over her last sentence. It was the nearest she had come to weeping. She looked at Mackinnon. 'People say you saw it happen, Doctor.'

'I'm afraid so. I was up by Kilt Rock at the time.'

'He jumped, did he not? I'll no believe anyone would ever have pushed him. The lad never hurt a soul.'

'But why on earth should he have jumped, Morag?'

At first Mrs Gillespie seemed unwilling to answer the question. Then, looking at Mackinnon and Mrs Tait defiantly, she said, 'He told me that he'd come home to die.'

'Oh, Morag, you must have misunderstood him! Either that or he was joking.'

'No, that's what he said. He came home so he could die among his own folk.'

Fewer patients arrived for surgery that evening than Mackinnon had expected, and they seemed less responsive and less ready to talk about themselves than those he had seen during the morning. He wondered whether it might be because people in and around Staffin knew that Jamie Gillespie was dead and that he had seen him die. Through superstition they might be linking his arrival on Skye with the lad's death. People who believed in fairy banners and water horses might believe anything. He told himself that the idea was absurd but could not shake off a feeling of unease.

Not long after the last patient had left, Kirsten came into the surgery. Since they had met that morning she had changed from her boiler suit, and though only into a jumper and skirt she looked more attractive than the previous evening at dinner and he supposed she had taken more trouble with her make-up or her hair. She flopped casually into the patient's chair on the other side of her father's desk and seemed totally at ease.

'Heavens! Sitting here reminds me of the days when I was little. I was allowed to run in and out of the surgery. No one minded and my father loved it. He said it helped the patients relax. "Look at my daughter," he used to say to them. "Isn't she a fine, strong girl?" I would get annoyed because I thought he meant I was fat, which of course I was.'

'Where is Mairi?' Mackinnon asked.

'She'll be in directly. I wanted to talk to you alone first.'

'Your mother tells me you believe she's pregnant.'

'Yes. I'm reasonably certain she missed her last period; perhaps the previous one as well.'

'Have you asked her?'

'Of course. First she denied it and then she said she wasn't sure. To be truthful I very much doubt if she would notice.'

'Does she show any other signs of pregnancy?'

'Only that she has complained of feeling sick a couple of times.'

'Has she had any opportunities to become pregnant? For intercourse, I mean.'

'I imagine so. I don't keep her a prisoner. She goes out with other young people.'

Mackinnon was not at all sure that he should ask the next question he had in mind. He would have been reluctant to ask it of Mairi's parents and as far as he knew Kirsten was not even the girl's legal guardian. He was also not sure of how, if he asked the question, it should be phrased.

Kirsten must have guessed the reason for his hesitation. 'I'm not saying Mairi's promiscuous, but I think she could be easily seduced.'

'In that case shouldn't she be taking contraceptive pills?'

'She is taking them, but sometimes she forgets. I've told her the facts of life but I often wonder whether she really understands the connection between menstruation and pregnancy.' Kirsten was silent for a time. Her concern was obvious and Mackinnon wondered whether she ever regretted taking on the responsibility of looking after a backward girl. Then suddenly her mood seemed to change. 'Poor Charles! We're giving you a hard time. I'm sure life on Skye is proving to be very different from what you imagined.'

Mackinnon laughed. 'You're right, but then I was always a romantic fool!'

'It isn't always as traumatic as it has been since you arrived. Once you've settled in we'll show you the real Skye.'

'I shall hold you to that.'

'Do you like walking? Or sailing?'

'More than anything I'd like to go up the Cuillins.' He remembered the photograph of Kirsten as a girl up on the mountains. 'Mind you, I've never climbed anything taller than a six-foot ladder.'

'In that case we had better start you off with some tough hill-walking. At the weekend, perhaps.'

She left the surgery, saying she would send Mairi in to him. While he was waiting Mackinnon found Mairi's medical record. She had been to Dr Tait several times in the past but for nothing more serious than childish complaints. If she had obtained her contraceptive pills from him there was no record of it. Her surname was McPhee and as he was putting her card back Mackinnon saw that there was another one made out in the name of Murdo McPhee. He wondered whether Murdo might be Mairi's father. His date of birth showed that he was forty-one, which would be about right. In the past ten years Murdo had only once been treated by Dr Tait, for a skin rash, but there was a note with his records stating that he had been discharged from Portree Hospital after treatment for gunshot wounds.

When Mairi came into the surgery he saw that she too had spent time on her appearance. She was wearing lipstick, her eyes had been made up and her hair looked as though it had just been washed and set. Although she was small and slight, her walk and her movements were clumsy, her head continually rolling slightly or dipping, as though she had difficulty in controlling her muscles.

When she was sitting in the chair on the other side of his desk he said, 'You won't mind if I examine you, will you, Mairi?'

She smiled, shook her head and at once began pulling off the sweater she was wearing. 'Hang on,' he said. 'Let's talk a little first. Kirsten tells me you've felt sick once or twice recently.' Mairi nodded. 'Anything else? Have you had any pains?' She shook her head. 'How long is it since you had your last period?' Mairi looked blank and shrugged her shoulders. 'You can't remember?' She shook her head.

The conversation stuttered on, Mairi saying nothing but answering Mackinnon's questions by either nodding or shaking her head. Her shyness was painful but he could see no way of breaking it down. A pad of paper which Dr Tait had used to jot down notes of his conversations with patients lay on the desk in front of Mackinnon. Suddenly Mairi reached out, pulled the pad towards her.

'Pencil?' she said to Mackinnon.

He found a pencil in one of the desk drawers and when he gave it to her she at once began drawing on the pad. Although he could not see what she was drawing he could sense her relaxing, and some of the tension in her eased. He continued to ask her questions and now she replied, though only in monosyllables. She did not appear to be aware of the purpose behind his questions nor to be in any way disconcerted by them. Since he had no evidence as yet that she was pregnant he did not ask her whether she had had sex recently. That might come later.

She was drawing all the time and presently she tore the top sheet from the pad and handed it to him. He saw then that she had sketched a landscape, probably a view of Skye that she knew well. There were hills in the distance and in front of them a trawler was making its way across a sea loch. On the edge of the loch stood a row of cottages with a road winding past them and a small hotel. The detail in the sketch was remarkable. One could see the nets of the fishing boat, the gulls that were following it, curtains in the windows of the cottages and a man unloading a van outside the hotel.

'That's very good,' Mackinnon told Mairi. 'You draw beautifully.'

She pointed at him. 'For you.'

'Thank you very much.'

After putting her drawing away in one of the desk drawers, he told Mairi to go behind the screen at the end of the surgery, where she could undress. She jumped up readily to do what he asked and when she came out from behind the screen Mackinnon understood why. Not only did she have a well proportioned body, but one could tell from her manner and her expression that she was proud of it. When she lay down on the bed and he began to examine her he realised too that she was ready for sex and wanted it. She did nothing coquettish or provocative, but her sexuality was so strong that he could almost feel it. In other circumstances and in another woman it might have disturbed him. He examined her gently but could find no physical sign that she was pregnant. When he told her that she could put her clothes on again she seemed disappointed.

After she had dressed he sent her with a sample bottle to the lavatory adjoining the surgery and when he had the specimen told her the examination was over and that she might rejoin Kirsten and Mrs Tait. It took him only a few minutes to test the specimen and learn that she was pregnant.

46

He was still thinking of what the implications of her pregnancy would be for Kirsten, as well as for Mairi and for Dr Tait when he returned to resume his practice, when Kirsten returned to the surgery. She looked at him anxiously and his expression must have told her what she had been hoping not to hear.

'Then she is pregnant? I knew it!'

'I'm afraid so.'

'Oh, God!' She flopped into the chair opposite him as she had done earlier, not casually this time but dejectedly. 'What will you do?'

'I don't know. Mairi would just about be able to look after the child, I suppose, with a lot of help and supervision, but how can we find out whether she really wants it? How can we make her understand what being a mother will mean? And, assuming that she didn't want it or that we decided she wouldn't be able to care for it, would one be justified in arranging an abortion?'

Charles knew he was not in a position to answer her questions. 'I can't advise you, I'm afraid.'

'I know. It wouldn't be fair to ask you to. We'll have to wait until my father can decide. He'll know what to do.'

'How is your father? Have you had any more news?'

'He's grand. The operation was completely successful.'

'I should have asked you before, I'm sorry,' Charles said, ashamed of his thoughtlessness.

'No need to apologise. You've enough on your mind.'

'Do you know who was responsible for making Mairi pregnant?'

'No. And she'll not tell me. I'm certain of that.'

'Have you no idea at all? Has she not talked of any man or have you seen anyone hanging around the cottage waiting for her?'

'No one at all. She has slipped out without telling me once or twice, but when I asked her where she had been she grew confused and would not answer.'

5

'Did you see any cars up by Kilt Rock, apart from your own, sir?'

'No.'

'Were there none parked at the view point where you stopped?'

'None. Nor were there any people there. The place was deserted.'

'You didn't see a car parked on the road nearby?'

'I'm afraid not.'

'In which direction did you drive when you left Kilt Rock?'

'Towards Portree. I went straight to the police station to report what I had seen.'

'After you left the station you must have driven past Kilt Rock again on your way back here. Did you notice a stationary car anywhere in the vicinity?'

Mackinnon shook his head. Detective Superintendent Grieve gave the impression of being content in his work; by no means a great intellect with his large, insensitive face and his large, capable hands, but clever enough to conceal his stubborn determination behind a mask of *bonhomie*. One felt that instead of asking tiresome questions what he would really like would be to invite one to go fishing or to a game of golf, which was totally untrue. Grieve was one of a team of three police officers who had come to Skye from the headquarters of the Northern Constabulary in Inverness to investigate the death of Jamie Gillespie. He had arrived at Dr Tait's house with Detective

Sergeant Mackenzie that morning, soon after surgery had ended.

'The way I see it, sir, is that the deceased must have driven to Kilt Rock.'

'It isn't too far to walk from Staffin, is it?'

'No, but we know that Gillespie was drinking in a pub in Portree from midday well into the afternoon.'

Mackinnon tried to remember his drive back from Portree to Dr Tait's home after leaving the police station. He could recall the shudder of horror he had felt as he passed Kilt Rock and how he had kept his eyes firmly on the road in front of him to avoid looking up at the cliff face. Had he passed a stationary car on the road at that point without really being aware of it? He began to believe that perhaps he had.

'What make of car did Jamie Gillespie own?' he asked Grieve.

'A Ford Fiesta.'

'And he was driving even though he was on drugs?'

'Aye, and even though he was a heavy drinker. The car has not been seen since his death. But we'll find it. One can't make a car disappear on Skye.'

'The man who threw him off the cliff may have used it to get away.'

'If there *was* another man,' Sergeant Mackenzie remarked.

Mackinnon had sensed that even though a body had been found at the foot of Kilt Rock the police did not entirely believe his story. None of them had said as much and Grieve looked at the sergeant sharply, as though to reprove him for his tactlessness.

'We can't be sure that what you thought you saw was not an optical illusion. Light can do funny things. After all, you did say at first that it was a woman you saw thrown off the cliff.'

'You believe that Gillespie fell accidentally, then?'

'Or that he may have jumped.'

'Have you been talking to his mother?'

'There may be some truth in what she said about his

coming home to die. As you yourself must have realised when you saw his body, he had the AIDS virus.'

'You know that for certain, do you?'

'Oh, aye. The post-mortem has not been completed yet but we made enquiries in Edinburgh and learned that Gillespie contracted AIDS there.'

'You haven't wasted any time, Superintendent.'

If Grieve took the comment as a compliment he did not show it. He was not a man who would bother to acknowledge compliments when he had other questions to ask. 'Does Dr Tait have any medical records for Gillespie, do you know?'

'There are none in his files.' Mackinnon had noticed that when he was looking through the medical records in the surgery the previous evening.

'Gillespie was his patient when he was a lad.'

'I know, but the records would have been sent to his doctor in Edinburgh after he had moved from Skye.'

'Dr Tait didn't treat him after he came back to Skye, then?'

'Not as far as I know. Why do you ask?'

'The man was a drug addict. He'd need to get his fix from somewhere.'

'You're not suggesting that Dr Tait might have supplied him with drugs? That's an outrageous suggestion!'

The force of Mackinnon's protest seemed to disconcert Grieve. 'Doctors do sometimes prescribe for addicts,' he said defiantly.

'Yes, Methadone. That's to help them break their dependence.'

'Could Dr Tait have done that for Gillespie?'

'If he had, then I'm sure there would be a record of it.' Mackinnon was beginning to lose patience with Grieve's persistence. 'Look, Superintendent. I'm not really in a position to help you. I've been on the island for less than forty-eight hours. You might learn more from Mrs Tait.'

'Possibly, but she's not here, is she, sir?'

'No, she's in Edinburgh visiting her husband in hospital. But she'll be back tonight.'

50

'Did you discuss Gillespie's death with her?' Grieve asked, reluctant to end the interview until he had extracted every possible scrap of information from it. Mackinnon was reminded of research students he had known who worked through the data they had assembled again and again, reluctant to believe that it had not revealed anything spectacular.

'Only in very general terms.'

'But the two of you did go to see Mrs Gillespie together?'

'Yes, because Mrs Tait wished to comfort her and felt she might need a sedative.'

'And what did Mrs Gillespie have to say?'

'Very little, except that Jamie had always been a good son to her.'

Grieve made a small, incredulous noise. 'She didn't tell you that he had been in trouble with the police in Edinburgh?'

'No. We just took a drink together in his memory.'

'These islanders are all the same.' Like many Scots from the mainland Grieve was intolerant of the people of Skye. He pulled some sheets of paper from the folder he had brought with him. 'I have here the statement that you made to the police in Portree, sir. Would you mind if we went over it together?'

For the third time Mackinnon described what he had seen at Kilt Rock and answered questions about it. The statement he had made to the police was so straightforward and so precise that one would have thought it left no room for ambiguity. He found himself wondering whether the motive of the police in repeatedly questioning him about it might be the hope of tricking him into proving he had lied. Then he told himself he must not become paranoid.

When at last the police left and he realised that he would be late in making his calls, he was unreasonably irritated. Unreasonably, because none of the calls was urgent and even in the few hours that he had been on Skye he had begun to realise that time did not have the same marshalling discipline on the island as it had in London.

Because her home was the nearest to Dr Tait's, his first visit was to Mrs Kennedy. He found the old lady sitting in the same chair as she had been sitting in the previous morning and wondered what proportion of her waking day was spent in it. She seemed pleased to see him, reinforcing his suspicion that there was little wrong with her health and what she wanted was not medicine but company. Even so, because she might expect it he had brought her some medicine which he had made up himself, little more than a placebo, and told her to take it three times a day.

'I've remembered your forbears,' she told him. 'They lived in Sleat.'

'Are you certain?'

'Oh, aye. The family had a small croft. They were well thought-of folk in those parts, hard working and members of the kirk.'

'How did you meet them?'

'I was in service in those parts then; in the same house which yon Swiss fellow bought.'

'Mr Short.'

'The people who stayed there then had lots of bairns – eight, maybe ten – and when I was no working in the house I had to mind them. One of the youngest was great pals with your grandfather, even though he was just a crofter's son.'

Mackinnon felt a surge of excitement. Out of an old woman's memory the past had reached out to him. He tried to picture Jeanie Kennedy, then a young woman, watching over children in Sleat. His father, had he still been alive, would have been in his mid-sixties now, so Jeanie was talking of more than eighty years ago. Victoria might still have been queen, another Englishwoman to meet with Jeanie's disapproval.

'Do you remember my father?' he asked Jeanie.

The old woman shook her head. 'I married a Staffin man and came to stay on the croft up here. I did hear your grand-dad had started this shop in Broadford.'

'You never saw it?'

'Goodness, no! We never journeyed further than Portree. There were no motorcars in those days.'

There would have been motorcars at that time, Mackinnon

52

knew, but probably not on Skye. Even if anyone on the island had been rich enough to own one, the hazards of transporting it from the mainland would have been considerable. He remembered reading that not all that long ago cars had been ferried from the mainland lashed to two planks balanced between two boats. And the roads in the early days of the century would have been no more than tracks. For Jean Kennedy a journey from Staffin to Broadford would have been almost as daunting as emigrating to Canada.

'And yon slip of a girl will no be any good for him,' Jean Kennedy said.

'Which girl?'

'You'll not have seen her yet, for she's away to the south. Gloria, they call her. She's bonnie enough if she'd only leave her face and her hair as the Almighty made them, but she'll soon tire of him if she hasn'a already.'

It took Mackinnon a few moments to realise that Mrs Kennedy was talking about Carl Short's wife. Her old woman's memory, which had spanned eighty years so effortlessly and with such clarity, was fickle in the immediate past and she had forgotten the subject of their conversation.

'Folks say she has an eye for younger men,' Jeanie said, 'just as he has for young girls.' The remark provoked another thought and she asked him, 'Why are you no married, Doctor?'

'I don't know. Too busy, perhaps.'

'Or enjoying your freedom too much?'

'Maybe.'

After leaving Mrs Kennedy he called on two patients in Staffin and then, before moving on to the outlying villages, dropped in on Morag Gillespie. She came to the door with reading glasses on the end of her nose and carrying a printed booklet.

'I thought I'd come round just to see if you're all right, Mrs Gillespie.'

'You need not have bothered yourself, Doctor. I'm fine. But as you're here maybe you can help me.'

'In what way?'

'It's this washing machine my lad bought me. I canna make head nor tail of it.'

She led him to the kitchen at the back of the house and pointed to a new automatic washing machine which she had loaded with clothes and washing powder. It was the row of push-buttons on the front of the machine, each marked with a symbol or a letter of the alphabet, which was puzzling her. Mackinnon took the booklet of operating instructions from her and began reading it, noticing as he did that it was stamped with the name and address of a retailer in Inverness. The instructions were clear and he explained to Morag how she should select the temperature of the wash to suit the fabric of the clothes she wished to wash and the length of spin drying they would need. Then, nervously, as though she were handling a sensitive detonator, she pressed the combination of buttons to start the machine.

'That's great, Doctor!' she exclaimed as she heard water gushing into the machine and the clothes beginning to swish around inside it. 'Jamie did show me, but I'm no one for handling machinery.'

She could talk of her dead son without emotion, but Mackinnon realised that this did not mean she felt none. Her resilience had allowed her to accept his death with the same fortitude as she had accepted the many privations and disappointments of her life. When he left her she was watching the wash spinning round through the glass window of the washing machine with an absorbed fascination.

Outside the cottage he found that the bonnet of his car had been raised and a man in worn corduroy trousers, a shabby green sweater and a brown trilby hat was examining the engine. The man looked up at him and smiled.

'That's a grand wee car you have here, Doctor,' he said, and then explained, 'I'm Willie.'

Willie Gillespie was older than Mackinnon would have expected he would be and a contrast to Jamie in his build, bigger, bulkier and in no way effeminate. Two or three days' growth of beard and gaps in his teeth gave him an appearance which would have been sinister, were it not for the disarming stupidity of his smile.

'You'll not mind my taking a wee peep at the engine, will you, Doctor?' Mackinnon said he didn't mind and Willie went on, 'My brother Jamie had a car no bigger than this, but it was older, you ken, second hand.'

'A Ford Fiesta, was it not?'

'How did you know?'

'The police told me. They're looking for it.'

The news that the police were looking for Jamie's car appeared to disconcert Willie. 'The police! Have they nothing better to do?' He let down the bonnet of the Toyota and thumped it till the catch snapped shut. 'Cars take an awful hammering on the roads here.'

'I've just been in to see your mother,' Mackinnon told him. 'She seems all right.'

'Aye. She would be. She'll grieve for Jamie right enough, but she's seen little of him these past years.'

'I must go and finish my calls,' said Mackinnon. As he got into the car, he remembered he had told Hilda that he would not need lunch that day. To have her cooking just for him seemed wasteful. So he asked Willie, 'Is there anywhere around here where I could get a bite to eat at lunchtime?'

'The inn along the road to Portree does bar lunches.'

The road leading north from Staffin was like most of the lesser roads on Skye, single track, wide enough for only one vehicle and widened every 150 yards or so to allow passing places, which were marked by posts. Drivers of two cars approaching each other from opposite directions had to decide which of them would pull in to the passing place and let the other go by. That morning Mackinnon, feeling that as a visitor he should at least match the islanders in courtesy, would pull in to the side of the road only to find that the approaching driver had already swung into the nearest passing place and was flashing his headlights as a signal for him to drive on. He had the feeling that the drivers whom he passed would be accepting the clumsy misjudgments of this stranger with a condescending tolerance and it irritated him. On the previous morning Mrs Tait had managed the same journey easily and fluently.

When he reached the last house on which he was to call that day in Flodigarry, he noticed from the temperature gauge of the car that his engine appeared to be overheating and, when he opened the bonnet, steam was hissing from the radiator's overflow pipe. He left the bonnet open while he made the call and after he had finished borrowed a jug of water with which he topped up the reservoir of the radiator.

On the short drive to Staffin the needle on the temperature gauge began creeping up again and when he reached the inn where he planned to lunch the same symptoms of overheating were apparent. Once again he left the bonnet open while he went into the inn to have a glass of beer and a plate of mince and tatties.

Three local men were drinking in the bar; an odd assortment, one lean and dark with a scarred face, another gross and so arthritic that he had difficulty in holding his glass, the third tiny but aggressive. In their conversation they had a common theme of complaint. They all did some form of work, part time, for a hotel on Trotternish and all of them felt that they were being exploited. Even so, they did not appear to be unduly short of money and each ordered when it was his turn three half-pints of beer with three whiskies on the side. Only once did Mackinnon hear any of them laugh, and that was a cynical sneer, and he began to wonder why on Skye – or at least in Staffin – he had seen so little good humour.

He had finished his lunch and was enjoying a Talisker whisky with a cup of coffee when Willie Gillespie came into the bar. 'That'll be your car outside, is it, Doctor?' he asked Mackinnon. 'I see the bonnet is up. Are you having trouble?'

'The engine's overheating.'

'Give us your keys, then, and I'll take a look at it for you. I know a thing or two about motors.'

'That's kind of you, Willie, but I'm sure you came here for a dram, not to work as a mechanic.'

'It's nae bother, Doctor.'

Mackinnon noticed the three men at the bar looking round at him and then at Willie with what appeared to be sardonic amusement. He had no great confidence in Willie's mechanical ability, but it would have been churlish to refuse his offer so he handed him the keys of the Toyota.

'You can buy me a dram, Doctor. I'll be back immediately.'

As he was ordering the whisky, Mackinnon heard the engine of his car start. Willie, one would have thought, must be forty or more, but Jamie, judging by what Mackinnon had seen in the mortuary and, discounting the ageing effects of AIDS on his appearance, would not have been much more than twenty-five. He wondered what the reason might be for the gap in their ages. Had their father been married more than once, making them half-brothers? Or had there been other children who had died? The infant mortality rate on Skye would probably have been high thirty or more years ago.

Presently Willie returned and told him, 'Sorry, Doc, it's nothing that I can fix. You'll need to take your motor into Portree.'

'Should I ring a garage and get them to come and tow it in, do you think?'

'I wouldn't. They'll likely be hours in coming. You'll make Portree all right if you drive carefully. Mostly it's downhill from here.'

'That's true.'

'If you wish I'll come with you, Doc. I was going into Portree later anyway and this way you'll save me the bus fare.'

As they drove south from the inn Mackinnon toyed with a suspicion that Willie might have engineered the whole incident, interfering with the car's engine earlier when it had been standing outside his mother's house, so that it would need to be taken to a garage. Could it have been no more than coincidence that he had arrived at the inn where he had advised Mackinnon to eat? He was unemployed and saving a bus fare would at least give him the price of another drink.

'Is it true you saw my brother Jamie go over the cliff?'
Willie's question sounded tentative, a chess player trying
out an opening move with which he was unfamiliar.

'I saw someone fall and it can only have been your brother.'

'You didn't recognise him?'

'He was too far away.'

'Nor the other man you saw up there?'

'In that light all I could make out was two figures.'

Willie seemed satisfied with the answer. 'Then you couldna'
tell if the one was pushed over or jumped.'

'He was tossed over. I saw that clearly enough,' Mackinnon
replied firmly. What he had seen on Kilt Rock, the whole
horrifying sequence, the larger figure's easy, casual swing as
he threw the other out into space, had returned to his mind
so often over the last two days, and with such clarity, that
he knew now it could not have been a trick of his imagination.

Willie was silent for a while, feeling perhaps that he had
reached his first objective and wondering what his next step
should be. They were passing the Old Man of Storr with
Mackinnon driving cautiously, switching the engine of the
car off to coast downhill whenever he could.

'Did they tell you Jamie was . . . ' Willie hesitated over
the choice of word. 'Did they tell you he was a queer?'

'Nobody told me but I assumed he was.'

'It was them hippies that made him that way.'

Mackinnon could have told him that no one could have
turned his brother into a homosexual if the latent inclination
had not been there, but he did not suppose that Willie would
be receptive to academic arguments. Instead he asked, 'Are
the hippies still on the island?'

'No. They set up this commune in Sleat when Jamie was
working in a hotel there as a barman. He fell in with them
and threw up his job. After a time they decided that life on
Skye was not as soft as they expected and moved back to the
mainland. Jamie went too but later we heard he had broken
away and gone to work in Edinburgh. Then without any
warning he turns up here, saying he's come home.'

'Was the hotel where he worked in Sleat the one Hector Monro used to own?'

'Aye. Why do you ask?'

'I just wondered. Why did Jamie come home?'

'To jump off Kilt Rock, my mother thinks.'

'And what do you think?'

'I wouldna' be surprised if he was in trouble with the police in Edinburgh.'

'What makes you think that?'

'I dinna ken.' Suddenly Willie was evasive and one sensed that he regretted what he had said. 'Just a feeling.'

'Was it because he seemed to be flush with money?'

'What money? I never saw any money.'

The money to run a car and buy his mother a washing machine and a new television set, Mackinnon might have answered. He said nothing, knowing it was none of his business. Willie also said nothing for a time and seemed to be brooding.

'Why did the bloody little poof come back?' he demanded angrily. 'He was nothing but trouble for me when he was a lad. You'd not know what it's like to have all your mates laughing at you for having a brother who's a poof. Then he comes home, not just a poof but a junkie.'

Mackinnon was startled by the venom of his outburst. 'Well, he's dead now, poor lad,' he said.

'Yes, and that'll no be the end of the trouble he's brought his mam and me, you can be sure of that.'

6

After dropping Willie off outside the Royal Hotel and watching him head for a pub down by the harbour, Mackinnon drove to a garage where a mechanic promised to take a look at the Toyota as soon as he could. Leaving the car there he wandered round the few shops in the town, bought a copy of a very early edition of a London newspaper and a bottle of Talisker whisky, planning to send it to his friends in Edinburgh who had put him up for the night on his way to Skye. Mrs Tait would be in Edinburgh by now, for she had left the island on an early ferry and with the vastly improved roads the drive from Lochalsh would not take much more than four hours. He realised that she must have done the journey twice on the day she took her husband to hospital, and was once again impressed by her energy and quiet determination. Running a single-doctor practice on Skye must be a partnership and there was no doubt that Dr Tait had chosen his partner well. He wondered how and where they had met.

When he returned to the garage he found the mechanic bent over the engine of his car with an apprentice beside him. Their manner suggested that they had solved the problem.

'It's no anything serious,' the mechanic told him. 'Just that the water pump's no working.'

'Then you can fix it?'

'Oh, no. She'll need a new pump.'

'How long will it take you to fit one?'

'We'll need to order one from the mainland. There's nobody here stocks one.'

'And how long will that take?'

The mechanic shrugged his shoulders. 'Two days, maybe three. You can no tell with any certainty.'

Mackinnon knew that he was experiencing just one of the problems of life on an island. Back in London he had friends who maintained their own cars. If they needed a new part they would go and collect one from a shop that specialised in stocking automobile parts. Many of the shops would be open late in the evenings and on Sundays.

'Can you get on the phone and order one straightaway?'

'Sorry, sir, the foreman will need to do that.'

'Where is the foreman?'

'He's no back from his dinner yet.'

Mackinnon knew that there were taxis to be found in Portree. One of them would take him back to Staffin, but he would still be left with a problem. A doctor in the country could not manage without a car and he did not know when Mrs Tait would be back from Edinburgh. He had pressed her to stay with her husband as long as she wished.

'Can I rent a car from you until mine is fixed?' he asked the mechanic.

'Surely. Just go and ask in the office.'

In the office at the back of the showroom a middle-aged woman was wrestling with a middle-aged manual typewriter, swearing every time the carriage jumped. Yes, the garage did rent cars, she admitted, but there had been a heavy call on their cars that week. One was expected to be returned later that afternoon and the only other one available had been in a collision with a sheep and was badly dented.

'Is it roadworthy?' Mackinnon asked.

'The hirer drove it back here so I suppose it is, but I doubt we'd wish to let it out in that condition.'

'I'm a doctor and I need a car urgently.'

'The manager will have to decide if we can let you have it.'

'Where is he?'

'He's away for his dinner.'

Not wishing to vent his frustration on the woman, Mackinnon left the office. As he came out into the forecourt of the garage a red Porsche swung in from the road and pulled up in front of the petrol pumps. The driver waved and it took him a few moments to recognise Carl Short. Climbing out of the Porsche, Short tossed the keys to the lad who came out to the pumps.

'Fill her up,' he said and then walked over towards Mackinnon. 'What brings you here, Doctor? Not having trouble with your car, I hope.'

He was wearing beige gaberdine trousers, a pale blue roll-neck cashmere sweater and tan brogues that were almost certainly handmade. Even in Sandwich, the Cotswolds and the other weekend haunts of investment bankers he would have looked overdressed. Mackinnon explained the trouble he was having with his car.

'Bloody nuisance, but not to worry. I'll run you up to Staffin.'

'I wouldn't dream of taking you all that way.'

'No trouble. The fact is that I'm just taking this red monster out for its weekly exercise. A Porsche is great when Gloria and I want to slip down to Edinburgh, but I don't drive it on the island; not on these roads.' He smiled. 'Besides, people might think it a bit ostentatious.'

'You're very kind, but getting back to Staffin is not the real problem. I need to rent a car and I've had no luck so far.'

'Of course! Fiona will have taken theirs to Edinburgh to see Donald.'

'I have to wait here until the manager returns from lunch.'

'Wait a minute. I've a better idea! You can borrow Gloria's little car. She isn't coming home till next week.'

'No, really!'

Short would not listen to any objections Mackinnon tried to make. Gloria's car was only standing idle in the garage, so he would be doing her a favour by borrowing it. He would drive Mackinnon down to Sleat, where he could pick up the

62

car and take it to Staffin. When Mackinnon pointed out that driving to Sleat and back would make him late for evening surgery, Short replied that in that case he would have the car brought up to the Taits' home.

'Nothing would be easier.' He waved Mackinnon's protests away. 'We are cutting timber on the estate just now and some of the men we're employing are from Staffin. Any of them would love an excuse to finish work early. I'll call my factor and he'll have one of them drive the car up to Donald's place for you.'

He went into the office to use the garage's telephone and came back shortly to say that everything was arranged. Meanwhile, the Porsche had been filled with petrol and the lad on the pumps had checked the oil and the tyre pressures.

'Now I'll drive you home,' Short said.

Inside, the Porsche had the smell of a new car, even though its numberplates showed that it was at least two years old. Mackinnon realised that Short would have people to look after everything for him: his house, his car, his clothes.

'We'll go by Uig, if you don't mind,' Short said as they climbed into the car. 'There's a stretch of fast road that way where I can give this monster a work-out.'

As they were pulling out of the forecourt of the garage Short stopped the car to allow a young girl who was walking along the pavement to go by. The girl, who must have been no more than sixteen and wore the burgundy-coloured blazer of Portree High School, gave Short a cheeky wave and laughed. He waved back and sounded the Porsche's horn in reply.

'That's Wilda,' he told Mackinnon, 'a little friend of mine.' He gave the knowing, confidential grin of one man to another. 'Those High School girls look pretty sexy when they wear black stockings, don't you think?'

He drove well, handling the car with assured, economical movements. On the stretch of road between Borre and Uig he accelerated up past ninety. In front of them was a white van, also travelling towards Uig, but so much more slowly that it gave an illusion that it was moving backwards towards them. As they overtook it Short sounded his horn in two sharp blasts and raised a hand in greeting. The driver of the van acknowledged the signal, but the sound of his horn was almost lost as the Porsche sped away from it. Mackinnon recognised the van as the one he had followed on to the ferry at Lochalsh on his way to Skye.

'Who's the fishmonger?' he asked Short.

'That's Tom Grant, but he's a bit more than a fishmonger.'

'How's that?'

'Tom and a friend got some money together and started an enterprising business up along the coast.'

'In fish?'

'Shellfish, mainly; lobsters, crabs and prawns, but other fish as well.'

They reached Uig and as they drove down the hill into the town with the bay and the harbour beneath them to their left, Short explained that Tom Grant would load up his van with the fish they caught and cross over to the mainland. There he would drive round calling at expensive country house hotels in Mallaig, Fort William, Culloden and Cawdor.

'He's away for two or three days on each trip,' he added.

'How does he keep the fish fresh?'

'They fixed up the van so that it would keep cool – not refrigerated, you understand, but cool enough – by improvising with a second-hand air-conditioning unit.'

'Does he have to travel so far? Is there no market for his fish on Skye?'

'Not many people are prepared to pay his prices. I have a standing order with him and so does the Skeabost House Hotel, but that's about the limit to it. Strangely enough, the people on Skye don't eat much fish.'

Mackinnon recalled reading in a book about Skye that fishing had never been a major industry on the island. Attempts had been made to encourage it and as long ago as 1787 the British Fisheries Society had founded a fishing village in Stein, providing the boats and all the equipment needed, but the enterprise had foundered. One reason given was that the catches had been too meagre and too irregular to make fishing viable, another that the people of Skye believed that fishing was not a dignified occupation for able-bodied men.

'Tom and his pals are making a good living out of the business,' Short remarked.

'I'm surprised someone didn't think of it before.'

'People on Skye will grow what they need to feed themselves and even fish for themselves, but beyond that work hasn't much appeal for them. It's not so much laziness as lack of ambition. For most of the work I had done to my estate when I first came here we had to import contractors from the mainland.'

When they had driven through Uig and were climbing the hill on the far side, Short said, 'Have you driven along the old road to Staffin past the Quiraing?'

'Not yet.'

'Then let's go that way. It's shorter and it's the nearest thing to the Corniche that we have on Skye.'

When they had left the last houses of Uig behind he swung the Porsche off the main road to Kilmuir. The road he took on their right was little more than a track, winding up the hill in a succession of hairpin bends. With plenty of passing places it was safe enough if one drove conservatively, but Short went up it at speed, swinging round the bends and skilfully correcting the skids as the back of the car drifted. It was pure exhibitionism but Mackinnon did not mind. He remembered showing off himself when he had bought a sports car soon after he qualified as a doctor.

They reached the top of the hill, sped along a fairly level stretch and then the road wound down between rock faces on both sides. Short almost lost control on one unbelievably acute, hanging bend but recovered and presently they were travelling normally along the last stretch of road before it rejoined the main road from the north.

When he dropped Mackinnon outside Dr Tait's house, Short kept the engine of the Porsche running. 'Don't forget that you and Kirsten are dining with us just as soon as Gloria returns,' he said and drove away before there was time to thank him for his kindness.

Mackinnon let himself into the house and began preparing for evening surgery. It would be some time yet before the first patient was likely to arrive, so he started writing up the medical records of those he had visited that morning. When that was finished he went through the file of records and found one for Willie Gillespie. Willie had been to see Dr Tait with surprising frequency for a man who seemed to be robust and reasonably healthy. None of the complaints had been serious: dyspepsia, nausea, backache, insomnia, migraines. Mackinnon found himself wondering whether Willie had a drink problem. Complaints like the ones in his records might be genuine enough, but very often they concealed a more far-reaching problem. He checked on the dates of Willie's visits to the surgery and saw that a very large proportion of them had been on Monday mornings. That was a classic symptom, the drinker coming in after a weekend binge to get a doctor's note excusing him from work. Perhaps it had been his drinking that had lost Willie his job at the distillery. And that may have been the reason why he had started distilling his own whisky.

Mackinnon was still speculating about Willie's drinking and wondering what he should do if his theory proved to be correct when he heard a knock on the surgery door. The man who came in must have been over fifty and had his hair cropped short, a tattoo on the back of each hand and a paunch. He might have been a boxer who had given up the ring for beer and a soft life.

'I've brought you Gloria's car,' he told Mackinnon and tossed a set of car keys on the desk.

'Thanks very much. You've been quick.'

'Aye, it suited me to get off from work early for a change. Mostly I'm not home till after dark.'

'Then you live in Staffin?'

'Aye. I'm Murdo McPhee.'

66

Mackinnon was not sure whether he should offer McPhee a tip for driving the car to Staffin. By reputation the people of Skye were supposed to be proud and independent, but he had also heard that they exploited tourists rapaciously. While he was hesitating, McPhee saved him from having to make a decision.

'Do you have a dram, Doctor? I'm awful drouthy.'

'Of course. Let's go next door.'

The decanter of whisky was standing on a table in the drawing-room with a jug of water and glasses. Mackinnon began pouring. 'I'd best not have one,' he remarked, 'with surgery just due to start.'

McPhee laughed. 'I'd not let that stop you. Dr Tait wouldn't. His patients would no trust a doctor who didn't take a dram.'

Thinking that the man was probably right, Mackinnon poured himself a weak whisky and water. 'Do you travel to work in Sleat every day?' he asked.

'Aye. There's a van picks us up in the morning and brings us back in the evening.'

'Even so, it makes a long day.'

Carl Short's new factor, McPhee told him, was trying to save the expense of bringing contractors over from the mainland on a simple job like cutting timber. Sleat was sparsely populated so he had to bring men down there from as far away as Portree and Trotternish.

'It's not work I would bother myself with mostly, but it brings in a few bob till summer comes.'

'What work do you do in summer?'

'I help in a pub in Portree.'

'As a barman?'

'Do I look like a barman?' McPhee asked indignantly. 'No, I'm there to help. Some of the tourists we get here canna hold their drink.'

Mackinnon was surprised that any pub on Skye should find it necessary to have a hard man around to sort out trouble. His impression of the visitors who toured the Highlands and islands of Scotland in summer was that in the main they were elderly or middle-aged couples who might go into pubs hoping to get a feel of local customs but who were unlikely to get fighting drunk.

'The police were round here this morning talking to you, Doctor, were they not?' Mackinnon wondered whether the mention of bars and barmen might have reminded McPhee of Jamie Gillespie and his death.

'They were, yes.'

'They were around Staffin all morning, asking questions in the shop, in the churches, knocking on folk's doors, everywhere.'

'That's normal procedure in a murder investigation.'

'It was yourself made them believe it was murder.' If McPhee intended a reproach there was no hint of it in his tone.

'I only told the police what I saw.'

'Did they ask you about drugs? Everyone knows Jamie was off the drugs when he came home, but the police'll not believe it.'

'Are you certain he had given up the habit?'

'Aye. The lad told me so himself. He'd no lie to me. I'm a good friend of the family, you understand. Jamie always looked up to me.'

McPhee's glass was empty but he was holding it in a way which indicated that he was not ready to stop drinking. Mackinnon refilled it from the decanter, telling himself that he must buy Mrs Tait another bottle to replace the one he was dispensing so liberally.

'Surely the police will have asked you if you know where Jamie was getting his stuff while he was on the island?' McPhee asked.

'As a matter of fact they did.'

'They'll be thinking of course that Dr Tait was supplying the lad.'

'That's ridiculous! He would never do such a thing.'

'Aye, we know that, but the police will surely know about the trouble the doctor was in once before.'

'What trouble?'

'When he was in London the authorities accused him of supplying drugs to junkies.'

'I don't believe it!'

'It's true, right enough. He was hauled up before the medical body. What do they call it? The General Medical Council?'

7

That evening Mackinnon had supper with Kirsten in her cottage behind the craft centre. She had invited him ostensibly so that Hilda would have the evening free as well as midday, but he had the feeling that her real reason was because she wished to talk to him about Mairi's pregnancy. His suspicion appeared to be confirmed when on his arrival he found that Mairi was out having supper with friends.

'The friends are going to a ceilidh at a hotel up towards Dunvegan and they are taking Mairi with them. I said I would go and collect her later,' Kirsten explained and then she added, 'Have you ever been to a ceilidh?'

'Never.'

'Would you like to go for the last hour or so?'

'Very much. I'd enjoy that.'

'There'll be Gaelic singing, I've no doubt, and some country dancing. And of course a bar. On the island we can't do without our dram.'

'Dancing?' Mackinnon said flippantly. 'If you'd warned me I would have worn my kilt.'

'Thank Heavens you didn't!'

'Why not? People tell me I've just the knees for the kilt.'

'You didn't really bring a kilt with you to Skye!' Kirsten exclaimed and when he nodded she laughed.

'Blame my upbringing. My father was the most ardent Scot that you could imagine; a fanatic.'

He told Kirsten how his father, who had been working for an oil company in the Middle East, had persuaded the company to send him and his wife on a visit to off-shore oil rigs in Scotland just so that his son could be born in the country. So Charles, after being born in Aberdeen, had been brought up as a true Scot, made to wear the kilt, learn the poems of Burns, read Walter Scott and take country dancing lessons.

'I was even named Charles Edward after the prince.'

'But your father didn't send you to school in Scotland.'

'No, my mother wouldn't allow that. They were living abroad almost all the time and I had to go to boarding school. My mother had a married sister living in Kent, so I was sent to school in Canterbury, where she could keep an eye on me, and I spent the school holidays with her. My old man didn't like the idea, but he had to agree. He was a real Scot, a Jacobite. I never actually heard him toast the little gentleman in velvet, but I bet he did.'

'Then you're in luck today. I've cooked you a real Scottish supper.'

The supper consisted of Clootie dumplings, Cranachan and Caboc cheese with oatcakes. The name of all the dishes began with a 'C', Charles noticed, and he wondered whether this was a little whimsy on the part of Kirsten. She admitted that she had cheated with the Cranachan, which should really be a harvest dish of cream, toasted oatmeal and fresh soft fruit, but she said she had used frozen fruit. Charles had eaten Clootie dumplings before, both savoury and sweet, for his mother loved cooking and he had to concede that Kirsten's were every bit as good as any he had ever eaten.

After supper they sat drinking coffee in the living-room of the cottage where, because the night was cold, Kirsten had lit a fire. The room was comfortably rather than tastefully furnished, with two paintings of Skye scenes on the walls, which Charles was sure must be the work of a local artist. A sculpture in green marble of the head of a young man, the same man whose head in bronze was on display in the craft centre, stood on a table next to a vase full of daffodils from Sleat, the garden of Skye, Kirsten told him, where spring had already begun. The rich aroma of peat smoke from the

71

fire and the flowers gave the room an atmosphere of rustic tranquillity which Mackinnon found strangely appealing and he felt relaxed and confident, freed of the minor frustrations which had irritated him earlier in the day. Kirsten too seemed happy, because she had heard good news from Edinburgh. Her father was making a splendid recovery and would be taken out of the Intensive Care Unit the following day.

'My mother would like to stay on there for one more night,' she said. 'Will that be all right, Charles?'

'Of course. Tell her to stay for as long as she wishes.'

'Did you manage to find your way around on your calls this morning?'

'Nae bother.'

'That reminds me, are you having trouble with your car?'

Charles explained what had happened to the Toyota and that Carl Short had very kindly lent him Gloria's car. 'The Mercedes?' Kirsten asked. 'I wondered whether it might be hers.'

'It's a grand little car. I drove here over the Quiraing and the way it held the road on those hairpin bends was out of this world!'

'Did you go down to Carl's house to fetch the car?'

'No. A man named Murdo McPhee brought it up to Staffin for me.'

Kirsten looked at Charles sharply, suddenly alert and wary. 'Murdo's Mairi's cousin, you know.'

'Her cousin?'

'A distant cousin. Did he talk about her?'

'No. He never even mentioned her name.'

Kirsten seemed only partly reassured. 'I pray to God he doesn't find out that she's pregnant.'

'Why? What would he do?'

'Stamp around, threatening to find the man who's responsible and beat the hell out of him.'

'Is he that fond of her?'

'No way. Mostly he ignores her but he'd feel obliged to make a gesture. Murdo tries to live up to his reputation as a hard man.'

'Is he a hard man?'

Kirsten made a small, scoffing noise. 'Not at all! The man's all sound and wind. But he's cunning as well. Everyone knows that when Willie Gillespie and some others were found making whisky by Fiskavaig, Murdo was involved, but he managed to keep his nose clean.'

As Charles had expected, they had begun to talk about Mairi, although Kirsten had not started the conversation; he himself had by naming Murdo McPhee. And yet he sensed that she was still worrying about the girl, preoccupied with the problem which faced her as well as Mairi. The pleasure she had shown when she was telling him of her father's progress in hospital had slipped away like the patches of sunlight he had seen on the hills on Skye and had been replaced by a sombre cloud of depression. Charles was reluctant to meddle, but for Kirsten simply talking about the problem might help.

'Have you told Mairi?' He tested her reaction tentatively.

'That she's pregnant? No, I'm afraid to. There's no knowing what effect the news might have on her.'

'Would she be frightened, do you think?'

'Very probably. Or she might think it was fun, a new kind of game. She certainly wouldn't comprehend all the implications. I don't want to tell her until I can advise her what we should do.'

'Shouldn't you tell her father?'

'I suppose so, but oh God!' Kirsten shuddered. 'He'd be of no help. Very probably he'd say she has disgraced him as he always knew she would. And the whole island would be told about it.'

'I wish I could advise you.'

'You can't be expected to, Charles. It's not your responsibility.'

'I realise that, but I'd like to help.'

She had been leaning forward in her chair, looking into the fire. Now, abruptly, she sat erect, squaring her shoulders as though to shake off a load that had been bowing them. Although her life had been sheltered from trouble she was sensitive to the misfortunes of others, but did not have the resilience of Morag Gillespie and the other island women.

'I'll just go and wash the dishes,' she told Charles, 'and then we'll be away to the ceilidh.'

'I'll help you.'

They washed and dried the dishes in a kitchen that would have been too small to accommodate Morag Gillespie's new washing machine. As they worked, Kirsten told Charles about the ceilidh which was being held in a hotel near Dunvegan to raise money for a retired schoolmistress whose cottage had been destroyed by fire. Owing to a misunderstanding with her bank the insurance on the cottage had not been renewed and the schoolmistress had been left homeless. She had been much loved as the headmistress of a local school and now her former pupils were arranging a whole series of fund-raising events to have her cottage rebuilt. On this occasion the hotel, which was not yet opened for the summer season, had offered its dining-room as a place to hold the ceilidh and was providing refreshments, while the band and the piper were giving their services free so that all the proceeds from the sale of tickets would go to the fund.

'The folk of Skye may not always make strangers welcome,' Kirsten remarked, 'but they know how to care for their own.'

They drove to the ceilidh in Kirsten's car and when they reached the hotel the dining-room was full of people but not of noise. A young girl was singing unaccompanied in Gaelic and although they must have heard the song she was singing scores of times before one could sense the appreciation of her audience as they listened to her sweet, fragile voice. Next she sang another Hebridean song, in English this time, and everyone in the room joined in the chorus.

Charles was struck by a wide range in the ages of those who had come to the ceilidh. Parties he had attended in Edinburgh as a medical student and in London later were almost always for people in roughly the same age bracket. At the ceilidh that evening he could see adolescents, married couples and a sprinkling of pensioners, schoolchildren, crofters, shopkeepers and professional people, all mixing and enjoying themselves.

When the girl had finished her songs, he and Kirsten, who since they had arrived had been standing just inside the entrance to the room, moved further in and began to circulate. Almost everyone seemed to know Kirsten, several stopped to talk with her and Charles realised that she was well liked. She introduced him to a number of folk and all of them were friendly, asking him questions about himself and whether, with his name, his forbears had come from Skye. There was no shyness or reticence and he supposed that seeing him in the company of Dr Tait's daughter reassured people, as though that were a guarantee that he was to be trusted. He wondered how long he would have to live and work on Skye to be accepted in his own right.

When the band, led by a young woman playing an accordion, began playing a modern dance, a man who Charles did not know came and asked Kirsten to partner him. Uncertain whether an invitation from him to dance would be welcomed by the many women and girls of all ages who were standing round the edge of the room, and feeling conspicuous standing there on his own, Charles went into the hotel bar, which led off the dining-room and which had also been specially opened for the ceilidh.

The bar was crowded, mainly with men, and among them he recognised Tom Grant, the driver of the white van and partner in the fish business. Grant was surrounded by a group of young boys who looked scarcely old enough to be in licensed premises and they were talking animatedly to him in Gaelic, their conversation punctuated by a good deal of what sounded like obscene laughter.

Charles was standing at the bar drinking the whisky he had bought himself when the man next to him said, 'Would this be your first ceilidh, Dr Mackinnon?'

'It is.'

'I'm Constable Martin. I was in the station when you came in with Mrs Tait yesterday.'

'I'm sorry. I didn't recognise you.'

'You would not have seen me. I was in the office at the back.'

'This seems to be a successful evening,' Charles remarked. He had little experience of making small talk with policemen off-duty.

'I'm no great one for dancing,' the constable replied, 'nor for singing. But my wife plays in the band.'

'The accordion?'

'Aye. It's no a great band, you understand; not one of your pop groups, but there's little competition on the island. Winnie picks up a little cash playing and it keeps the lass out of mischief, I always say.'

Charles smiled. 'You're not on duty this evening, then?'

'I'd no be very popular if I was.' Charles may have glanced towards the boys at the far end of the bar, for Martin went on, 'You'll be thinking those lads should not be in here. Maybe you're right but there are times when I'm awful shortsighted. I canna make out their faces at this range.'

'Do you have the Gaelic?' Charles knew that one did not ask people if they spoke Gaelic.

'Aye. I'm Skye born and bred. Why, are you curious about what the lads are saying there?'

'I just wondered.'

'They're teasing young Tom Grant. "I'll bet you've had more screws than there are crisps in this packet," one of them said to him.'

'What was Tom's reply?'

'He only laughed. Mind you, it could well be true,' the constable said and then he added, 'Tom's a bit of a hero to the boys around here. He's one who has made good without leaving the island and that's uncommon.'

Portree High School, the constable explained, had an excellent reputation but its brightest pupils knew that they would have to leave Skye to find worthwhile careers. The island offered scarcely any opportunities for the professions; a handful of doctors, one or two lawyers and accountants, and it had no industry.

'Tammy's made good,' he concluded. 'Not like poor Jamie Gillespie.'

'You knew Jamie, then?'

'Aye. We were at school together.' The constable's glass was empty and he allowed Charles to buy him a dram. As he added water to the whisky he said thoughtfully, 'Jamie's is the second death at Kilt Rock. Fifty years ago folks would have been saying it was the work of the fairies.'

'What was the other death?'

'A woman killed herself by jumping off the cliff. At least the conclusion was that she had committed suicide.'

'When was this?'

'About a couple of years back.'

The woman had disappeared, he told Charles, and her car had been found above the cliff by Kilt Rock. It had been in winter with snow on the ground and next morning near where her car was found they had seen her footmarks, plenty of them, as though she had been walking backwards and forwards, distraught and trying to steel herself for suicide. Her body had never been found, but had she jumped into the sea the currents around that part of the coast might have carried it out into the Atlantic.

The constable may have had more to add to his story, but suddenly he stopped speaking as he looked over Charles's shoulder. Charles turned to look too and saw that Kirsten had come into the bar and was walking towards them. He was surprised, for he had not noticed that the band had stopped playing, and equally surprised to see that Kirsten was accompanied by Hector Monro.

'I didn't expect to find you at a ceilidh,' he said to Monro. 'Are you sure it's wise?'

'I'm fine. Fully recovered. That champagne we drank did the trick!' Monro grinned. 'I opened another bottle today. But don't worry. I shan't be dancing tonight.'

'Hector has donated the prizes for the raffle,' Kirsten explained, 'and he's here to present them. Have you bought any tickets for it?'

'No. Should I have?'

'Of course. There are two wee girls selling them in the other room. But hurry! The next dance is an eightsome reel and I intend to find out if you're really as Scottish as you claim.'

A kilted piper played for the eightsome reel. Kirsten took Charles on to the floor and they formed a set with three other couples, none of whom Charles recognised. The reel was danced very differently from the polished dances he had been taught and sometimes performed with country dance societies in Edinburgh. On Skye, he was learning, people danced vigorously, exuberantly and with humour. By the end both he and Kirsten were out of breath and she leaned on him for support, laughing.

'There's Mairi.' Charles nodded towards a far corner of the room where Mairi was standing among a group of girls. 'Should we go over to her?'

'No, not now. The more she enjoys herself alone with other kids the better. I don't want to seem too protective.'

Charles had noticed Mairi while they were dancing and had waved to her. She had returned the wave, half-heartedly, and had not given the impression that she was enjoying herself. It was possible, he supposed, that Kirsten over-valued the therapeutic effect on Mairi of being with other people of her own age. At a ceilidh or a dance the others might find her a drag.

As he and Kirsten were going back into the bar, Tom Grant came out. He stopped briefly, said something to Kirsten in Gaelic and laughed.

'Cheeky sod!' Kirsten exclaimed indignantly.

'What did he say?'

'It's best you don't know.' Surprisingly, Kirsten appeared to be blushing. 'He fancies himself, does our Tammy. Once he even made a pass at me!'

'Perhaps his wealth has gone to his head.'

'What wealth?'

'He's wearing a Rolex Oyster watch.'

Kirsten laughed. 'It's an imitation. He says it fell off the back of a lorry. As you know they make imitations of everything now in Hong Kong and Korea - watches, calculators, Scotch Whisky, everything.'

'Still, Tom seems to have done pretty well.'

'He has, even though when he was a lad at school everyone said he was lazy and a trouble-maker. But I'm surprised to find him here. One would not have thought that he's into ceilidhs. Night clubs would be more his line.'

The only person in the bar was Hector Monro, for everyone else had left for the hall of the hotel where refreshments were being served during an interval in the ceilidh. Tables had been laden with sandwiches, pork pies, ham and cheese rolls and generous slices of fruit cake, plenty of them, for most of the people at the ceilidh would have had their evening meal some hours ago when they arrived home from work and, after the exertion of dancing, would be ready for a substantial supper.

Hector was drinking mineral water. 'I despair of this island,' he grumbled. 'Do you know the hotel has no champagne on ice?'

'They wouldn't be expecting any demand for it.'

'I should have brought a bottle with me. The hotels on Skye know nothing about wines and how they should be served.'

'You should stick to whisky,' Kirsten advised him. 'Everybody knows it's much better for one.'

'I don't believe that for a moment.'

'It's true,' Charles told him. 'One or two glasses of Scotch a day helps to protect against heart disease.'

In less than fifteen minutes all the food on the tables in the hall had been eaten and people began coming back into the dining-room where the raffle was to be drawn. Charles had bought tickets for himself and Kirsten, so they went in to watch. The prizes had been laid out on a table at one end of the room, together with a large biscuit tin, which two small girls had been filling with the stubs of the tickets which had been sold under the supervision of Mrs Williamson, the wife of the hotel proprietor. Monro went to join them. When everything was ready, he picked up the biscuit tin, gave it a vigorous shake, withdrew one of the tickets and called out a number. The main prize, a huge bottle of Mackinlay's Scotch whisky, was won by a post office engineer who was on Skye only to repair some telephone lines and the tepid applause when he went to collect his prize showed the general disappointment that it had not been won by an islander. More prizes were drawn: a presentation pack of six whisky miniatures, a plaid scarf, a celtic brooch. Every time, Hector shook the tin before drawing out a ticket stub.

Then the number of one of the tickets that Charles had bought was called out. He showed it to Kirsten and she told him, 'Then go and get your prize.'

People clapped as he crossed the floor and somebody shouted 'Good old doc', which he felt was reassuring. The prize which Mrs Williamson handed him was a packet of ten small cigars of a brand often advertised on television. While he was thanking her, Hector suddenly interrupted.

'You've given the doctor the wrong prize, Mrs Williamson!'

'Surely not?'

'Yes, yes! The box of chocolates was due to be the next prize.' Hector seemed upset. 'Those silly girls have made a mistake.'

Reaching out, he took the packet of cigars from Charles and handed him a box of chocolates which he had quickly grabbed from the table behind him. 'You don't mind, do you, Doctor? After all, you don't even smoke.'

'Of course not!'

After Charles had rejoined Kirsten more prizes were distributed: another, smaller box of chocolates, a pair of knitted gloves, the cigars and a tie with matching hand-kerchief. Charles noticed that Tom Grant won the cigars. He seemed pleased with his prize and lit one immediately. After the prizegiving the ceilidh continued. A bank clerk from Portree with a fine, light tenor voice, who had won medals at the Mod, the annual festival of Gaelic music, sang two songs and there was more dancing. Charles allowed himself to be persuaded to join in three Scottish dances – the Dashing White Sergeant and the Duke of Perth, which he had known in Edinburgh as Clean Pea Strae, and the Machine Without Horses, a dance popular in Skye that he had not danced before but which he found easy to follow.

Soon after midnight Kirsten went to call Mairi and the three of them broke back to her cottage. Mairi scarcely smiled when Charles presented her with the chocolates he had won and she sat silently in the back of the car on the drive home.

The mist which hung over the lochs had lifted and the evening was cold and clear. There had been a little snow during the previous night which, like all late snow, had quickly melted in the morning except on the hills.

'The last snow before the summer,' Kirsten told Charles. 'We often have a flurry at this time; a taut little warning from winter that he'll be back next year.'

'The new soft-fallen mask,' Charles replied. 'It adds a new beauty to the hills.'

'Now, we'll have none of your erotic verse, please!'

'Erotic?'

'You'll be banging on about your fair love's ripening breast next,' she teased him.

'Sorry. I quote snatches of poetry without thinking.'

'Do you read much poetry?'

'Hardly any. It's just a legacy of my schooldays. I had an uncanny facility for memorising verse. If I read any poem twice I could recite it perfectly. Now, even after all these years, the words come bubbling out.'

'Don't be ashamed. It proves that in spite of all that grisly medical training you've retained a soul!'

Charles knew she was laughing at him, but not unkindly. He might have teased her in return, feigning incredulity at finding a former nurse in the middle of a Hebridean island who could match him in quoting Keats, but he decided to keep any comment for another occasion. Intuition told him that Kirsten might yet surprise him in many more ways.

When Kirsten stopped the car in front of the cottage and switched off the engine they heard a muffled noise coming from behind them. Mairi was crying, her stifled, convulsive sobs sounding like the noise of an animal in pain.

'What's the matter, darling?' Kirsten called out anxiously, turning to look at the girl.

Instead of replying, Mairi jumped out of the car and ran into the cottage, still holding her box of chocolates, her sobs, no longer checked, becoming a doleful wailing. They heard her run up the stairs of the cottage and the door of her bedroom slam.

'I must go to her,' Kirsten said. 'What on earth can have happened?'

'I'll be off, then.'

'No, come on in. See if you can rescue the fire and I'll be down presently.'

Charles found that there was still a dim red centre of fire in the ashes and after careful raking and coaxing brought it to life and added blocks of peat from the stack in the hearth. As he did, he wondered what might have provoked Mairi's tears. He had seen her dancing at the ceilidh with a man who had been pointed out to him as a local schoolmaster and again with an elderly crofter whose kilt revealed boney legs but who danced nimbly in spite of them. Only to be asked to dance twice might be a disappointment but not strong enough for tears as among other girls, prettier and more lively than she, Mairi surely would not expect to receive attention and flattery.

When Kirsten came downstairs again she poured him a whisky. 'Only a small one,' Charles warned her. 'I've to drive home, remember.'

'You'll not take the road over the Quiraing, will you?'

'Not on your life! Not at this hour and in a borrowed car. Did you find out what's upset Mairi?'

'No, she refuses to say. I've never known her to be like this. She has moods, yes, but usually, like the moods of a small child, they are brief and passing. She's a happy little soul.'

'Perhaps she'll tell you in the morning.'

'I hope she'll have forgotten whatever upset her by then. I gave her some Valium.'

Charles had not seen any Valium prescribed for Mairi in Dr Tait's medical records. He supposed it was possible that Kirsten might have her own supply, but he had not thought she was a person who would ever need sedatives or tranquillisers. Like her mother she gave the impression of having inner resources that would enable her to cope with any emotional or nervous crisis.

They sat for a time in silence, staring into the fire. Then Charles asked her, 'Did you know that Jamie Gillespie had AIDS?'

'Yes, my mother told me.'

'Do you suppose that may have been the reason why he was murdered?'

'What do you mean?'

'Many people have an almost superstitious fear of AIDS. Sufferers are treated with hostility and disgust. They are shunned and sometimes even abused and attacked.'

'Are you suggesting that Jamie was killed because he brought AIDS to the island and the islanders wanted to get rid of him?'

'I think it's possible.'

'Charles, I can't believe it!' Kirsten was appalled. 'I won't believe that!'

'Skye is a close, strongly knit community.' Charles wanted to use the word 'tribal', but he was afraid Kirsten might misconstrue and resent it.

'That may be true but the islanders are not vicious. You saw tonight how they look after anyone in trouble. They are kind, caring folk.'

'I'm probably wrong. It was just a theory.'

'No, I won't believe it.'

Soon afterwards, when Charles decided he must leave, she went out to the Mercedes with him. The night was really cold now, with frost in the air. Kirsten shivered.

'The hare limped trembling through the frozen grass,' she quoted. 'I can understand how he felt.'

Charles felt a sudden impulse to put his arm around her shoulders to warm her. 'Get inside before you catch pneumonia,' he said in a doctor's brusque manner, in case she might sense what he was thinking.

'What are you doing tomorrow afternoon?' she asked him. 'There's no evening surgery on a Wednesday.'

'Nothing. Why?'

'Would you like to go walking in the Cuillins? It's high time we showed you the better face of Skye.'

'Sounds great!'

'Then come round and pick me up as soon as you've done your morning calls. I'll have sandwiches ready for both of us.'

8

'Folks say you're a lively dancer,' Mrs Kennedy told Charles.

'You'll have heard about last night's ceilidh, then?'

'Aye, and they say you danced as well as anyone.'

'Not really. My dancing's a little rusty. I don't get much practice down in London.'

'And whose fault is that?' the old lady demanded belligerently. 'You should be living and working among your own folk.'

As he chatted to Mrs Kennedy, Charles found the irritation which had soured his mood for most of the morning gradually subsiding. The annoyance had been prompted by another visit from Superintendent Grieve. He had arrived at the house before surgery and his visit had begun with a request that he and his sergeant should be allowed to check Dr Tait's register of dangerous drugs. Like some other general practitioners in rural areas, Tait dispensed medicines and under the Dangerous Drugs Act he was obliged by law to keep such drugs locked in a cupboard and to keep a record of all the quantities he bought and dispensed. Charles had protested that, as a locum, he could not be expected to allow the police access to the drugs, but when Grieve pointed out that he could easily get a search warrant and any other authority that might be needed he had given way, although under protest. The police had checked the drugs in the cupboard and the register and then locked them away again. Grieve concealed his disappointment at not finding any discrepancies. The outer veneer of his *bonhomie* may have been stripped away, but nothing more.

'Have you any reason for believing that Doctor Tait may have misused his drugs?' Charles asked him.

'I'm sorry, sir. At this stage I am not in a position to answer that question.'

Grieve smiled as he spoke. The smile may have been intended to reassure Charles, or it may have been a mild rebuke, an assertion that the police were in control and knew what they were doing. Whatever its purpose, it only intensified Charles's irritation and to make sure that he was not venting it on his patients, he was almost excessively polite and tolerant at surgery and during his calls. He had left his visit to Jeanie Kennedy to the last and was amused when he noticed his mood lighten. Was it she who was providing therapy for him, he wondered, and not he for her, as he had supposed.

'I won a box of chocolates in the raffle,' he told her.

'What were the other prizes?'

He listed as many of the prizes as he could recall and then added, 'Mr Monro was very generous.'

Jeanie sniffed. 'He likes playing the laird, that one. He was never very generous to his wife, the poor soul. She used to work all hours to keep that hotel of theirs going, while he fished and stalked and drank whisky.'

'Mrs Tait told me the hotel was very successful.'

'That was only after the Italian came to work for them. Master Hector was never one for running a hotel, but his wife, she had hotels in her blood.'

The hotel which Hector and his wife Phyllis owned, Jeanie explained, had originally belonged to Phyllis's parents. Hector himself was from Dundee and he had met his wife when on holiday in Skye. She had been captivated by him and, as he worked only as a clerk in an insurance company, after they married he came to live with her family and help run the hotel. When her parents died they had inherited the business, but running a hotel on Skye was always a struggle. Theirs had been poorly situated and was open for only six months of the year. While Phyllis's parents had been alive they had managed well enough, but after their death increasingly the work and the responsibility had fallen on her.

'Then one day out of the blue this Italian arrives, looking for work. Happens he's a cook and in no time he turns their dining-room into a proper restaurant and people from all over the island start to eat there.'

'What kind of food did they serve there?'

'I dinna ken. It wasn't folks like me went there. Those that did said the portions were so small they wouldn'a satisfied a wee mouse. Laid out on the dish in bonnie colours and everyone was given a thimbleful of some foreign drink when they arrived by a local lass whom they dressed up in a frilly dress.'

'It sounds like nouvelle cuisine to me.'

'Whatever it was, the visitors liked it. And Mrs Monro did the dining-room up with fancy curtains and polished tables and chairs that wouldn'a take the weight of a real man, but no tablecloths. Did you ever hear the like of it? No tablecloths; not even a piece of oilcloth. For all that it must have cost a pretty penny.'

'It must have been a good investment. Mr Monro seems comfortably off now.'

'Aye. Giving the prizes. But those dances they call ceilidhs are not real ceilidhs, not like the ones we had when I was a lass.'

Jeanie Kennedy began telling Charles about the ceilidhs of past years. In those days when there was no public entertainment, no cinemas, no television or radio, people made their own entertainment in their homes. They would gather together in somebody's cottage, sit round the peat fire and take it in turns to sing or recite or tell stories. That was how the songs and legends of the Gaelic language, the tales of Ossian and Cuchullin and the Fiennes, the giants from Ireland, were handed down through the centuries.

When Charles decided it was time for him to leave,

Jeanie Kennedy asked him, 'Are you calling on Morag Gillespie today?'

'I was not intending to. Why?'

'Maybe you should. The poor soul was up for most of the night.'

'How do you know?'

'I saw lights in her house and not just in her bedroom; first upstairs and then downstairs. Someone was not sleeping at all.'

On his way to Morag Gillespie's house Charles reflected that Jeanie Kennedy herself must have been awake for most of the night, watching the lights go on and off in the Gillespie house. Could she have seen them from where she lay in bed, he wondered, or did she sit up in the same chair as she sat in during the day, gazing at the windows of her neighbours' cottages – for there would be nothing else to watch – trying to guess what the neighbours might be doing? As a boy, when travelling by train at night, he had done the same, looking at the lights of solitary houses in the black countryside, trying to imagine what domestic dramas of passion or anger were being played out behind the curtained windows. He wondered how much Jeanie Kennedy slept. She did not complain of insomnia, aware perhaps that all there was left for her was the role of a lonely spectator watching life being played on a stage from a distant seat on the fringes of death. Charles felt a sudden compassion for her age and for her loneliness.

When Morag Gillespie opened her door to him he saw at once that she had been weeping. Her eyes were red, her face drawn and pale, her hair still in curlers.

'Are you all right, Mrs Gillespie?' he asked her.

For a moment he thought she was not going to let him into the house and was ashamed that he should see her in a moment of emotional weakness. Then she stepped aside and as he passed her in the doorway Charles repeated the question.

'My money's gone,' she said. 'All the money my lad gave me.'

'Are you saying that someone stole it?'

'Aye. It was there when I last looked.'

'Where were you keeping it?'

'Under the floor in my bedroom.'

With a succession of questions Charles extracted a fumbling, inarticulate account of what had happened. Her son Jamie, besides buying her a television set and the washing machine, had given his mother money. Mrs Gillespie could not say exactly how much money, but hundreds of pounds anyway, perhaps thousands. She had never seen so much money, all in notes, many of them fifty-pound notes. Jamie had packed the notes carefully in a number of cellophane bags so that she would be able to take them out, one at a time, as she needed money. Then, together, they had placed the bags in a plastic shopping bag and hidden it beneath a floorboard in her bedroom.

'Was anything else stolen?' Charles asked her.

'No, but the room had been searched, drawers pulled out and emptied, clothes thrown on the floor. Maybe whoever it was thought I had nothing else worth taking.'

'How long ago did you and Jamie hide the money?'

Mrs Gillespie shook her head. 'Two weeks back, maybe. Maybe a little more.'

'And did no one else know the money was there?'

'Not a soul. Jamie said it was to be our secret.' She looked at Charles. 'What should I do, Doctor?'

'There's only one thing you can do, Mrs Gillespie. Tell the police.'

'How can I? Who knows how he got the money. It wouldn'a be legal; one can be sure of that.'

The path along Glen Sligachan was rough and stony and, after the rains of winter, still boggy in places, so that Charles was glad that he had stopped off in Portree on his way to Kirsten's cottage and bought himself a pair of boots. They had left Kirsten's car by the Sligachan Inn, crossed the road and taken the path which led to Loch Coruisk. The loch, Charles knew, was the most famous on Skye, painted by

Turner and described by Walter Scott – a solitary sheet of water lying in a deep basin and surrounded by mountains of savage beauty. They would not go as far as the loch that day, Kirsten had decided, for the walk was almost eight miles and they would not have enough time to reach it and return. Charles suspected that she was concerned not so much about time as about him, feeling that an unfit creature from the soft south of England would find a fifteen-mile walk too much.

After they had covered two miles or so she pointed ahead of them and to the right. 'That's the entrance to Harta Corrie,' she said. 'The scene of one of the many bloody battles between the Macdonalds and the Macleods. But we're looking at nature today, not history, so let's turn off here and climb Marsco.' She pointed towards a mountain which towered above them on their left and then, confirming Charles's suspicions that she had doubts about his stamina, she added, 'It's not a difficult climb; not much more than a stiff walk, but we'll get a fine view from the summit.'

As they started walking up the lower slopes of the mountain Charles asked, 'What's Mairi doing today?'

'Spending the afternoon with friends in Edinbane. There'll be no one wanting to call at the shop and I don't like leaving her alone in her present mood.'

'She's still upset, then?'

'Very. More tears at breakfast and then suddenly she was away upstairs and locked herself in her room.'

'Have you no idea what the trouble is?'

'No, but of course it could be connected with her being pregnant.'

'In what way?'

'When she came to live with me, Mairi had never experienced sex. I'm sure of that. Perhaps when she was a girl boys may have interfered with her, you know the sort of thing, but nothing more. Then, quite recently, some man must have seduced her. She may have liked the experience.'

'Very probably.' Charles remembered how he had been aware of Mairi's sexuality when he had been examining her.

'She's a very affectionate little creature. What if she trans-ferred all her affection to that man, became obsessed with him, wanted him to make love to her again? And what if he would have nothing more to do with her? Ignored her? Would Mairi understand? She would be hurt, terribly hurt and upset.'

'If this were true perhaps she would tell you.'

'Perhaps. If I asked her the right questions. I'll try but at the right moment.'

'I wish I could be of help.'

'I know you do, Charles. You're very kind.' Kirsten reached out and squeezed his arm.

As they climbed on they stopped talking, for the slope became much steeper and the going hard. Kirsten led and Charles followed her as she picked her way surely over the rough ground, avoiding loose stones and boggy patches. As they ascended, it grew colder and Charles could feel a sharp wind around his neck and ears. His legs were beginning to ache now and he was relieved that they appeared to be approaching the top of the mountain.

'At last!' he exclaimed, pointing ahead of them. 'Now we'll be able to stop and admire the view.'

Kirsten laughed. 'Not yet. That's a false summit and there are at least three more before we reach the top.' Charles groaned and she laughed again. 'I'll take pity on you. Let's stop for lunch. I'm starving.'

She had brought sandwiches for both of them in a shoul-der bag, some of beef and some of cream cheese, and a flask of coffee. After they had eaten and were sharing the coffee, she produced another flask, of whisky this time, and two small silver cups. They drank the whisky neat, as malt whisky should be drunk, she told him, when one was on the mountains or the moors or out fishing or stalking. At home she would always take it with an equal amount of water. The water must be cold and soft, though, for the hard chlorinated water that flowed from taps in London and the other cities of the south would ruin the flavour of the whisky.

'Have you always drunk whisky?' Charles asked her.

'Ever since I was about sixteen. When I left home to be a nurse my father made me promise only to drink whisky when I went to parties, either neat or with water. That way no scheming medical student would be able to doctor my drink without my knowing.'

'That's rather a harsh judgement of medical students.'

'Oh, I don't know. My father had been one too.'

'Have you had any news of him, by the way?'

'Yes, my mother rang me before she left Edinburgh at noon. Dad's fine. He's out of the ICU and will be moved into a private hospital in a few days.'

The summit of Marsco was covered with a light, powdery snow. When they reached it and were admiring the view Charles noticed that there was snow on most of the peaks of the Red Cuillins to the east of where they stood, but none on the Black Cuillins to the west, even though the range was higher with several mountains of well over 3000 feet. When he pointed this out to Kirsten she told him that legend had an explanation.

A million years ago there were no mountains to the west of them, only a lonely heather-covered moor where Winter, the fearsome Cailleach Bhur, would roam. Spring hated her and fought with her but she was too powerful for him, so he invoked the help of the Sun. The Sun hurled his spear at the hag and where it struck the moors they exploded, throwing up a molten mass of rocks and earth which became the Black Cuillins. Centuries passed before they cooled and even now the snow of Cailleach Bhur never lay long on their fiery hills.

Listening to Kirsten telling the story as they descended the mountain, Charles recalled the irritation that had infected much of his morning. He had deliberately not mentioned the cause of his irritation to Kirsten but now he knew he must risk spoiling the pleasure they had shared that afternoon by telling her. He waited until they were at the foot of Marsco and had set out along Glen Sligachan towards the hotel.

'The police came to the house this morning,' he told her.

'Again? What for?'

'They insisted on checking the dangerous drugs in your father's surgery.'

'Why on earth should they wish to do that?'

Charles knew he must be frank. Nothing but the truth would satisfy Kirsten and she would not expect it to be diluted for her. 'Superintendent Grieve appears to believe that your father might have been giving drugs to Jamie Gillespie.'

Kirsten stopped walking and turned to face him. For several seconds she stared at him as though trying to decide whether he was being serious or teasing her. Then she said dismissively, 'He's mad!' and started walking along the glen again.

Not until they were in the car driving towards Portree did she come back to the subject. 'My mother will be furious when she hears that the police have been checking Dad's drugs.'

'And well she might be. I protested but Grieve wouldn't listen. He threatened to get a search warrant if I refused.'

'But people said Jamie had given up taking drugs.'

'If he hadn't, could he have been getting them from another source on Skye?'

'If he had, we would have heard about it. There are precious few secrets here.'

They drove on in silence for a while. Then Kirsten said, 'Charles, I have a feeling that you've something more to tell me.'

'About the police?'

'Not necessarily. It's just that I feel you've something on your mind.'

Charles paused. She was right. He had a question he felt he must ask but it would have to be carefully phrased, dispassionate, not implying any judgement on his behalf. Finally he said, 'Might it be that the police believe your father has been in trouble over drugs before?'

Kirsten's hesitation was no more than momentary and her tone when she replied was calm and measured, but Charles sensed the flaring alarm which his question had ignited, an alarm which needed all her self-control to prevent becoming panic.

'Why should they believe that?'

'It would explain their behaviour in this business.'

They were on a straight stretch of road, probably the best and widest stretch on the island and immediately in front of them it had been widened still further to provide a place where cars could be parked. Without warning and without comment Kirsten swung the car off the road and into the lay-by, drew it to a halt and switched off the engine.

'Did the police tell you that was their reason for coming to check up on the drugs?'

'No, but it was the obvious inference to draw.'

'You're not being honest with me, Charles. That may be the truth but it isn't the whole truth. Somebody must have told you this – this story about my father. Who was it?'

'I think it's best I don't tell you.' Charles had no wish to sour relations between Dr Tait and one of his patients.

Kirsten shook her head in disbelief. 'But nobody on Skye knows!'

'Then it's true?'

'Of course it isn't true! Dad was never in trouble. He was falsely accused but completely exonerated.'

She told Charles the story. Years ago, when he was a young doctor, Tait had gone to do a locum in a country practice in Wales for a GP who, he had been told, was taking an extended holiday to visit his son in Australia. As Tait did in Staffin, the GP dispensed his own medicines and after he had been running the practice for a time an anonymous complaint had been made to the Disciplinary Committee of the General Medical Council that Tait, as the locum, was selling dangerous drugs to street operators. The enquiries that followed showed in the Dangerous Drugs Register discrepancies that had been cunningly concealed. Patients came forward to give evidence against Kirsten's father and it was only after prolonged investigations that the truth was learned. The GP had been a drug addict for years and was not in Australia but taking a cure in Austria. In spite of

94

his addiction he was a good doctor and his patients, who were devoted to him, had hoped that by incriminating the Scottish locum they would forestall the likelihood that he would discover the discrepancies in the drugs register and expose him.

'Do you find that hard to believe?' Kirsten asked Charles when she had finished telling him the story.

'No way. Plenty of doctors are protected by their patients and continue to practise even when they are hopelessly addicted or alcoholic.'

'This happened years ago; forty years, maybe. I don't see how anyone on Skye could know of it.'

'Your father told your mother, of course.'

'Of course, and the three of us daughters. The whole affair frightened him horribly. He could see himself being struck off, his career ruined, even though he was innocent. It left him with an unforgiving prejudice against the Welsh and I believe he told us about it as a kind of warning. But he would not have told anyone else.'

'There are ways of finding these things out. Minutes of committee meetings and press reports are never expunged and the damage that the skeleton of a scandal can do to innocent people is always there, waiting to be exhumed.'

'But who would wish to do that? Who hates my father enough for that? I can't believe it, unless— ' She stopped in mid-sentence and then, leaning forward, restarted the car's engine.

After they had driven through Portree and were heading for Staffin it was dark and the lights of isolated cottages reminded Charles of his conversation with old Mrs Kennedy that morning and of the loneliness of life on Skye. Loneliness one could endure and even enjoy if, beyond the lighted windows, one could sense a waiting warmth and kindness and sincerity, but more and more the solitude of Skye was beginning to seem as no more than a mask behind which he found, increasingly, a cynical selfishness that was ready to tolerate violence and corruption. When they reached the Taits' home, they saw the Rover standing outside the house.

'She's back!' Kirsten exclaimed, her uneasiness melting instantly in the warmth of pleasure.

Mrs Tait had heard the car pulling up and she was already standing in the open doorway when they reached it. 'How's Dad?' Kirsten asked at once.

'Great! He's doing splendidly,' her mother replied, but there was concern in her eyes and she kissed Kirsten's cheek almost absentmindedly. 'Morag Gillespie's inside. You'll need to give her a sedative, Charles. She's hysterical.'

'Why? What's happened?'

'Willie has been arrested. The police believe he killed Jamie.'

9

As he looked at the two people who sat facing him across the table, Detective Superintendent Grieve showed no signs of the indecision that was irritating him. For several minutes he had been stalling, but he knew that soon he must make up his mind on how he should respond to their questions. The woman had asked him their main question already – why had he arrested Willie Gillespie? – and he had replied correctly but evasively that Gillespie had not been arrested but was merely being questioned.

'Oh, yes. He's helping you with your enquiries. Isn't that how you phrase it? And in due course he will be charged and arrested.'

'Not necessarily.'

The reason for Grieve's indecision was that away from his home patch he found it difficult to assess the level of co-operation that the two people should be given. Co-operation in his way of thinking was synonymous with respectful subservience. He was not much concerned about the young doctor. Clever, he might be, and determined, but as an incomer and one from the south of England he would carry no clout on Skye. The older doctor's wife was something else. Tait might not be the most important medic on the island but he was the most senior in experience; the kind of man whom the Government, in the form of the Scottish Home and Health Department, might consult. As such he might have influence and he was certainly well liked and respected on the island. Grieve did not attach much importance to the anonymous tip-off he had received to the effect that Tait had been involved in drug offences before. In his experience anonymous tip-offs were made through malice and were often exaggerated, if not actually false.

'Surely you can tell us why you're holding Willie?' Mrs Tait asked him.

'He can have a lawyer if he wishes one.'

'We'll get him a lawyer,' Mrs Tait said firmly, 'if and when he needs one. Surely it would do no great harm to tell us why you have brought him to the station for questioning?'

Grieve decided reluctantly to give in. 'As far as we know, he was the last person to see his brother alive.'

'Or was I?' Charles asked. Mrs Tait had asked him to come with her to see the police. He did not know why, but if she wanted moral support then he ought to contribute what he could.

'Let me put it another way,' Grieve replied. 'Willie Gillespie was seen with his brother, in his brother's car, driving away from Portree on the afternoon when Jamie died.'

'What's so surprising about that?'

'Nothing, except that when we first questioned Willie he told a different story. The two of them had been drinking in a pub in Portree from about midday. Willie told us that when his brother left in the afternoon he stayed on. We know differently now, so why did he lie?'

'What does he say now?'

'That it was the drink which made him forget he left the pub with Jamie. Now that his memory has returned, he claims that they drove back to Staffin together, where Jamie dropped him off in the village. He says he doesn't know where Jamie went after that.'

'You sound as though you don't believe him, Superintendent.'

'We've found no one who recalls seeing him in Staffin that afternoon.'

Grieve did not feel obliged to tell them what he knew

about Willie Gillespie's movements on the day of his brother's death, that he had been recognised by a police sergeant coming out of a pub in Broadford at around nine that evening, that his mother had reluctantly admitted that she had seen nothing of him all afternoon and evening and he had not come home when she went to bed well after midnight.

'And where does he say he went after Jamie dropped him in Staffin?' Mrs Tait asked.

'He's hazy about that. Says he went drinking in an inn below Staffin and can't recall what happened after that.'

'It sounds to me as though you've made him so frightened that he's saying the first thing that comes into his head.'

Willie Gillespie was frightened, badly frightened. Grieve knew that and he was going to make sure that the man remained frightened. If Willie had thrown his brother off Kilt Rock it was going to be hard to prove. Mackinnon's account of what he thought he had seen would be valueless as evidence, for he could not identify either of the figures he had seen on the top of the cliff. The forensic people had begun work but Grieve did not believe they would find anything that could be used as scientific proof. There had been no fight so there would be no blood or scratches and if fabric from the dead man's clothes were found on Willie's it would mean nothing, as they had been living in the same house and riding about in the same car. The best hope for a quick end to the business was a confession, and a frightened man could be cowed into making one.

'There's also the question of the money,' Grieve said.

'What money?' Charles asked quickly.

'Since Jamie died, Willie has been spending freely, on drink, mostly, brandishing ten-pound notes. As he's unemployed and generally skint, we'd like to know where the money came from.'

'What does Willie say?'

'That Jamie gave him a hundred pounds when they were driving back from Portree on the day he died.'

'He says he gave him a hundred pounds? Just like that?'

'Willie claims he wondered at the time if it might be a goodbye present and that Jamie intended to return to Edinburgh.'

Soon afterwards Mrs Tait and Charles left the police station. They realised that if Grieve had any further reasons for suspecting Willie of having murdered his brother he was not going to disclose them. Their visit had achieved little, but Charles had expected no more and they had only gone to see the police because Mrs Tait had promised Morag Gillespie that she would do all she could to help Willie.

As they were driving back to Staffin, Mrs Tait asked Charles, 'Do you suppose that Jamie might have given Willie that hundred pounds?'

'Why should he have?'

'If he had money to spare, he might well have. Like many homosexuals he was kind and gentle and considerate. As long as he was living at home he did his best to help his mother and he was always very sweet with Mairi. He would play with her, take her out for walks, try to teach her things. Yes, I honestly believe that if he had money he would share it with his mother and brother.'

'Did you know he bought his mother a washing machine?'

'Yes, and that television set.'

Charles wondered whether Mrs Tait knew about the money that Morag Gillespie and Jamie had hidden beneath the floorboards of their home. Morag had told him, so surely she would have told Mrs Tait, but making her promise not to tell the police. He recalled how late in the night when he arrived on Skye he had seen Mrs Tait leaving the house. She had gone to see Morag Gillespie, he was sure of that, but why? Because she had guessed that it had been Jamie whom Charles had seen thrown off Kilt Rock? Or had there been another reason? As an incomer he could not expect to understand the nuances of a relationship between two Skye women.

'I refuse to believe that Willie could possibly have killed Jamie in that horrible way.'

100

Although he scarcely knew the man, Charles was inclined to agree. 'It doesn't seem very likely.'

'Willie's not very bright, and he's inclined to be lazy, but there's no malice in him. He could never kill anyone in cold blood.'

'Has he a temper?'

'No more than most of us. His main weakness is that he's easily led. He would never have thought of distilling whisky illegally on his own.'

'Who did, then?'

'Murdo McPhee, and he was cunning enough to let the other two take the blame and the consequences.'

'One gets the impression that Murdo's a bad lot.'

'Not really.' Mrs Tait smiled. 'My trouble is that I can never find any wrong, any real wrong, in our patients. As Donald is always saying, all my geese are swans. Though, mark you, he's as bad as I am.'

The day was fine and as they approached Kilt Rock they could see the face of the cliff with its long, vertical grooves. In the bright mid-morning sunshine its proportions had an ecclesiastical majesty which reminded Charles of the vast ceiling of the cathedral in Canterbury where he had spent so many hours. The macabre, silent pantomime he had seen performed on the cliff's top was still etched in his memory, but it was losing its horror.

'I was told that a woman killed herself by jumping off Kilt Rock,' he remarked to Mrs Tait.

'Yes. At least, one has to assume it was suicide.' Mrs Tait shuddered. 'Even now I can't bear to think about it.'

'Who was she?'

'Phyllis Monro.'

'Hector's wife?'

'Yes.'

That afternoon Charles went for a long walk around Staffin Bay. Hilda, perhaps to welcome Mrs Tait home after her brief visit to the mainland, had cooked them an enormous meal of Cullen Skink, a fish soup that had been a favourite

101

of his when he lived in Edinburgh, with a thick mutton stew to follow. Charles told Mrs Tait that he needed exercise after a meal much larger than any he would usually eat in the middle of the day, but he had another reason for wanting to go. A stiff walk of several miles would help to prepare him for his next visit to the Cuillins. Kirsten had promised him they would go again soon and he was determined to tackle a more strenuous walk this time, climbing high enough to enjoy the exhilaration and full splendour of the mountains. She had seemed to take pity on him for his lack of fitness during their walk the previous afternoon and his pride had been dented.

As he walked he found himself thinking of Willie Gillespie. Nothing the police had said that morning had changed his opinion that Willie would never have murdered his brother. Working in a London hospital and especially when on duty in casualty on a Friday or Saturday evening, Charles had met many violent people. He had learned that the victims of violence and those who handed it out had much in common. He had begun to believe that he could recognise – though not understand – the compulsion that drove them, almost unwillingly in many cases, to club with their fists, butt with their heads, thrust their knees into groins or to the mayhem of machetes, Stanley knives and bicycle chains or to the ultimate in self-expression, the sawn-off shotgun. Violent men were brutish, unfeeling, stupid and more often than not physical cowards. Willie might be all of those but he was not, Charles felt sure, violent, and certainly not a murderer.

Thinking of Willie Gillespie made him wonder at the way he was gradually becoming involved in the lives of Dr Tait's patients; in Willie's arrest, if it could be called that, in the problem of Mairi's pregnancy and in the loneliness of Jeanie Kennedy. The medical student friends with whom he had kept in touch and who had gone into general practice did not appear to have become so involved with their patients. Mostly they practised in health centres, working with several other doctors and centralised services, sharing duties on a rota and seeing patients in much the same way as bank managers interviewed prospective borrowers. On Skye, by contrast, GPs had to be more than doctors; they had to be confessors, chauffeurs, legal advisers and even washing-machine technicians. He wondered whether, if he had to live and work in a rural practice, he would like this close, personal relationship and decided that perhaps he might, though not on Skye.

He walked for two hours at a good pace, around the bay and back, trying to convince himself that his calves and thighs were not stiffening up as they had the previous afternoon. Approaching Staffin on his way home, he decided impulsively to call on Jeanie Kennedy. His trip to Portree with Mrs Tait that morning after surgery had delayed him, obliging him to make his calls in a hurry, and as there was no medical reason for seeing Jeanie he had not stopped at her house. Now he would pay her at least a social visit. Her manner when he arrived was brusque.

'I was no expecting you, Doctor.'

'I know, but I was passing and surely on Skye a door is always open to a friend?'

'Away with you! You can save that blathering for your fancy patients in the south,' Jeanie replied but she pointed to a chair and Charles knew she was pleased he had come.

'I had a busy morning,' Charles explained.

'Aye, with you and herself trying to get Willie Gillespie out of jail.'

'How did you know?' Jeanie only smiled so Charles added, 'Anyway, he's not in jail.'

'Not yet. Is yon policeman from Inverness daft, thinking Willie would kill his brother?'

'I think he feels he must be seen to be doing something. He wants to impress us.'

'No doubt, but he'd be better spending his time figuring out why anybody should want poor Jamie dead.' Charles sensed that there was an innuendo behind the remark and he would have liked to find out what it was, but once again Jeanie was ahead of him, switching to another subject. 'I see you've been driving around in that fancy toy car of the Swiss fellow's wife.'

'Yes, my own car broke down and Mr Short was kind enough to lend it to me.'

'Then you'd best look for another. She'll be home tomorrow.'

'Mr Short said she wouldn't be returning until next week.'

'Then she will have changed her mind.' Jeanie chuckled maliciously. 'It will no be that she's rushing back because she's missing him. And he finds others to keep him company when she's away.'

This time it was Charles who changed the conversation, deliberately, for he felt he should not allow himself to be drawn into local gossip. To sustain any coherent conversation was in any case difficult, for Jeanie kept hopping from one twig of a subject to another, and he wondered whether it might be because her mind was beginning to wander, the first symptom of impending senility. When he was about to leave her, Jeanie looked at him with an amused tolerance.

'Poor Dr Mackinnon! Did you suppose that life on Skye would be all climbing and shooting and fishing?'

'I never imagined it would be a holiday,' Charles replied and wondered whether he was being completely truthful.

'You've had more than your share of trouble, with seeing Jamie going over the cliff, Morag's grief, Willie in prison and a feeble old woman like myself to look after. And there's likely more trouble no very far ahead.'

'What makes you think so?'

'For you and that Kirsty Tait, bless her.' Jeanie was not looking at him but gazing into the distance, her own expression troubled. 'And all on account of poor, timorous Mairi McPhee.' Charles made no comment, fearful that Jeanie, who knew everything, had somehow found out about Mairi's pregnancy. She went on, 'I'm afeared the bairn will do something feckless, if she hasn't already.'

'What sort of thing?' Charles asked but Jeanie only shook her head.

When he reached the Taits' house he found that Mrs Tait was out but she had left a note where he would find it, underneath a paperweight on the desk in the surgery.

Charles
Carl Short phoned. Gloria is coming back tomorrow and he wants you and Kirsten to dine with them. You need only call him back if you can't make it. He has spoken to Kirsten and she says she'll go.
See you at dinner.
Fiona.

Charles smiled. Jeanie Kennedy had been so confident that Gloria Short would be returning to Skye the following day and she was right. How she was able, alone in her room, to gather news from all over the island so quickly amazed him. He would accept Short's invitation, for it would give him a chance to return Gloria's Mercedes. Kirsten and he could drive to Sleat separately and return after dinner in her car. Kirsten would have thought of that already, he was certain. He resolved to ask Mrs Tait if she would speak to the garage in Portree about renting a car, for she seemed capable of achieving anything she wished on Skye.

Surgery was busy that evening, an unusually high number of patients arriving with minor injuries, cuts, sprains and burns, many of which they could have treated quite easily themselves. Charles decided that it was a sign that the suspicion people may have felt towards him after the death of Jamie Gillespie had abated, and he was glad.

After surgery he found Mrs Tait in the drawing-room and she poured him a whisky. As he relaxed in an armchair enjoying it he said, 'This is the best dram of the day, don't you think?'

Mrs Tait nodded in reply, but she seemed scarcely to be listening to him and he sensed that she had withdrawn into a preoccupation with some personal problem. He hoped it did not mean that her husband's condition had worsened. For a long time they sat in silence sipping their whiskies, for he had no wish to intrude on her thoughts. Then he felt he must speak. If there was a problem he might be able to help.

'Is anything worrying you, Fiona?'

'A little, yes. It's probably nothing; a false alarm.'

'What's happened?'

'Mairi has disappeared.'

That morning Kirsten had sent Mairi to shop on her own in Portree. She allowed her to go on little errands from time to time because she believed it encouraged her to become more self-reliant. After putting her on a bus bound for Portree with a list of what she was to buy, Kirsten would telephone the shopkeepers telling them to expect the girl and repeating her order. The shopkeepers all knew Mairi and would help her, for they all liked her.

This time she had walked with Mairi to the bus stop at about ten o'clock and had seen her leave, expecting that she would be back home in good time for their midday meal. When by one o'clock she had not returned Kirsten had not been unduly concerned, thinking perhaps the bus bringing her back to the craft centre had broken down, a not uncommon occurrence. At two she had phoned the bus station and been told that they had no report of any bus failing to complete its journey, so then she had phoned each of the shops on Mairi's list and was told that she had been in none of them that day.

Now thoroughly alarmed, Kirsten had taken her car and driven to all the homes of friends whom Mairi sometimes visited. The girl had been depressed and moody that morning and Kirsten supposed it was possible that she might have rebelled, deciding to defy Kirsten, ignore the shopping and go off on her own. She had never rebelled before, but she was maturing, so there probably had to be a first time. Alternatively, she might even have forgotten why she had been sent out and wandered off to call on friends.

None of the friends had seen or heard anything of Mairi that day, so Kirsten had driven to her mother's home and Mrs Tait had quietly but unobtrusively taken charge. They had driven together to Portree, callinnng first at the hospital, even though if Mairi had been in an accident they would certainly have been informed by that time. From the hospital they had gone to the police station where the local officers, who were not engaged in the investigation of Jamie Gillespie's death, had been very helpful, telephoning the sub-station at Broadford, and then one by one all the single-man stations on the island. No one had seen Mairi but now at least she was posted as missing.

Not until they went to the bus station did they even find a clue to where they might start looking for Mairi. The driver of the bus that she had boarded near the craft centre had finished work for the day but he had been tracked down drinking in a pub. He remembered seeing Mairi on his bus and remembered too that she had not travelled as far as Portree but had left not long after she had boarded it at a stop near the Skeabost House Hotel. When the bus pulled away she appeared to have been walking towards the entrance to the hotel.

'So we drove to Skeabost,' Mrs Tait told Charles. 'The hotel isn't open for the season yet but the owner was most helpful. He questioned members of the permanent staff who live on the premises and found one who, as he was leaving the hotel by car, had passed a girl who can only have been Mairi, walking down the drive from the road.'

'No one saw her actually at the hotel?'

'No. That's as far as we got, for today at least.'

'Has Kirsten gone home?'

'Yes. She wants to be there in case Mairi returns. That's what she's hoping; that Mairi will just walk in the door.'

'Do you think she will?'

'I don't know what to think, Charles. Mairi has never acted in this way before.'

During dinner Mrs Tait was tense. She gave the impression that she was waiting for the telephone to ring, for news of Mairi. It did ring once, but it was a call from a patient who was worried about her little daughter. The girl had been sick twice that evening and would not eat her supper, although she was not complaining of any pain and her temperature was normal. Charles advised the mother what she should do and promised to go and see the child if her condition grew any worse.

When he returned to the dinner table he asked Mrs Tait, 'Do you suppose that Mairi's disappearance could be connected with her pregnancy?'

'In what way?'

'From what Kirsten told me it seems unlikely that Mairi had experienced sex before. For a simple girl it might have had a disturbing effect.'

'Are you saying she must have been raped and is suffering from delayed shock?'

'No, that isn't what I mean; rather the opposite. Let's suppose she was seduced, more than once in all probability, and that she enjoyed it. Perhaps she hasn't seen the man for some time and has gone to find him.'

Charles could see that Mrs Tait was not convinced by his theory, even though she did not immediately dismiss it. She may have thought of Mairi as a simple, retarded child and not even have stopped to wonder what psychological effects puberty might be having on her. The powerful sexuality which Charles had noticed would not be so obvious to a woman.

'Have you no idea who might have seduced her?' he asked.

'Not the slightest.'

'What will you do tomorrow if she doesn't return tonight?'

Mrs Tait and Kirsten had planned what they would do in that eventuality. Kirsten would telephone all the police stations on the island to see whether they had any news. Meanwhile, Mrs Tait would drive to Kyleakin where she would speak to the men who operated the ferry to Lochalsh, in case Mairi had for some reason taken it into her head to cross over to the mainland. The men would certainly have recognised her for she loved the ferry and sailed on it whenever she could. Not very long ago Kirsten would take her to Kyleakin, just as a treat, and they would cross over and back on the ferry, very often twice.

While Mrs Tait was talking Charles suddenly remembered what Jeanie Kennedy had said to him just as he was leaving her home earlier that evening. He said to Mrs Tait, 'On my way back from my walk I dropped in on Mrs Kennedy.'

'She's not ill, is she?'

'No, but I think she enjoys company.'

'You're spoiling her, Charles. You're as bad as Donald. He goes round just to gossip with Jeanie and then grumbles that he can't get away and she's stopping him working.'

'Do you suppose she might know where Mairi has gone?'

'How could she possibly know?'

'She told me she was afraid Mairi was going to do something foolish, if she hadn't already done so, something that would cause us all trouble. Those were the words she used.'

'She was just blathering! You know what Jeanie's like,' Mrs Tait protested. 'And she's the world's greatest pessimist; always prophesying doom and gloom.'

'She also told me that Carl Short's wife would be returning to Skye tomorrow.'

'Come on, Charles! You're as bad as some of the old wives of Staffin. They believe that Jeanie has second sight.'

Although Mrs Tait was laughing at the suggestion that Jeanie might know what Mairi had done, Charles sensed that she had not completely dismissed it. Her face might be smiling but her eyes were thoughtful. When they were having coffee in the drawing-room and the telephone rang she jumped up nervously to answer it, but once more it was a patient asking for advice.

'What are the police doing about Mairi?' Charles asked her. 'Apart from putting all their people on the alert?'

'If she hasn't turned up by breakfast time tomorrow, they will collect volunteers and organise a search in and around the hotel grounds. It backs on to Loch Snizort, you know.' Mrs Tait shuddered and one could feel her distress. 'And I suppose they'll drag the loch.'

10

'Skye in summer is the bottom. The pits!' Gloria Short complained.

'Because of the tourists?' Charles asked.

'Yes. They swarm everywhere, in the hotels, the bars, the shops, all over the countryside. Do you know we've even had them walking on to our estate, peering into the windows of the house, picking flowers, pissing in the flowerbeds?'

'Come on, darling! It isn't as bad as that.'

'Oh, yes it is! And another thing I can't stand is the midges.' Gloria turned to Charles. 'The island's OK at this time of year but come back in summer and you'll be eaten alive by midges.'

'I agree with you about the midges,' Kirsten said, 'but one learns to live with them.'

'Not me. I insist that Carl takes me away during the worst of the summer.'

'Where do you go?' Charles asked.

'We do the season in London: Ascot, Wimbledon, Henley. I love it. And last year I went to a May ball in Cambridge. My brother used to be at Magdalene College. Carl wouldn't come to the ball.'

'I'm too old for May balls,' Carl said, smiling.

Although Charles had supposed that Gloria would be younger than Carl Short – and in fact she could not be much more than half his age – in appearance she was very different from what he would have expected from a

110

young woman brought up in the middle-class respectability of Cheltenham. Her hair, dyed to a light brown and streaked with gold, hung heavily crimped to her shoulders, and her face, undeniably pretty as Mrs Kennedy had said, was made spectacular with purple eyeshadow and patches of purple blush. She was wearing a very short black silk dress which would have been more suited to a slimmer woman.

The Shorts had invited four other guests to dine with them that evening: David Buchanan, the manager of Talisker Distillery, and his wife, and a couple named Innes, friends of the Buchanans who were staying with them for a few days. Innes also worked in the whisky trade as the chief blender for a company based in Glasgow.

The dinner, served by two wee girls wearing tartan skirts and white blouses, was impressive, the food well cooked and beautifully presented, and wines that most people would only choose for a major celebration: a 1979 Pouilly Fumé and a 1966 Léoville Poyferré. Gloria, however, complained about the salmon trout which was served as a first course.

'Why didn't you take a couple of lobsters from Tom Grant?' she asked her husband. 'He must have called here yesterday.'

'He didn't. I told him not to come as you were not here and I wasn't expecting you until next week.'

'Was that the reason?' One could sense the malice in Gloria's question. 'Or was it because you were on one of your romantic little expeditions to the mainland?'

'Don't be absurd!'

'Who was it this time? Not Wilda. She'll have been at school.'

'Gloria never stops teasing me.' Carl's laugh could not have been more forced. His guests smiled to hide their embarrassment.

'Tom always saves the best of everything they catch for us,' Gloria told the others brightly. 'Because he fancies me, I think.'

During dinner Charles glanced from time to time at Kirsten. Mairi had still not been traced and it was only with difficulty that Mrs Tait had persuaded Kirsten to come to Sleat. The grounds of the Skeabost House Hotel had been thoroughly searched and men had gone in boats out into the loch but had found nothing. Mrs Tait had questioned all the men who worked on the Lochalsh ferry, but they were certain that Mairi had not crossed to the mainland. Comparatively few people made the journey at that time of year and they were sure that had Mairi been on one of the ferries they would have recognised her. Throughout the meal Kirsten appeared composed, joining in the conversation, but Charles had the impression nevertheless that she was fighting an anxiety that could easily have made her morose and depressed. So that her cottage would not be empty if Mairi should return, Mrs Tait had agreed to spend the evening there and the police would telephone her if they had any news of Mairi.

'What do you think of Sleat?' Short asked Mrs Innes.

'We've seen nothing of it yet. When we arrived this evening it was already dark.'

'People call it the garden of Skye. One finds trees and plants and hundreds of different wild flowers that won't grow elsewhere on the island.'

'You must drive up to Tarskavaig,' said Kirsten. 'It's beautiful and from the coast there you'll get a grand view of the Cuillins.'

'We've been here almost a week,' Innes grumbled, 'and we've not really seen the Cuillins.'

'You'll see them tomorrow, whatever the weather,' Buchanan told him.

'David and Meg are taking us on to the hills,' Mrs Innes explained.

'You couldn't have better guides,' Kirsten said. 'David knows every inch of the mountains.'

'Don't exaggerate!' Buchanan protested. 'There's many folk know them better than me.'

'David is a stalwart of the Mountain Rescue Team,' Short explained to Charles. 'How many people did you bring down off the Cuillins these past twelve months, David?'

'Let's not talk about mountain rescues,' Gloria said. 'Think of poor Kirsten's feelings.'

'Don't be silly! Of course we can talk about them!' The impatience in Kirsten's tone suggested that she did not appreciate Gloria's solicitude.

'I suppose you're right, dear. Life must go on and it was a very long time ago.'

While Charles puzzled over this enigmatic reference, Buchanan told them of some of the most dramatic and difficult rescues that the Mountain Rescue Team had effected over the past year or two. He needed prompting by Carl Short, for he was a modest man who often went out in vile weather and late at night to rescue people in trouble on the mountains, but did not see it as a cause for boasting.

'My father once climbed the Matterhorn singlehanded to rescue two injured Italian climbers,' Gloria said. 'He was awarded the Légion d'Honneur.'

'Did Willie Gillespie work for you at the distillery?' Charles asked Buchanan.

'He did, yes.'

'Have you heard that the police have taken him in for questioning?'

'Over his brother's death? Surely they can't believe that he killed Jamie?'

'Put it this way. They're not convinced that he didn't.'

'That's preposterous!'

'You don't think he could have?'

'I'm certain of it. Willie has his faults, but he's never a violent man.'

'He's too fat and lazy to be violent,' Gloria said.

'And at heart he was fond of his brother. The only time I ever saw him lift his hand to another man was in defence of Jamie.'

Buchanan told them of an incident that had occurred when Willie had been working at Talisker. One of the other workers had made an allusion to Jamie's homosexuality, only marginally offensive and half in jest. Willie had immediately turned on the man and lashed out, striking him in the face.

'The man was so surprised,' Buchanan concluded, 'that he didn't fight back. In fact I heard later that he had apologised to Willie. I think the other men respected Willie for what he had done.'

'Was Gillespie the man you told me about who was distilling whisky illicitly?' Innes asked.

'He was one of them. The others were using him for his knowledge. He knew his way around the distillery and I'm fairly certain they were stealing our malt.'

'Why should they do that?' Charles asked.

'Because malt is difficult to make without being detected. You need a fire and that means smoke.'

One of the problems in illicit distilling, Buchanan explained, was avoiding detection. One needed a fire to make malt and another to heat the still. In the old days when whisky was being made illicitly all over the Highlands and islands of Scotland, more often than not it was smoke rising from a lonely moor or a hideaway in a glen that told the revenue men that a whisky smuggler was at work. Smugglers went to great trouble to conceal their stills and other apparatus, but it was generally smoke that betrayed them.

'Is there much illicit distilling now?' Charles asked.

'I doubt if there's any on Skye and there'll not be much on the mainland. You're more likely to hear of someone making whisky in his kitchen in Glasgow than in the north today.'

'If Willie didn't push his brother off Kilt Rock, then who did?' Gloria asked.

No one had any names to suggest for the murderer. As Buchanan said, crime of any kind was rare on Skye and murder was totally outside the experience of anyone living on the island. Even Innes and his wife, who came from the mainland, found it hard to accept that there might have been a murder on Skye.'

'Are you sure he was pushed over?' Innes asked. 'Could he not have just lost his footing and fallen?'

'Not again!' Gloria protested. 'That's really too much!'

'What do you mean, again?'

'When Phyllis Monro threw herself off Kilt Rock they tried to tell us it might have been an accident.'

'We don't know she killed herself,' Carl said.

'Of course she did! Why else would she have gone up there at night in the middle of winter?'

'But what reason could Phyllis have had for wishing to kill herself?' Mrs Buchanan asked.

'The poor thing was out of her mind. She was on drugs, you know.'

'Gloria! What are you saying?'

Everyone stared at Gloria; Carl, the Buchanans and Kirsten in disbelief, the rest in surprise. She appeared to be enjoying the reaction that her assertion had provoked. Because she had been away she had missed the stir that the death of Jamie Gillespie had caused on Skye and now, Charles decided, she was creating a sensation of her own. Gloria was clearly a woman who liked and expected attention.

'What possible reason can you have for thinking Phyllis was taking drugs?' Kirsten asked her.

'She told me so herself. As you know, the hotel they used to own is near here and I would often meet Phyllis when she was taking a walk. Twice just before she died when I met her she was distraught; crying and talking to herself. When I asked her what was wrong she started ranting on about drugs, broke into floods of tears and rushed away.'

'You must have misheard her.'

'No, she said it was drugs, quite definitely.'

'There was no hint in the papers that drugs might have been her trouble,' Buchanan remarked. 'Her doctor said she was on the point of a nervous breakdown.'

'He would say that, wouldn't he? No doctor is going to destroy a patient's reputation after she's dead.'

'Doctors don't lie,' Kirsten said and one could sense her simmering irritation.

'No, but they bend the truth. A hopeless alcoholic dies and what do they put down on the death certificate? Pneumonia.'

'I can see nothing wrong in that,' Carl said. 'Not morally

wrong, anyway. What does it matter whether a man dies from pneumonia or alcohol? In the end it is no more than a statistic and a useless one at that.'

Skilfully he turned the conversation away from Phyllis Monro's death into broader issues of medical ethics. He may have felt that debating whether Phyllis had been taking drugs or not might embarrass his guests. Charles suspected that if this were the case it would not be the first time Carl had tactfully massaged the feelings aroused by Gloria's provocative statements.

At the end of the evening Kirsten drove him home, for he had come to Sleat in Gloria's Mercedes. On the way she asked him, 'Well, what did you think of the siren of Sleat?'

'Gloria?' Charles hesitated over his reply, feeling that the question may not have been as flippant as it sounded. 'To tell you the truth, I didn't know what to make of her.'

'Oh, come on, Charles! Stop being diplomatic! You're not in London now. Here on Skye we speak our minds.'

'I'm not being diplomatic. Gloria is so different from what I expected Carl's wife to be that I'm wary of making harsh judgements. Much of what she said this evening seemed to be only for effect.'

'You realised that, did you?'

'Did her brother really go to Cambridge? She didn't even pronounce the name of his college correctly.'

'I doubt if he did. And her mother doesn't live in Cheltenham but in a humble terraced house in Islington. I found that out by chance.'

'Is she a pathological liar, then?'

'I suppose so.' Like her mother, Kirsten was reluctant to accept that any person living on Skye could be even partly bad. 'But there's always some basis, however tenuous, for her lies.'

Gloria's mother, she told Charles, had worked in a post office in Cheltenham and moved to London when she married. Her father, a sous-chef in a hotel, was Swiss Italian and he had got Gloria a job as a croupier in one of the gambling clubs run by Carl Short. That had been how Gloria had met Carl.

'Is that how Carl made his money? With gambling clubs?'

'Yes. Exclusive, expensive gambling clubs. His son by his first marriage runs them for him now.'

They were passing the hotel that Hector Monro had once owned and Charles remembered what Gloria had said about Monro's wife. 'No one seemed inclined to believe Gloria when she said that Phyllis Monro had been taking drugs.'

'They didn't and nor do I.'

'Then what possible reason could Gloria have for thinking she might be?'

'I've no idea. Mind you, Phyllis was saying some very odd things at about the time of her death.'

'Was she unbalanced?'

'I don't know. She was certainly neurotic. Religion seemed to have affected Phyllis in a strange way.'

'Religion?'

Religion, Charles had learned, dominated the lives of many people on Skye. In even the smallest village of a few houses one would find two churches staring aggressively across the road at each other, the Free Presbyterian Church and the Free Church of Scotland. Known derisively on the mainland of Scotland as 'Wee Frees', they managed to keep all shops and places of amusement on the island closed on Sundays, and thundered from their pulpits against tourism as a corrupting influence. Charles had heard, though, that their influence was not so strong in Sleat.

Phyllis Monro, Kirsten told him, had been religious as a child but had become less devout after marrying Hector. Then, late in life, perhaps to find consolation for the disappointment of a childless and loveless marriage, she had turned to the church again. Hector had not treated her badly. He had not been unfaithful, nor had he abused or neglected her, but he had given her little attention and seemingly little affection. She had grown bitter, retreating into a melancholy, which no amount of prayer and religious duties had been able to dispel. She began talking to herself a good deal and would go off alone on long walks from which she would return exhausted.

'The church did not seem able to help her,' Kirsten concluded.

As they drove northwards and drew nearer to Kirsten's cottage Charles thought he could feel her tension return. She had not spoken of Mairi all evening and had seemed to shake off the worry that her disappearance had caused, but now anxiety returned, bringing the uncertainty of hoping and yet not daring to hope that all would be well.

When she stopped the car outside the cottage she said dejectedly, 'Mairi hasn't been found.'

'How do you know that?'

'My mother would have come out at once to tell us.'

Mrs Tait was sitting in front of the fire in the living-room of the cottage, working on a piece of embroidery. All she said to them was, 'Did you have a good evening, dears?'

'Very pleasant,' Kirsten replied and then she added, 'There's been no news, I suppose?'

'I'm afraid not. The police telephoned. They intend to start another search tomorrow, covering a larger area. Since it will be Saturday, they expect to get scores of volunteers.'

'I'll join them,' Kirsten said at once.

'Much better you didn't, dear.'

'I must do something. I can't just sit here waiting.'

'You did say that you would drive down to Edinburgh. Your father will be looking forward to seeing you.'

'He'll not mind if I don't go.' Kirsten sighed and then looked at Charles. 'Don't think me rude, Charles, but I think I'll be away to my bed. Today seems to have lasted for ever.'

'Of course. You must be tired.'

She kissed her mother and as she smiled wearily at Charles he saw the strain in her face. How much longer would she have to wait and worry, he wondered. It might be days, even weeks. One read of people who simply disappeared, leaving no trace, starting a new life for themselves in another part of the country, although it seemed unlikely that a backward girl would have the inner resources to be able to do that. He wondered too whether Kirsten might be regretting having taken on the responsibility of being a surrogate mother to Mairi.

They heard her footsteps, heavy and tired, going up the stairs and across the room above them. When the footsteps stopped Mrs Tait said, 'Would you mind very much driving yourself home in the Rover, Charles dear? I'd rather not leave Kirsten on her own tonight.'

'Of course I don't mind.'

'Did you drink much at dinner?' Mrs Tait looked at him anxiously. 'The police are rather strict on drinking and driving on Skye.'

'I drank more than I normally would if I were going to drive. Carl is a good host. But it's more than an hour since I had my last drink.'

'Then don't go immediately. I'll make us both a cup of coffee.'

'That might be sensible.'

As they sat drinking coffee in front of the fire, Mrs Tait asked Charles about the dinner party, questioning him on what they had eaten and drunk, the other guests, the talk. She was not making conversation or being inquisitive, but trying to share the occasion. Social life on Skye would be limited and the chance of enjoying a dinner party, even vicariously, should not be missed.

'Gloria made a remark during dinner,' Charles said, 'which sounded as though it were meant to be tactful but which I sensed was actually intended to embarrass Kirsten.'

'What was that?'

'A suggestion that it might hurt Kirsten's feelings if we were to talk about climbing in the Cuillins.'

'What did Kirsty say to that?'

'She dismissed it but I suspect that it irritated her.'

'That Gloria!' Mrs Tait exclaimed in exasperation. 'Yes, she would be trying to embarrass Kirsten. It was perceptive of you to realise that.'

119

Charles made no comment. Mrs Tait hesitated, as though uncertain whether she should explain the meaning of Gloria's remark. Then she said, 'She was reminding everyone about Bruce.'

'Who was Bruce?'

'Kirsten's young man. Oh, it was years back, when she was nursing. Bruce was an architect in Inverness. She used to bring him home at weekends. They were planning to marry.'

'What happened?'

'He was killed on the mountains.'

Although Bruce had been an experienced climber, he had not followed the advice which everyone climbing in the Cuillins was given. He had gone out with only one companion in diabolical weather and started their climb too late to finish it in good light. His companion had been injured by falling rock and, instead of waiting with him to be rescued, Bruce had lashed him to a ledge and set out for help. On the way down he had lost his way, slipped over a precipice and been killed instantly.

After telling him the story Mrs Tait was silent. She must have known that had it not been for the accident life would have been richer for Kirsten but lonelier for her and her husband, since after marrying Kirsten would have lived on the mainland. There was little work for an architect on Skye. And had Kirsten not come back to live on Skye she would have been spared Mairi's disappearance and the long anxious wait.

'I shall insist that Kirsten goes to Edinburgh,' she said at last. 'Staying here, joining in the search and waiting for news can only upset her. And if the news is bad, as I fear it might be, it will be so much worse if she's here.'

Charles was not sure if he accepted the reasoning behind her statement. 'Maybe it would be best if she were to go and see her father,' he said. 'That would take her mind off Mairi.'

'It's a long journey for her to make alone, though, especially if she is worried and anxious.' Mrs Tait looked at Charles.

'You wouldn't think of going with her, would you?'

'What about the practice?'

'The two of you could leave after morning surgery. There's no evening surgery on a Saturday. And one of the other doctors could take any calls there might be over the weekend.'

Now it was Charles who hesitated, wondering whether he really wished to be drawn into what was a family matter. In her present mood Kirsten might be a responsibility that he was not eager to shoulder. Then, remembering Mrs Tait's many kindnesses to him since his arrival on Skye, he was ashamed of his reluctance. He reasoned too that it would suit him to go to Edinburgh, where he would certainly be able to buy the new water pump for his car, which the garage in Portree seemed unable or unwilling to procure.

'It's a lot to ask, I know,' Mrs Tait said.

'Of course it isn't. I'll gladly go with Kirsten.'

11

Next morning there had been a mist on the hills, but as they left for Edinburgh it was lifting and the soft clouds above it began to slip away. Charles recognised the promise of a fine day to come, but he was unprepared for what lay ahead. Approaching Sligachan from Portree, they rounded a bend in the road and suddenly they were imprisoned by mountains. When he had passed that way before he had been aware of the distant Cuillins, shadows in mist or rain. Now they towered above them, dwarfing the valley so that the inn and the bridge over the burn and the winding stretch of road were no more than toys.

Kirsten must have noticed his astonishment, for she said, 'Stunning, aren't they? You could be here for weeks and not get a view like that.'

'They're majestic! Overwhelming!'

The mountains were overwhelming in their grandeur but Charles did not find them intimidating. He remembered thinking on the day when he arrived on Skye that the island had put on its worst face to welcome him. Now, seeing him leave, she was showing all her beauty, enticing him to return. He was aware of a sharp pang of regret as they drove away towards the ferry, and wondered what he would feel in three weeks' time when the day came for the final goodbye.

After crossing to Lochalsh they drove along Glen Shiel and then turned south, heading for Invergarry and the Great Glen. Kirsten spoke little and, trying to take her mind off Mairi, Charles told her about his friends in Edinburgh,

Alistair Ross and his wife Kate, with whom they would be spending the night. He had telephoned Alistair that morning to cadge beds for the two of them and had also asked him to track down and buy a new water pump for his car. Alistair, who had qualified at the same time as Charles, was now a psychiatrist working at the Royal Edinburgh Hospital and he and Kate had recently bought a large, old house in Morningside.

Even though the day was fine, the roads were not crowded and after stopping for a bar lunch in a hotel just short of Spean Bridge, Charles took over the driving, turning inland in the shadow of Ben Nevis to join the main road round to the south at Dalwhinnie.

As they were nearing the top of Drumochter Pass, Kirsten asked him, 'Did you hear that the police allowed Willie Gillespie to go home?'

'Does that mean they've decided it was not he who killed Jamie?'

'No, only that they're not charging him with murder; not yet, anyway.'

'His mother will be glad to have him home.'

'She'll not see much of him. Willie will be doing a round of honour in the pubs, boasting how he made the police look foolish. There will be plenty ready to buy him drinks just to hear his tale.'

'Does he do no work at all?'

'Only casual work when he can get it. He potters around on the croft, but more often than not it's the neighbours who have to help Morag out.'

'I'm surprised she can get a living out of it.'

'She barely does, but there are grants and subsidies from the EEC.'

Charles was glad that she should be talking about Jamie Gillespie. That must be a sign that she was beginning to forget the depression that had hung over her ever since Mairi had disappeared. They would be spending the evening with Alistair and Kate in Edinburgh and she was not likely to enjoy it if her mood of guilty anxiety persisted.

'Do you think we might be able to find anyone who knew Jamie when he was living in Edinburgh?' she asked. 'If, as people say, he had kicked his drug habit, he probably had treatment.'

'I would think so, and for AIDS as well.'

'We might learn something that would help to explain why he was murdered.'

'We can try, certainly. Alistair is working mainly with alcoholics, but he'll know the drug scene, I'm sure of that.'

When they reached Edinburgh Charles dropped Kirsten off at the hospital and then drove to Alistair's house. Edinburgh had changed remarkably little since the time when he was a medical student there, for the City Fathers, because Edinburgh was so rich in history, had not allowed either the winding cobbled streets, tiny courtyards and narrow alleys of the Old Town, or the elegant Georgian crescents and squares of the New Town, to be pulled down and replaced with modern architecture. Charles was glad for in the years he had spent there Edinburgh had become, as Canterbury had during his schooldays, a substitute for the home he had never had, a place for which he would always have a nostalgic affection.

'Where's this Kirsten of yours?' Alistair asked him as soon as he had opened the door.

'Visiting her father in hospital. I told you he was in the Royal.'

'We've given you separate rooms. Is that all right?'

'I should hope so!'

'You didn't say anything about her when you rang.' Alistair sounded disappointed to know that separate rooms were what Charles wanted.

'Her mother was in the room when I spoke to you.'

'But you have hopes at least, haven't you? Who knows? After a few jars and a bottle or two of wine over dinner?'

'Alistair, you're on the wrong track. I've only known Kirsten for a week.'

'As far as I can recall a week used to be more than enough for you.'

Charles was amused that Alistair should be slotting him into the role of philanderer, but not surprised. He had noticed before that whenever they met, no matter how many years had intervened, Alistair and his other Edinburgh friends slipped immediately into the attitudes and behaviour of their student days, invoking the same memories, using the same outmoded slang and telling the same jokes. In a way he found it reassuring that the past could be recreated so readily, proving that the impressions which time had made on them were not indelible.

'You're in the same room as you were on your last visit,' Alistair told him. 'Throw your bag in there and come into the kitchen for a beer. Kate's out shopping.'

'I hope she hasn't gone to any trouble on our account.'

'She's not intending to cook for you, if that's what you're thinking. You know Kate. What sort of food does Kirsten eat, anyway?'

'Only boiled oatmeal and an occasional turnip.'

'No, be serious! We'll be eating out tonight and I wondered if Kirsten liked Indian food.'

'I would think it's very likely. She used to be a nurse.'

Nurses were not well paid and when they ate out more often than not they ate cheaply. Charles had often seen nurses in the Nepalese restaurant near his hospital in London where he frequently went himself.

As they drank beer in the kitchen they talked about Skye. Charles told Alistair about Doctor Tait's practice and the patients in his care, trying to give him an impression of what life on the island was like. Alistair had never been to Skye and, like so many Scots, was surprisingly ignorant about its culture and beyond a hazy knowledge of its associations with Prince Charles Edward he knew nothing of its history. Like many doctors he had few interests outside the closed world of medicine except, in his case, a passion for golf.

'Have you ever wished that you had opted for general practice?' he asked Charles.

'Not really. One has a closer and more personal relationship with patients as a GP, but that is not necessarily an advantage.'

'One would have a far more peaceful life than in a hospital job, I should think, especially in a place like Skye.'

'Don't you believe it! In a hospital one sees all life's dramas, but at a distance, without becoming personally involved. On Skye one can't keep aloof. I've even been tangled up in a murder.'

'What murder?'

Charles described what he had seen happen at Kilt Rock on his first afternoon on Skye and what he had come to know of Jamie Gillespie, his mother and his brother. He told Alistair that Jamie had been a homosexual and, at one time, anyway, on drugs, that he had been suffering from AIDS and had lived for a time in Edinburgh.

'I wonder if we could find anyone who knew Jamie when he was living here. He must have had treatment for AIDS, I should think.'

'We could ask Maggie Wilkie. She's been working with addicts at the City Hospital.'

'Where can I reach her?'

'Why don't we ask her and her husband Gordon to join us for dinner this evening? Kate's very fond of Maggie and Gordon is good news.'

'Fine, but only if you allow me to pay.'

'We'll argue about that later.'

Over dinner that night Charles and Kirsten learned that although Maggie Wilkie had not known Jamie Gillespie, she knew of him. Maggie was a consultant physician at the City Hospital where people infected with the AIDS virus were treated and Jamie had been a patient of one of her colleagues. They had often discussed their cases and Maggie knew that after discovering he had AIDS Jamie, with the help of a GP in Muirhouse who had more than 200 patients on drugs, had managed to kick the habit. Then, realising that he was likely to die within months rather than years Jamie had resolved to make some use of the time that was left to him. He had nursed his homosexual partner, a lad named Andy, until Andy had died and had joined a voluntary association which tried to help drug addicts.

'I hadn't heard he had gone home to Skye,' Maggie said.

'So you have no idea why he decided to go?' Charles asked her.

'No, but I can tell you who might know. Jamie and Andy shared a flat with two girls who were also on drugs.'

'Wasn't that a rather unusual arrangement?'

'It suited all four of them. Andy had a regular job as a hotel porter and Jamie got casual work from time to time in hotels. The two girls were on the game.'

'They were prostitutes?'

'Not regularly. They would go out and pick men up in pubs along Leith Walk when they needed money to buy drugs. That was how Jamie and Andy got into trouble with the law. They were charged with living on the girls' immoral earnings.'

'Were they found guilty?'

'No. They were able to prove that they were contributing as much as the girls to the expenses of the household.'

From Jamie the conversation turned to drugs in general and then to AIDS. Kirsten had read that the incidence of AIDS was higher in Edinburgh than any other city in Britain and wished to know the reason for this. The prevalence of AIDS, she was told, was explained mainly by the sharing of needles by heroin users, but no one could put forward a convincing reason for why there was such a disproportionately large number of drug addicts in Edinburgh. Unlike Glasgow, the city had not seen widespread unemployment resulting from the collapse of major industries and there was not the urban decay that one could see along the Clyde. Alistair had a theory that drug-taking in Edinburgh was a legacy of the annual Festival. Scores of young people, many of them aspiring actors or musicians, were attracted to the 'Fringe' Festival and came to the city, sleeping wherever they could, flaunting their permissive lifestyles and often deviant behaviour. Many of them stayed on in Edinburgh, others left a model for local young people to imitate. Maggie, who had liberal views, did not subscribe to this theory, but believed that it was the legal and social sanctions which society imposed on the so-called 'hard' drugs that were responsible for the crime and vice associated with heroin. Countries in which the use of heroin was not illegal, she maintained, had no such problems.

They were dining in the Shamiana, an Indian restaurant in Brougham Place, where the food was excellent and the décor bright and cheerful, with none of the gloomy red wallpaper much loved by Indian restaurant proprietors. One could see that Kirsten was enjoying the evening. She and Kate had made one of those instant friendships, slipping into intimacy, and the bond between them was not only that they had both once been nurses. Charles had noticed a change in Kirsten's manner and mood when she had come to join them after visiting her father in the Infirmary. She was more positive, more ready to join in the conversation and give her opinions. It was as though she had drawn some inner strength from seeing her father again and from their affection for each other.

After the meal they all went back to Kate and Alistair's home for coffee. Gordon Wilkie, who worked for a whisky company, had brought a bottle of Glenmorangie Malt Whisky with him and they drank it from brandy glasses, comparing its dry, delicate flavour with the full-bodied malt whiskies from Speyside. The reason for the difference in flavour, Gordon told them, was partly that at Glenmorangie, a distillery just outside Tain in Easter Ross, they used a hard water and not the soft, peaty water used by most other distillers, and partly because the copper pot stills at Glenmorangie had much taller necks.

'It's quite different from Talisker,' Kirsten remarked.

'Talisker is an island whisky,' Gordon replied. 'They all have a flavour of their own, too.'

When the Wilkies left, soon after midnight, almost immediately Kate and Alistair said they were going to bed. Kate kissed Charles and then Kirsten on the cheek. 'Breakfast is as late as you like,' she said, 'so long as you make it for yourselves.'

Kirsten smiled as she watched them leave. 'They seem in a hurry to leave us. Have we been boring them?'

A more likely reason, Charles thought, was that Kate wished to leave him and Kirsten alone together. At heart Kate was a dedicated romantic. 'I know they both enjoyed the evening as much as I have. You made a hit with them, Kirsten.'

She was silent for a time and he wondered whether she was thinking of Mairi. She had telephoned her mother shortly after they had returned from dinner, but there had still been no news. Presently she said, 'You've been very good, Charles, putting up with my gloom and my moods.'

'What are you talking about?'

'You've been made to shoulder all our family burdens and you've never complained once.'

They were sitting next to each other on a sofa and before he could reply she leaned over and kissed him on the lips. She seemed to have surprised herself by the gesture and they stared at each other. Then with unspoken consent they kissed again, Kirsten cautiously, as though she were experimenting with a new sensation. Then she sighed.

'I suppose if I were one of your trendy London birds I'd let you take me to bed.'

'But you're not?'

'I'm afraid not.'

'I know and I'm glad.'

His reply may have been what she expected, for she was ready to tease him. 'Have you no poetry for the occasion?'

'Poetry?'

'An apposite quotation. I would have thought Andrew Marvell would fit the bill. Something to the effect that had we world enough and time my coyness would be no crime. Isn't that how it goes?'

Charles took her hand in his. 'You could never be coy.'

129

'I know.'

'And you'll have heard the old Hebridean saying, "When God made time, he made plenty of it".'

They walked upstairs hand in hand, kissed once more on the landing and went to their separate rooms.

12

'What's Jamie to you?' Ruth asked aggressively.

'I'm a doctor on Skye. Jamie's mother is one of my patients.'

'So what do you want?'

'Only to ask you a few questions. Jamie's dead.'

'He would be, wouldn't he?'

'He didn't die of AIDS. He was murdered.'

Ruth stared at Charles, uncertain of whether she should believe him. 'You'd better come in.'

The basement flat which Ruth and Annie shared was in a dilapidated terraced house not far from Leith. Maggie Wilkie had found out the address from her colleague at the City Hospital and given it to Charles that morning over the telephone. He had driven to the house after dropping Kirsten off at the Royal Infirmary and promising to pick her up from there later in the day.

Ruth led him into the kitchen of the flat. To reach it they passed through the living-room in which a man was sleeping, naked as far as one could see, on a sofa. The curtains were drawn, shutting out what little grey light might have seeped through the basement windows, and the air in the room was heavy with the smell of sweat, stale cigarette smoke and stale beer. The one table in the kitchen was stacked with a few dirty plates and a much larger number of the rectangular foil containers used for carry-out Indian and Chinese food. The crumbling remains of a giant pizza was smeared across a dish.

'Want a coffee?' Ruth's accent was unmistakably from London.

'If it's not too much trouble. Thank you.'

'I've just made some.'

She emptied the dregs of a brownish liquid from a mug decorated with a motif of hearts, put a teaspoonful of instant coffee granules in it and added water from an electric kettle which not long ago had been boiled. After offering Charles a cigarette which he refused she lit one for herself. She was a small, fragile girl who in other circumstances Charles might have thought was anorexic, but her thinness and pallor, he decided, were more probably the result of malnutrition.

'Did you say Jamie was murdered?'

'Yes. He was thrown off a cliff.'

'Jesus Christ! What bastard would do that?'

'That's what we'd like to find out.'

'Bloody hell!' Ruth stubbed out the cigarette she had just lit. 'What sort of shit would do that to Jamie? The poor sod never hurt anyone.'

'Everyone says that about Jamie.'

'Tell me about what happened.'

Charles told her what he had seen on Kilt Rock, briefly and starkly because it was beginning to be no more than a recital, a story in words which lost a little of their impact every time he repeated them. Ruth's face showed no sign of shock or any other emotion as he described how Jamie had died. In her eighteen or nineteen years she had seen enough violence, he supposed, to become immune to horror.

'What a shitty way to die,' she said when Charles had finished. 'But perhaps Jamie would have liked it that way. He was proper cut up watching Andy die slowly from AIDS.'

'Have you any idea of who might have wished to kill him?'

Ruth shook her head. 'Poor little sod! He never hurt anyone.'

'Where did he get the money from?'

'What money?'

'To buy a car for himself and a TV and washing machine for his mother.'

'He didn't have no money when he left here, I can tell you. He was skint. Me and Annie we lent him a fiver to set him on his way. He was going to hitch to Skye, he told us.'

'Did he say why he was going home?'

'No. Could have been because he got the sack from the hotel, though he didn't seem too bothered about that.'

Ruth told Charles that not long after Andy died Jamie, with the help of his GP, found work in the kitchens of a hotel in Princes Street. It was the first permanent job he had held in years, but it had not lasted for long. Then, not long after he left the hotel, he had told Ruth and Annie that he was going home to Skye.

'Do you think he really wanted to go?'

'Yes and no. He loved Edinburgh, Jamie did, but he seemed quite excited about going to Skye.'

While they were talking another girl, who Charles assumed must be Annie, came into the kitchen. She was taller and looked older than Ruth and she was wearing jeans and a crumpled tee-shirt which looked as though she had slept in it. Her arms were covered in bruises and from another bruise on her lower lip a little blood had trickled down and congealed on her chin.

Ruth reached out and touched the lip gently. 'Did that bastard do that?' She nodded in the direction of the living room.

'Yeah. He's one of them what thinks it's macho to knock girls around. Don't worry. I made him pay for his fancy – in cash,' Annie replied carelessly. Then she looked at Charles. 'Who's he?'

'Remember Jamie? He's Jamie's mum's doctor. Some bastard shoved Jamie off a cliff. He's dead.'

Annie seemed unconcerned. 'I told him he shouldn't go back to that crummy island.'

She began hunting among the debris on the kitchen table and eventually found a bottle with a couple of inches of vodka in it. After pouring most of the vodka into a dirty coffee mug she topped it up with the dregs of Cyprus sherry

133

from another almost empty bottle, swallowed a gulp of the mixture and seemed to feel better for it.

'This place is the pits,' she said, looking around her at the kitchen. 'A pity Jamie left. He always left things tidy. A proper little housewife, was our Jamie.' She looked at Charles. 'A lot of poofs are like that, aren't they? Tidier than us women.'

'So they tell me.'

'Jamie never said why he was going home, did he?' Ruth asked Annie.

'No, he never did. Funny that, 'cause he wasn't shy of talking about hisself, wasn't Jamie. He could be a proper little bag of wind most times, but he wouldn't say why he was going home. "Better you don't know" was all he said when I asked him.'

'That pal of his at the hotel might know,' Ruth suggested. 'And he might know who would want to do poor Jamie in. What was his name, Annie?'

'Sandy,' Annie replied. 'Sandy Reid.'

Sandy Reid was a junior porter in the hotel where Jamie had worked for a time. With the help of Ruth and Annie, Charles had been able to contact him and they met in a pub in Rose Street when Reid came off duty later that morning. He was from Dundee, a nicely spoken lad with a pleasant manner who, one felt, should do well in the hotel business. Hearing that Jamie was dead obviously upset him.

'Poor Jamie! How did it happen?' he asked, and when Charles told him he was incredulous. 'That's awful!'

'How well did you know him?'

'We were good friends. First when he came to work in the hotel I thought he was just another poof, but when I got to know him he was all right.'

He began talking about Jamie, explaining that when he had been taken on in the hotel kitchens the management knew he had been on drugs but had kicked the habit. Jamie had soon become popular with his workmates. He was a good worker, conscientious and always willing to do a dirty job that no one else wanted to do and always ready to change shifts or work overtime if that would help another member of the staff.

'He and I became good pals,' Reid said. 'Used to meet for a drink with the other lads and once or twice on a Saturday we went to watch Hearts play. Then one day Jamie was given the boot.'

'He was fired? Why?'

'Of course he was in the wrong, but it wasn't fair. They couldn't prove that he'd stolen anything and the guest didn't make a complaint.'

'A guest at the hotel?'

'Yes. This foreigner bloke. Good looking, he was, and rich, but a real ponce; wore silk shirts with the initials AC on them, gold cufflinks as big as dinner plates, Gucci shoes and smothered himself in aftershave, so he smelt like a whorehouse. Jamie was found in his room one morning when the bloke was out. He'd borrowed a pass-key from one of the maids.'

'What was he doing?'

'God knows. The management thought he was on the prowl, meaning to nick something, but Jamie was no thief. He may have gone into the man's room just to take a look at his gear; all those suits and shirts and stuff. Jamie loved clothes, the trendier the better. Not that he ever had anything flash himself, poor little bugger.'

Charles remembered that it was Jamie's pink sweater that had led him to believe that it was a woman who had been thrown over Kilt Rock. 'And he was fired for this?'

'Yes. There'd been some nicking going on in the hotel so they decided Jamie must have done it. After all, he had been on drugs. They knew that.'

'Did he find another job?'

'Not as far as I know. We only met a couple of times after that. Jamie always seemed to be busy; either that or he was avoiding me. I think that after being sacked he may have gone back on drugs.'

'What makes you think that?'

'Another mate of mine who knew him and who's in on the drug scene told me he'd seen Jamie more than once in pubs and other places talking to men who he knows are pushers.'

There seemed to be nothing more that Reid could tell him and shortly afterwards Charles collected Kirsten's car from where he had parked it in George Street and drove up through the Old Town to the Royal Infirmary. During their conversation it had become clear that Reid did not know that Jamie had been infected with AIDS and Charles had decided not to tell him, thinking that it might in some way tarnish his memory of a man who had been his friend. Hostility and prejudice towards AIDS sufferers was as strong in Edinburgh as anywhere else.

He remembered seeing Jamie's body in the hospital at Portree. It was a body, not remarkably different from many other bodies he had seen, noteworthy only because he had witnessed its death. Now the body had taken on new dimensions, as people told him about Jamie, his behaviour, his feelings and his virtues. Jamie was beginning to live again, stirring feelings of pity and sympathy. At the same time Charles could not help wondering why it was that he had become involved.

He found Kirsten in her father's room at the Infirmary, a room with two beds, one of which was empty. A table in the room was covered in vases of flowers, fruit, cards and bottles of Scotch of various sizes. Although he was always wary of looking for stereotypes, Charles could not help thinking that Dr Tait was in many ways a typical Scot, short but sturdy, with a high colour in his face that owed more to fresh air and the sun than to whisky, his sandy hair liberally shot with grey, a natural reserve in his manner even when he was being friendly.

'I owe you an apology,' he said to Charles as they shook hands. 'You should never have had to take the practice over cold, as it were.'

'That was not your fault, sir.'

'Not really. I had the greatest difficulty in finding a

136

locum and by the time I found you the operation wouldn't wait any longer. And do please drop the "sir", Charles!' Tait said, although one sensed that he was pleased that Charles had offered him the token of respect.

'Mrs Tait made it all very easy.'

'Fiona's a marvel, isn't she? She could run the practice on her own. But you haven't done badly yourself. Jeanie Kennedy is telling everyone you're a better doctor than I am.'

Charles laughed. 'That's only because I've been spoiling her.'

'He goes to see her every day,' Kirsten said.

'I enjoy chatting to her. I really do. Do you know, she can remember my grandfather.'

They began talking about Jeanie Kennedy and then about the practice. Dr Tait wanted to know about the condition of other patients, some of whom were virtually permanent invalids. They discussed in detail the case of a man who was recovering from hydatid, a singularly unpleasant complaint, which originated in the infected tapeworms of dogs and in humans caused cysts in the liver, lungs or brain. Charles had never come into contact with hydatid before, but Tait seemed satisfied with the answers to the questions he asked. As he made no mention of Mairi McPhee, Charles concluded that Kirsten had not told her father that the girl was pregnant, nor that she had disappeared.

'I'm really enjoying doing this locum for you,' Charles said. 'It's been fascinating to live on Skye and see the island from the inside, as it were.'

'You're one of those who fall in love with Skye. I did, the moment I set foot on the island. Though, mark you, I never imagined then that I would spend my life there.'

'How did that come about?' Charles asked him.

'Now, you two!' Kirsten interrupted. 'This is not the time for swapping life stories. Charles and I should be leaving if we're to arrive home in time for dinner.'

Before they left, she kissed her father and he held her for a moment, reluctant to let her go. Once again, as he

137

had sensed between Kirsten and her mother, Charles was aware of the power of their family affection, a bond so strong that one could not imagine it ever being ruptured or even weakened. He had never shared that experience with his own parents, for during most of his boyhood and adolescence they had lived abroad and infant love had gradually diminished into a distant affection as they had become for him almost strangers. Now, watching Kirsten kiss her father tenderly, he felt an emptiness and was sad for what he had missed.

As they left Edinburgh and were crossing the Forth Bridge, Kirsten was still thinking of her father. 'Did you see all the gifts and cards in his room? They were all from Dad's patients. Four wee kids even clubbed together and bought him a miniature bottle of his favourite Scotch!'

'He must be a very good doctor.'

'A good GP. He's no medical genius and he knows his limitations, but his patients come first for him.'

'Not first,' Charles corrected her. 'Second, after his family.'

'Does it show?' Kirsten asked and she smiled when he nodded.

She began talking about Edinburgh, about Kate and Alistair and the dinner the previous evening, recalling the conversation, some of the jokes and the more outrageous comments that had been exchanged. Charles would have liked to tell her what he had learned that morning about Jamie Gillespie and the events that had led up to his return to Skye, but he could see she was happy and he had no wish to remind her of the depressing events whose aftermath would be waiting for them when they arrived back in Skye. Only when they had turned off the A9 and were heading west did he sense her mood change. It may have been the declining sun which reminded her of home, for sunsets of a dazzling beauty were a part of Skye.

'My mother phoned while I was with Dad,' she said. 'They've not had any news of Mairi.'

'You didn't tell your father about her?'

'No. We decided it would only upset him.'

'Mairi will turn up soon, I'm sure of that.' Charles hoped that his words would carry a conviction which he did not feel. 'People don't disappear.'

'They do. All the time, I'm told,' Kirsten replied. She said nothing for a time, then, thoughtfully, as though she were speculating aloud, 'I wonder whether she had arranged to meet someone that morning without telling me.'

'What makes you think that?'

'She seemed excited. The previous evening, you remember, after the ceilidh, she was so upset and next morning she was still in the dumps. Then after breakfast she seemed to cheer up. Before going out she brushed her hair and put on make-up and insisted on putting on her best coat. It was a coat I had bought her for the winter, and she wore it that day even though the weather was really too warm.'

Charles recalled suggesting to Mrs Tait that Mairi's disappearance might be in some way connected with her pregnancy, and what Kirsten had just told him seemed to support his theory, but he decided against pursuing that line, for the time being, anyway. Instead he said, 'Do you think Mairi's disappearance could be linked with Jamie Gillespie's death?'

'I can't see how it could be.'

'Nor can I, but when there are two unexplained events within a few days of each other, two traumas, on Skye of all places, one can't help believing that they must be connected.'

'You may be right. I've given up speculating.'

'But don't give up hoping.'

'I won't, but I feel so helpless.'

As they drew nearer to Skye their conversation became sparse, a desultory exchange of trivial remarks with Charles trying to prevent Kirsten from slipping back into a silent melancholy. On the ferry crossing to the island they left the car to ease the stiffness of a long drive, and stood, mindless of the cold wind that was sweeping across the sea, looking at the lights of Kyleakin as they drew nearer.

139

'This is the first time I have ever wished I wasn't coming home,' Kirsten said.

'Why?'

'I'm afraid of what will be waiting for us.'

As he could think of nothing he could say to comfort her he put his arm around her shoulders and she leant against him. At the same time he wondered whether they were unthinkingly slipping into a kind of intimacy and whether that was what he wanted. It was the secret sympathy, Walter Scott wrote, the silver link, the silken tie, which bound people together, and he could not deny the sympathy he felt for Kirsten, even though he believed she had been wrong ever to have shouldered the responsibility of looking after a retarded child.

He had driven all the way from Edinburgh and when the ferry touched shore Kirsten took the wheel, driving fast but nervously, as though she were steeling herself for her arrival home. When they reached her cottage they saw two cars standing outside: her father's Rover and a dark green Range Rover.

'That's Hector's car,' Kirsten remarked. 'I wonder why he's here.'

'Perhaps he's brought a little champagne with which to welcome us home.' Charles knew that the remark was frivolous, but he felt bound to say something to ease the tension that was building up in Kirsten.

They had stopped the car and were taking their bags out of the boot when Mrs Tait came out, followed by Monro. She went up to Kirsten and, even before she kissed her, asked anxiously, 'How was Dad?'

'Wonderful! Full of life!'

Mrs Tait looked towards Charles, as though waiting for confirmation. 'Was he really? Give us your professional opinion.'

'He looked like a million dollars. The man's a marvel! He might have spent the last week on a health farm, not a hospital.'

'Thank you.' Unexpectedly, Mrs Tait reached up and kissed

Charles on the cheek. Then she laughed self-consciously. 'Sorry, Charles. I really am turning into a sentimental old woman!'

The four of them went into the cottage which, with its warmth, the smell of peat burning on the fire and the reassuring familiarity of its furniture and ornaments, seemed to offer a refuge from the tensions of the world outside, but when Kirsten took her travel grip upstairs Mrs Tait's pleasure at the return of her daughter seemed to be replaced by concern. She looked at Charles anxiously.

'We've had no news of Mairi, poor creature.'

'I know. Kirsten told me.'

'The search was abandoned when darkness came. The police seem to believe that she must have fallen into one of the sea lochs and drowned.'

'Couldn't she swim?'

'No. We tried to teach her but she wasn't able for it.'

'Fiona and I made our own search,' Hector Monro said. 'With so many hunting in this area, we decided to search the whole island, trying all the places that Mairi liked, woods and beaches where she had been taken to play or close to where her friends lived. We spoke to everyone who might have known her.' Mrs Tait looked at Monro gratefully. 'Hector has been wonderful. He drove everywhere and was so patient, but we learned nothing.'

'It must have been very disheartening.'

'We mustn't give up hope,' Hector said.

When they heard Kirsten coming downstairs Mrs Tait immediately changed the subject. It seemed to Charles that she was being too protective of her daughter. He understood how harrowing uncertainty and the fear of anguish to come could be, but Kirsten was mature enough to accept and live with it. She showed no signs that she had been permanently scarred by the death of the young man she had been going to marry and did not need to be sheltered from what might have happened to Mairi.

'Pour us all a drink, Charles, will you?' Mrs Tait said when Kirsten came into the room.

141

As he was pouring the whiskies, Kirsten remarked, 'Charles met some people in Edinburgh who knew Jamie Gillespie when he lived there.'

'Really? Who?'

'One of the women who had dinner with us was a psychiatrist who worked at the hospital where Jamie had treatment and through her Charles met two girls with whom he had been sharing a flat.'

'Did you learn anything which would explain why he was murdered?' Hector asked.

'Not really. I did find out that he had given up taking drugs and found a job in a hotel.'

'He worked in my hotel for a time, as you probably know, but the lad was unstable. He could never have stuck long in any work.'

'I was also told he was broke when he left Edinburgh, but he appears to have had money here on Skye.'

'Do you know where he got it?'

'No. It occurred to me that he might have been selling drugs; that this was his reason for returning to Skye.'

'Jamie would never do that, not to his own folk.' As always, Mrs Tait was unwilling to believe that any patient of her husband was capable of evil.

'I agree,' Hector said. 'And it seems unlikely that having managed to give up drugs he would risk exposing himself to temptation by becoming involved in drug trafficking.'

'You may be right, but the police seem to think that drugs are being made available on Skye.'

'They do,' Mrs Tait agreed. 'Superintendent Grieve came and questioned me about it again this morning.'

'That's monstrous!' Kirsten said angrily.

'We can't allow that,' Hector said. 'The man must be put in his place. I'll have a word with his Chief Constable, who's an old friend of mine.'

They began criticising the police who, they felt, were mishandling the case of Jamie's murder, blundering around looking for suspects without logic and even without commonsense. Mrs Tait believed this was because they were

142

from the mainland and either did not understand the people of Skye or despised them or both. The islanders were better able to deal with their own problems and should be allowed to do so.

Presently Kirsten said, 'Can I smell food cooking? Charles and I had no lunch and the poor man must be starving.'

'Yes,' her mother said. 'There's a casserole in the oven and soup which only needs heating.'

Hector stood up and as he did so finished what was left of his whisky. 'Time I was going.'

'But, Hector, you said you would stay for supper!'

'Sorry, Fiona, I really can't stay. I had forgotten that my nephew said he would be phoning me tonight. He appears to have problems – money problems, no doubt.'

While Kirsten was seeing Hector to his Range Rover, Mrs Tait told Charles that she wished to spend the night at the cottage and asked him if he would again mind driving himself back to Staffin in her car. Charles told her that of course he did not mind, but wondered anew whether Mrs Tait were being too protective. Kirsten seemed composed and relaxed and not in need of a mother's comforting.

His manner or tone may have betrayed what he was thinking, for Mrs Tait said, 'You'll think me foolish, but I feel certain that soon we're going to have bad news about Mairi and I would like to be with Kirsten when it comes.'

Charles did not stay at the cottage long after they had finished supper, for he could see that both Mrs Tait and Kirsten were tired and he too was ready for his bed. A lane, not much more than a track, led from the cottage and as he swung the Rover out of it into the main road to Portree he noticed a car parked by the side of the road a couple of hundred yards or so along the other way. He wondered whether it had broken down or been abandoned, for there were no houses or cottages nearby, but glancing in his driving mirror he saw that as he moved off the car's lights were switched on and it pulled out into the centre of the road, moving in the same direction as himself.

His curiosity stirred now, he watched the car as it followed behind him, which was not difficult as on a Sunday evening there were few cars on the roads. The car followed him past Skeabost and when it reached the junction of the main road from Sligachan to Portree turned and followed him into the town. That in itself was nothing to be surprised about, but he began to wonder if the driver of the car was following him and for a sinister reason. He laughed at the notion but decided anyway to find out if it might be true.

Reaching Portree, he turned into Somerled Square, swung the car into the parking area in the centre of the square and stopped, switching off the engine but leaving the lights on. He saw that there were only two other cars in the park, both empty. Leaving the Rover, he walked out of the square fifty yards or so in the direction of the post office. As he did so the car that had been behind him also swung into the square. He deliberately did not look towards it, not wanting the driver to think he had even noticed it. At the post office he went through the motions of dropping a letter in the posting box, read one of the notices in the window, which encouraged saving, and then walked back to the Rover.

Now there were three cars in the square beside the Rover, all parked and with their lights off, but he could make out a figure seated behind the wheel of the new arrival. In a leisurely and natural manner he climbed back into the Rover, started the engine and drove out of the square to join the road to Staffin.

When he was about half a mile along the road he saw headlights appear behind him. Convinced now that it was the same car that had been waiting for him outside Kirsten's cottage, he slowed down, but only gradually, so that the driver of the car would not suspect what he was doing. The car began to draw nearer at first, then it also slowed down and kept its distance. As he approached Kilt Rock, Charles saw the inn where he had stopped for a bar lunch one day. He turned off the road and into the car park of the inn, stopped the Rover and got out as though intending to go into the inn for a drink.

He was locking the car door when the other car appeared.

144

The driver seemed to hesitate for a moment, looking towards him, and then drove on along the road to Staffin. The night was clear with a fine moon, giving Charles enough room to see the driver's face. He was almost, but not absolutely, certain that it was Murdo McPhee.

13

Mairi's body was found on the mainland in the woods above Loch Garry. A middle-aged couple from Fort William had driven up there on Sunday afternoon to walk and it had been their dog that had nosed out the naked body that had been partly and probably hastily concealed in a thick bank of bracken.

At first no one knew who the dead girl was. The police had been called and the body had been examined and photographed where it lay, before the area had been cordoned off for a search which would be started the following morning. At police headquarters in Inverness they had noticed that the body resembled the description of a Mairi McPhee, who had been reported as missing on Skye some days previously. Late on Sunday night Inverness had telephoned Skye and early next morning a helicopter had been sent to take Mairi's father to Inverness. No one on Skye had been told about the body until he had identified it as that of his daughter.

Charles did not hear the news until Mrs Tait telephoned him from Kirsten's cottage just after he had returned to the house from his morning calls. 'I'm only glad that Kirsten wasn't asked to identify her,' she said.

'How was she killed?'

'By a blow on the head, they say. Apparently, she had not been sexually assaulted, but they haven't found her clothes, which is rather curious.'

'Is there anything I can do?'

'Not really.'

'Shall I come round? I've finished my calls.'

'I don't think so, dear. I believe Kirsten would prefer to be alone and I shall be leaving myself directly.'

'How is Kirsten taking it?'

'Pretty well.'

'Will you be home for lunch?'

'No, I thought I would drop in on Hector, and I might have a snack with him.'

As Charles lunched alone he thought of Mairi and realised how little she had left him to remember of her. She had shown the same visible signs of her emotions as anyone else would – laughter and tears, smiles and pouting, but one could not share them with her nor feel their intensity. It was as though her mental underdevelopment had acted as a filter, holding back any expression of an individual personality. He was filled with pity for her and for the grief that Kirsten must be experiencing.

He found himself contrasting Mairi's death with that of Jamie Gillespie. Both had been violent and ugly and, at first sight, motiveless, and both had brought to an end lives that many people might have thought to be incapable of ever achieving any real fulfilment. Motiveless murders could only be committed by a psychopath or someone deranged enough to find satisfaction in the act of killing. In this case it might be the satisfaction of killing victims whose lives the murderer considered valueless or even an affront to society. Charles could think of another possibility. The people of Skye were in many ways a backward community, their lives in the twentieth century shadowed by age-old superstition. He remembered the uneasiness, bordering on fear, which he had experienced when he had realised that he was being followed in his car the previous night, the feeling that he had been unwittingly drawn into a sinister ritual of primitive savagery and vengeance.

After lunch he drove round to Mrs Kennedy's home. Surgery had been long and busy that morning, as it usually was on a Monday, with patients coming in for notes which would excuse them from work, some of them only because they were suffering from the effects of a weekend's heavy drinking. The number of calls he had to make was also larger than usual, so, since Jeanie Kennedy was not in the real sense of the word ill, he had decided to postpone visiting her until the afternoon. He had in any case another reason for wishing to see her. He had questions about Murdo McPhee he wished to ask and Jeanie was as likely as anyone to know the answers.

When he reached her house she was sitting in her usual chair and he had the impression that she had been waiting for him to arrive. 'You're back from your holiday with Miss Kirsty, then?' she asked him.

'Some holiday! We were only in Edinburgh for twenty-four hours.'

'And you saw himself? How was he?'

'Grand! He was asking after you, Jeanie.'

'And well he might, neglecting us all this while,' she replied with feigned grumpiness. 'Still, you've done as well as he ever did, I'll say that.'

'Have you heard about Mairi McPhee?'

'Aye, poor wee mite! But maybe that's God's way and it's best for her.'

'Do you remember last week when I was here you told me you were afraid Mairi would do something rash, something that would cause Kirsten and me trouble?'

'Aye, I remember. Why? Do you think my mind's going?'

'What did you mean when you said that?'

'Just what I said, that she'd be bringing you trouble and pain.'

'But what reason did you have for saying so, Jeanie?'

'I knew the lass was in some kind of distress. I could tell by the cut of her that she was suffering.'

Charles realised that he would have to be satisfied with her answer. It told him nothing but probably for Jeanie it was the truth. Her intuition of what people might do was based not on reason but on observation and instinct and she would find it impossible to explain or justify. In any event, she might as easily be wrong as right in her premonitions.

'And Andrew, Mairi's father,' she went on scornfully, 'he'll be saying he's grieving for the lass and pouring whisky for his friends, but he gave her nothing but hurt while she was alive.'

'Is Murdo McPhee his brother?'

'A cousin. He's worse than her father, that one. Never minding his own bairns nor his wife, spending his days and his nights in Sleat.'

'He's working there, isn't he? On Mr Short's estate?'

'Some might call it work, but he'll be spending more time warming the bed of that widow woman than working, I'm thinking.'

A woman in Sleat, according to Jeanie, had lost her husband some months previously and, not wishing to marry again, had looked around for a man to relieve the loneliness of her nights. One day when she was walking her dog on Carl Short's estate, she had met Murdo McPhee. Murdo, bored with the monotony of cleaning out ditches, had been easily seduced and she had him home and in bed within the hour. The chance meeting had rapidly developed into a liaison that had become a scandal. Now Murdo was spending more nights at the widow's home than at his own, an arrangement which suited him, saving him the long journey home to Staffin after he finished work.

'Her minister has spoken to the widow woman,' Jeanie said, 'but there's no making her change her ways. Shameless, the creature is!'

'Murdo told me that Jamie Gillespie was devoted to him.'

'Aye, the lad looked up to him, though I canna think why. And his brother Willie would do anything Murdo asked him to. The pair of them should have more sense. Murdo has never given them anything but trouble.'

In the turmoil created by Mairi's disappearance, Charles had forgotten Willie Gillespie. He had heard that the police were no longer detaining him, but had told him he was not to leave the island. Jamie's car had still not been found and the police believed it had been taken off the island, suggesting that Jamie had been murdered by someone from the mainland.

'How is Willie?' he asked Jeanie Kennedy.

'Puffed up with pride. He's in and out the pubs boasting how he was too cunning for the police and they had to release him.'

After leaving Jeanie's home, Charles drove to the garage in Portree where his car was waiting to be repaired and gave them the replacement water pump that Alistair had bought for him in Edinburgh. The foreman promised that fitting the pump would take no time at all and that once the job was finished the car would be brought up to Dr Tait's home. On his way back to Staffin, as he approached Kilt Rock, he recalled the police asking him whether he had seen Jamie Gillespie's car parked on or off the road nearby on the evening of the murder. There had been no other car in the parking area at the view point just south of the cliff and if Jamie had gone there in his car then he must have left it on the road between Kilt Rock and Staffin, but when he was driving on that stretch of road Charles had seen no car. He was sure of that now and began speculating on where, if he had been the murderer, he would have taken the car. Not back through Staffin, surely, for there it would have been seen and recognised.

When he reached the Taits' home, he found that Mrs Tait had returned. He had expected that she would wish to talk about Mairi's death, telling him more of the circumstances in which her body had been found. Instead, he sensed almost at once that she wished to avoid the subject. So he asked her, 'How was Hector?'

'Grumbling about his health, but otherwise fine.'

'I hope he gave you champagne.'

'He did, and smoked salmon for lunch. He always spoils his guests.'

'Was he joking the other day when he said you were the girl he would have liked to marry?'

Mrs Tait made a small, contemptuous noise. 'He likes

to pretend that now, but when he first came to Skye on holiday he only had eyes for Phyllis. She was much prettier than me and a better catch.'

'You make it sound as though he were an adventurer.'

'Not at all. Hector was unfortunate, that's all. He had a good war, you know, won a medal at Anzio, but when he came home no one was interested. All he could find was a clerk's job in Dundee.'

'People say he and his wife were not very happy.'

'They were not well suited. Phyllis was a very serious and intense person, while Hector – well, you've met him. He's fond of the good life, too fond, I would say. He was complaining of his dyspepsia again today.' Mrs Tait hesitated before she added, 'It isn't my business, but perhaps you should drop in and give him a check-up, Charles, just in case it's the beginning of something serious.'

'I'd be glad to. I could go now.'

'Why not go after supper? We'll be eating early this evening as Hilda's son and daughter-in-law are over from the mainland to see her. I wanted her to take the evening off, but she wouldn't hear of it, but if we have supper early she can get away.'

'Of course. Whenever you like.'

At evening surgery Charles realised that even though she came from Staffin Mairi's murder had made little impact on the local people. Not one of his patients mentioned it and he could sense none of the heightened tension, a combination of fear and excitement, which a sudden, violent death usually arouses in those close to it. A life had been extinguished but other lives went on. He found it sad that the girl's death had passed unnoticed.

Not until they were at supper did Mrs Tait mention the subject and then objectively and without emotion. 'I cannot understand how Mairi could have left the island without anyone knowing,' she said. 'I talked to the lads on the ferry myself and they were certain that they hadn't seen her.'

'It would not have been difficult for anyone to have smuggled her out.'

'Smuggled her?'

'She was so small, poor thing! If she were lying in the back of an estate car and covered with a blanket, no one on the ferry would have seen her.'

'You must believe then that she was . . . ' Mrs Tait, shying from the word 'murder', hesitated. 'You believe she met her death on the island, then?'

'Probably. It would make sense for whoever killed her to take her body and hide it on the mainland. Weeks, months might have passed before it was found, by which time any clues on the island would have been erased.'

Mrs Tait seemed satisfied with his answer and did not mention the subject again over supper. Instead they talked of routine matters concerned with the practice, the condition of some of the patients, the stock of medicines for dispensing, the possibility that surgery hours might be changed when Dr Tait returned to work. After supper, when Charles was about to leave the house, Mrs Tait said, 'After you've seen Hector why don't you drop in on Kirsty?'

'Didn't you say she wished to be alone?'

'That was hours ago. She'll be glad to see you, I know she will. And it isn't very far out of your way.'

In her own undemonstrative way she was begging him to go, for she could not bear the thought of Kirsten grieving alone. Did parents always worry about the feelings of their children, even when they were mature adults? Charles supposed that they must.

'I'll be glad to go,' he said and smiled as he added, 'I'm worried about her too.'

'Whenever you appear,' Monro grumbled, 'the pain disappears.'

'That's customary among my patients. Their fear of what I might do is greater than the pain.'

'No, seriously. I've had quite a deal of pain, but intermittently.'

'I believe you.'

Charles gave him as thorough an examination as he could.

Although Monro was overweight, his blood-pressure was good for a man of his age and his heart sound. In all probability he was suffering from nothing more serious than the effects of a sedentary and cosseted life, but since this was the second time he had complained it would be best to arrange for him to have tests at the hospital, even though it was unlikely that they would tell Charles anything.

'Your diet doesn't help,' he said as Monro was putting his shirt on again. 'Cutting down on alcohol would certainly be advisable.'

'Could it be stomach cancer, do you think?'

'What possible reason can you have for thinking that?'

'My father died of cancer of the prostate.'

'That doesn't mean you will. I'm reasonably sure that what is bothering you is no more than indigestion but I'll arrange for some tests to be taken just to reassure you.'

The room they were in at the back of the house overlooked Loch Snizort and as he waited for Monro to dress Charles looked out on to the water and the hills of Waternish beyond. A breeze from the west was breaking up the sheet of cloud that had persisted for most of the day, allowing a hard, bright moon to appear and disappear fitfully. In such a night as this, he thought, then checked himself, feeling guilty for the ineptness of the quotation on a night when Mairi's lonely body was lying in a distant mortuary. He felt a sudden crushing pity for the girl who had held only a tiny, ill-wrapped parcel of life so briefly in her hands.

'You said yesterday,' Monro remarked, 'that Jamie Gillespie seemed to have money when he arrived on Skye.'

'Yes. Enough to buy himself a car as well as a television set and a washing machine for his mother.'

'Did he pay cash for them?'

'I've no idea. Why?'

'He may have bought them on hire purchase.'

'Even then he would have had to put down a deposit.'

'Yes, but the amount would be trifling. Everyone is encouraged to live on credit now. And Jamie would have been drawing the dole.'

'Would he have been able to pay the instalments?'

'I would think so, but I hope he hasn't left debts for his mother to pay. She's a patient of yours. Do you think you could find out tactfully if he did, so I could help her if she needs help?'

'I'll do what I can.'

The sky was clear by the time Charles left Monro's house and the moonlight had softened, shrouding the hills with a ghostly stillness. The constantly changing moods of Skye, he realised, were closely linked with the sudden, unexpected changes in the light. On a night like this he could understand why people believed in fairies and fairy bridges and fairy banners.

When Kirsten opened her door to him she smiled, not at him but as though amused by some private thought. She offered her cheek to be kissed with an air of good-natured resignation and he followed her into the living-room of the cottage.

'My mother asked you to come, didn't she?' she asked, but without resentment.

'She did, but I came because I wished to see you.'

'Why?'

'Do I need a reason?'

'To comfort me?'

'If you need comforting, yes.'

'Then I'm glad you came. Now, will you take a dram?'

'I don't think so, thanks.'

She looked at him defiantly. 'I'm going to.'

'In that case I'll keep you company.'

Watching Kirsten as she poured two glasses of Scotch from the decanter that stood on a table next to the marble head of a young man, Charles realised that she had been drinking already, not a great amount, not more than a whisky or two perhaps, but the drink had smoothed the stiffness of tension that would have shown in her face, brightened the dullness of grief that would have shown in her eyes.

She handed him his whisky and sat down beside him on the sofa, lifted her glass to him in an empty gesture of conviviality and then put the glass down on the coffee table beside her.

'Comfort me, then,' she said and held out her arms.

He took her in his arms, thinking to kiss her gently and then let her head rest on his shoulder while they talked and he spoke what words of consolation he might find. But when their lips met hers were open and demanding. The fierceness of her passion surprised him. While they kissed she seized his hands and thrust them up under her jumper. She was wearing nothing underneath and when his fingers touched her breasts she trembled. As he drew his face away to look at her she reached up, loosened the knot of his tie and began unbuttoning his shirt. Her eyes were bright and hard.

'Take me to bed, Charles.'

'I don't think that's a very good idea.'

'Why not?'

'Not now, not today.' He could not explain to her the inner constraints that were putting a brake on his inclinations, restraining desire, for he did not understand them himself.

'Take me to bed, darling, comfort me! Now!' She was imploring him but he could see no passion in her eyes, only pain.

Still he hesitated. Impatiently she sat back, pulled her jumper off and then swooped down on him, pressing her naked breasts to his face and trying at the same time to entwine her legs with his. Coming from any other woman, her clumsy attempts to seduce him would have been irritating and distasteful, but Charles found himself strangely moved.

'Take me to bed, darling,' she repeated. 'Comfort me!'

When he shook his head she took it in her hands and held it still, as though to immobilise any objections he might make. They kissed again and Charles felt his resistance subsiding. Jumping to her feet, she grabbed his hands and pulled him up off the sofa.

He followed her up the stairs, feeling guiltily that he was taking advantage of her confused emotions. In the darkened bedroom she quickly slipped off her remaining clothes, pulled back the blankets and top sheet of the bed and lay down.

Once more he hesitated, but knew that this would be the last time. Her naked body astonished him for he had only seen her dressed in the prosaic and unflattering clothes of island life and he was unprepared for the beauty of her throat and breasts, her tiny waist and long, slim thighs. In the darkness her skin had an almost luminous silkiness.

Her arms when she held them out to him seemed fragile and immature, the arms of an adolescent, and for that reason their entreaty had a curious poignancy. He undressed and lay down beside her.

When he began to caress and kiss her, her breath quickened and she moaned quietly. She would not kiss him, turning her face away. Was there an emotion in her eyes, Charles wondered, which she did not wish him to see. Her excitement, as it grew, matched the pace of his own and began to outstrip it, her breath erupting in great, half-strangled gasps. He thought she was going to have an orgasm, although he had not touched her in any way that would provoke one. Then suddenly she gave a single, piteous cry, more mournful than any he had ever heard. Twisting in her bed she threw her arms around him, pulling him to her, and began weeping in great, convulsive sobs that shook her whole body.

He tried to comfort her, stroking her hair and her cheeks, kissing her gently, feeling her hot tears coursing down his chest, holding her to him and whispering consolation, but aware of the miserable inadequacy of any words he could say. After a long time the storm began to abate, the sobs grew less violent, the roar of the waves subsiding slowly to little more than a sigh of water sliding back over sand. Then the sighs were no more than breathing, calm and regular, and he knew that she was asleep.

'Still, still to hear her tender-taken breath.' He mouthed the words soundlessly and smiled, remembering how she had teased him when he had first quoted from the sonnet.

Carefully, gently, he withdrew his arm from her shoulders, slid off the bed and drew back the blankets and sheets to cover her. There was a full-length mirror in the hall and when he saw his reflection in it, naked, holding his clothes in one hand and his shoes in the other, creeping down the stairs like an escaping lover, he laughed.

He dressed in front of what was left of the fire and then left the cottage, closing the front door quietly behind him.

14

When Charles arrived at the Shorts' home the following afternoon he was told that Carl was out shooting on the estate and he could hear the distant sound of gun shots. He wondered what it might be that Carl would be shooting at that time of the year, and when he followed the directions he was given he discovered that it was clay pigeons. Carl, dressed in breeches and a shooting sweater, was firing at the pigeons while a man in a tweed suit was pulling the traps.

As well as his reason for calling on the Shorts that afternoon, Charles had an excuse. That morning a lad from the garage in Portree had brought his car up to Staffin for, with the unpredictability that Charles was beginning to recognise as typical of Skye, the new water pump he had brought back from Edinburgh had been quickly fitted and the repairs completed. When he had looked in the glove compartment of the car he had found that the sunglasses he sometimes wore when driving on bright days were not there and, remembering that he had once worn them when driving Gloria's Mercedes, he realised that he must have left them in it.

When he saw Charles arrive in the field, Carl stopped shooting and introduced the man who was pulling for him as his factor, Angus MacDougall. Then he added, 'Why didn't you come earlier and lunch with us?'

Charles explained the reason for his visit and Carl said, 'That's a bore. Gloria has gone out in her car.'

'I can come again some other time. The glasses are not important.'

158

'No, hang on. She might well be back soon.' Carl held the shotgun he was holding out to Charles. 'In the meantime, why not have a little shooting practice?'

Charles explained that, apart from one or two visits to the rifle range at school, he had never shot. Shooting had never been a sport that interested him, even though his father had shot and hunted in many countries where he had worked.

'Never mind,' Carl said. 'Have a try. You might enjoy it. I'll show you.'

He first explained the shotgun to Charles, showing how it was loaded and demonstrating how it should be held and swung to follow the flight of a bird. When firing at clay pigeons one should aim well in front of them so that, in effect, the clay disc flew into the concentration of pellets. Several stands had been marked out in the field from which one could fire at the clays when they were released. In this way one could get practice in shooting at different angles. Carl picked one that would give a relatively easy shot for Charles's first attempt.

'Beginner's luck,' Charles exclaimed when to his surprise the clay pigeon was shattered by his first shot. His second and third attempts failed miserably with the clays sailing away into the distance, but the next two shots were on target.

'You could be a useful shot,' Carl commented. 'You've a good eye and good co-ordination. That's all it takes.'

He told Charles that he shot clay pigeons regularly two or three times a week at that time of year, just to keep in practice till the shooting season began. Taking back his gun, which was one of a pair that had been made to his measurements by Purdeys, he was about to continue with his practice when they heard the bleep of a cellular telephone and Charles saw that Carl had brought one with him and placed it on the ground up against the hedge behind them.

Carl took the call and what he was told must have annoyed him for he began talking rapidly and angrily in German. Charles knew no German, for Latin and French were the only languages he had studied at school and the only words he could understand in what Carl was saying were the names of places: London, Edinburgh, Milan. As the conversation continued, Carl's anger grew and he began shouting until presently he broke off the call abruptly.

'That was my son, the bloody fool!' he told Charles. 'I'll have to go and phone him from my study where my papers are.'

'Then I'll be leaving.'

'No, hang on. I'll only be a few minutes and then Angus and I will show you round the estate.' He turned to MacDougall. 'Give him some more instruction, Angus, while I'm gone. We'll have him shooting with us when the season starts.'

Carl walked off in the direction of the house and MacDougall pulled a few more clays for Charles. He shot reasonably well, missing only two, and decided it was a sport that he could learn to enjoy, although he doubted whether he would feel the same satisfaction from shooting if instead of shattering a clay disc, success was rewarded with the body of a bird falling out of the sky in the ugly finality of death.

'That's enough, thanks,' he said to MacDougall, for his shoulder was beginning to feel bruised from the recoil of the gun.

MacDougall took the shotgun from him and they stood chatting, waiting for Carl to return. The factor told Charles that he had studied agriculture at Aberdeen University and had managed estates in several parts of Scotland but never before on one of the Western Isles. He was responsible for the upkeep of Carl Short's property, including the farms that were let to tenants, and he had to organise and supervise a whole range of activities, from the maintenance of buildings to keeping the small loch stocked with fish. He mentioned some of the improvements that Carl was having made.

'Is it true that you are employing only local labour?'

'Yes. Mr Short insists on it, although it would be cheaper in the long run to bring men in from the mainland.'

'Surely you would have to pay them more?'

'Yes, but they would get through twice as much work.'

'Are you saying that the locals are lazy?'

MacDougall shrugged. 'That's partly true but there's more to it. The people of the Western Isles have always been crofters, working their own land. It's a tradition that goes back for centuries. They seem to get no satisfaction from working for other people and take no pride in it.'

'They tell me you bring men to work here from as far as Staffin.'

'Aye, I've no choice, for I can't get enough men in Sleat. And it means providing transport for them, morning and evening.'

'Was it not one of your men who drove Mrs Short's car up to Staffin for me the other day?'

'It was. McPhee.' The thought of McPhee seemed to be as unwelcome to MacDougall as an infestation of vermin on the estate would be. 'Aye, he works here, if one can call it work. Arrives an hour late most mornings, even though it's no more than a mile from the cottage of that widow who's he's shacked up with, and he slides off whenever it suits him.'

'Why do you put up with him?' MacDougall did not strike Charles as a man who would suffer laziness lightly and immorality even less. One could feel a streak of the Presbyterian in him.

'I wouldn't if it was up to me, but yon Murdo has friends up there.' MacDougall nodded in the direction of the house behind them.

'Carl likes him, then?'

'It wasn't Mr Short I was meaning,' MacDougall replied.

As soon as he left Carl Short's estate Charles stopped his car by the side of the road and, from the pocket in the door beside him, pulled out the two Ordnance Survey maps of Skye that he had bought in London and brought with him to the island. The Sleat peninsula was covered by the map of south Skye and, unfolding it, he spread it out in front of him. With its scale of one and a quarter inches to the mile, the map gave a wealth of detailed information, showing not

161

only roads, rivers and lochs, but buildings and houses, the contours of the hills and outcrops of rock and woodland. The patches of woodland were divided into conifers, mixed and others.

Charles decided he could afford to ignore the conifer woods because on Skye these were largely plantations created by the Forestry Commission, in which the trees were closely planted in neat rows and difficult to penetrate. Along the road which led to Broadford there were a number of mixed and other woods but these, he felt, would not be remote enough. He noticed that a few miles north of the pier at Ardvasar, from which the ferry to Mallaig sailed, there was a small road leading off the main Broadford road. It was marked in yellow on the map, which indicated that it must be extremely narrow, and in and around the township of Tokavaig it passed through several patches of mixed woodland and by a number of small lochs.

Putting the map away, he drove in the direction of the road and when he reached the turning saw a notice warning drivers that it was unsuitable for caravans. As he soon found out, the warning was an understatement, perhaps a typically laconic Skye joke. Narrow, tortuous and undulating, with unexpectedly sharp, winding drops followed by equally unexpected sharp ascents, the road had to be driven at little more than walking pace. This suited the search Charles was making and from time to time he stopped, leaving the car to explore patches of woodland, outcrops of rock and several small lochs.

After driving and searching for several miles he had found nothing, when he noticed tyre tracks skirting a copse of trees. An attempt had been made to obliterate the tracks, possibly by dragging a branch of a tree across them, but at a point where the ground was marshy the wheels of the car had sunk in and Charles could make out the tracks quite clearly. He followed them round the trees and between them and a platform of rock, well concealed from the road, he found the car.

It was a dark green Ford Fiesta, some years old, Charles

judged, and, like many cars on Skye, scarred by the ravages of poor roads, a surfeit of wet weather and neglect. Both the front and rear numberplates had been removed and the tax disc had been peeled from the windscreen. Charles tried the handle of the door on the driver's side, found it was locked, and peered through the mud-spattered windows to see whether there was anything inside that might suggest the identity of the owner. He saw nothing and the inside of the car seemed to have been scoured clean. He walked right round the car examining it but, apart from a generous sprinkling of dents and scrapes, found nothing.

Returning to his own car, he drove on towards Tokavaig where surely he would find a telephone. Before he found one he reached the shore of Loch Eishort and was so dazzled by the view in front of him that he was almost distracted from his purpose. The mist of the early morning had lifted, the sky was clear and the sunshine unbelievably bright. Across the loch stood the Cuillins, their peaks still capped with snow, silent and remote in their majesty. It was the sort of day and the sort of view that people said one never found on Skye and Charles wanted to stay and stare until it was etched for ever in his memory.

When, reluctantly, he went into the phone box, getting through to Superintendent Grieve was not as simple as he had expected, for the police station in Portree appeared to have installed a new telephone system and he was passed from one policeman to another before, finally, he heard Grieve's voice.

'Good afternoon, Dr Mackinnon. What can I do for you?'

'I've found what I'm almost certain is Jamie Gillespie's car.'

'What made you think of looking down in Sleat for the car?' Grieve asked Charles.

'You might call it a hunch, I suppose.'

'Was it because Sleat is just about as far away from where the lad was killed as anywhere on the island?'

'Sleat is also probably one of the places on the island where it would be easiest to hide a car.'

'With all its trees? Yes, I can see that.'

Charles thought that to anyone who knew the island there were many places on Skye where one could more safely have hidden a car, deep lochs in which a car would sink and disappear, caves along the shores of sea lochs near Monkstadt where no one would go at least not until summer when the island would be dissected by inquisitive visitors. He was glad that Grieve did not press him on his reasons for looking in Sleat for Jamie's car.

He was talking to Grieve not in the police station but in the Royal Hotel, where the police had set up what they described as an incident room to deal with the two murders, for, although Mairi's death was being investigated by police on the mainland where her body had been found, information about her disappearance was also being collected on Skye. A room adjoining the incident room had been adapted to serve as an office for Grieve.

The car that Charles had found in Sleat the previous afternoon had been towed, with some difficulty, from its hiding-place and brought to a disused workshop on the outskirts of Portree for examination. Already the police had established that it was Jamie's car by checking the engine and chassis numbers.

'I wonder why whoever took the car went to the trouble of removing the numberplates,' Charles remarked.

'That copse would have been meant as only a temporary hiding-place. Later, when the heat was off, the car could have been resprayed a different colour and fitted with new numberplates. Then it could have been driven away and off Skye with no bother at all.'

'Then my finding it may not have been of much help to you.'

'We shall have to see. Now that we can issue a photograph of the actual car and a detailed description of it, someone may come forward who saw it that evening when it was being driven to Sleat. The driver may have been recognised.'

That did not seem very likely to Charles. The days were still short and within no more than an hour, at the most, of the time when he saw the murder at Kilt Rock it would have been dark. The murderer could have driven the car to a lonely place, the Quiraing perhaps, and waited for darkness before he drove to Sleat.

'Did you find nothing in the car that would show who had driven it after Jamie's death?' he asked Grieve.

'Nothing so far. The forensic people have been working on it since first light this morning. There was nothing in the car; not a cigarette end, a scrap of paper, mud or grass, nothing.'

'What about fingerprints?'

'They found prints, all right, plenty of them, and a good number of them we were able to match at once: Willie Gillespie's, Murdo McPhee's and those of another local man named Barclay. They've all been smalltime villains so we have their dabs on record. But all the prints were in parts of the car where a passenger would have left them. They must all have ridden with Jamie at one time or another.'

'You found none on the steering wheel?'

'No, nor on the brake lever, the gear shift, the ignition lock or the inside and outside handles of the driver's door. Obviously all those must have been wiped clean.'

Charles was disappointed. The callous and brutal murder on Kilt Rock and the sight of Jamie Gillespie's flailing arms as he was thrown into space had sickened him. He also felt a growing sympathy for Jamie. From what he had heard in Edinburgh, he realised that there had been no malice in the lad and he had hoped that by finding the car he would have helped the police to prove who had murdered him.

'Did your people test the driving mirror for prints?' he asked Grieve.

'I don't know. Why?'

'From what I saw on Kilt Rock, the man who murdered Jamie was a good deal taller than him. If he drove the car away afterwards he might well have adjusted the driving mirror, automatically as one does, and forgotten that he had done it.'

Grieve looked at Charles, impressed. The young doctor

was showing that he had a good brain. Without commenting he picked up the telephone on the table in front of him and, speaking to whoever was examining the car, gave instructions that the driving mirror should be checked for fingerprints.

'You've clearly been giving the death of Gillespie a good deal of thought,' he remarked.

'Not really, but what I saw happen that evening has left a memory which keeps recurring. The business of the car puzzled me.'

'In what way?'

'Killing Jamie by throwing him off Kilt Rock must have been meant to make people believe that he had committed suicide, because he was dying of AIDS. If I had not been at the view point quite by chance, that is what people would have thought, but only if his car had been found in the road alongside the cliff. So why did his murderer take the car?'

'Because he needed to get away.'

'Maybe, but surely he could have waited until it was dark, walked up to Staffin and caught a bus from there or hitched a lift.'

'Then what is your theory?'

Charles shrugged. 'Perhaps he needed to get wherever he was going as quickly as possible to establish an alibi for himself.'

Grieve sighed. The whole world was a detective these days. Everyone knew how a murder was planned, evidence concealed or faked, alibis arranged. Everyone knew how to handle investigations better than the police and more often than not the help they volunteered was only a hindrance. Television was to blame. With a dozen or more murder mysteries, private eye series and police squad series screened every week it was only to be expected.

He and the doctor chatted for a while. Charles did not wish to leave until he had heard whether any more fingerprints had been found in the car. Eventually the call came and when Grieve answered it and heard what his colleague had to say he laughed with satisfaction. He was growing tired of being stuck out on this unfriendly island, and back in Inverness his wife was becoming restless and nagging him over the telephone. All he needed was a stroke of luck to break this case and now Dr Mackinnon had provided one.

'You were right, Doctor,' he said as he put down the telephone. 'Good for you! They've found a print on the driving mirror, all right; a beautiful thumb print.'

'Do you know whose print it is?'

'Aye, we do. That villain Murdo McPhee.'

15

The case against Murdo McPhee was assembled without much difficulty. Until Jamie Gillespie's car was found the police had been concentrating their investigation in and around Staffin. Now, switching to the Sleat peninsula, they soon found the accumulation of evidence they needed.

When he was questioned McPhee claimed he had been in the home of his widow friend throughout the afternoon and evening of Jamie's death, but a married couple taking an early holiday in a small hotel at Ardvasar remembered picking him up as he was hitching a lift to Broadford that afternoon. A nurse from the Doctor Mackinnon Hospital in Broadford, who had been friendly with McPhee until he took up with the widow, had seen him climbing into a van belonging to a firm of builders from Inverness as she was cycling home from the hospital. The van was traced and its driver identified McPhee as the man to whom he had given a lift, dropping him off on the outskirts of Portree in the middle of the afternoon.

The widow from Sleat at first confirmed McPhee's story but, pressed by the police, she had eventually admitted that she had not seen him all day. Finally, the missing number-plates of Jamie's car were found where McPhee had hidden them, in a shed on the widow's croft.

The police had 'lifted' McPhee and interrogated him aggressively for the full six hours that were allowed under Scottish law before he might be charged. McPhee had defended himself, equally aggressively, with blustering denials, a good deal of swearing and protestations that people were ganging up on him, perjuring themselves to destroy him. Superintendent Grieve continued questioning him, unwaveringly, with the blinkered focus of a determined Scot. He had heard of the subtle technique of brainwashing used in Communist countries, in which interrogators alternated between bullying their prisoner and treating him with an almost loving kindness, but he had no faith in it. Nor did he believe in playing a victim as one might a hooked salmon, gradually reeling him in to within reach of the landing net. He preferred to bludgeon a suspect, without pity and without humanity, confident that eventually his resistance would break.

McPhee surprised him for he did not break, at least not in the way that Grieve might have expected. When finally he knew he was about to be charged with the murder of Jamie Gillespie, his whole attitude changed.

'Aye, all right,' he said. 'I did toss the lad off the cliff, but it was no murder.'

'I see. It was just a wee mishap, an accident.' Sarcasm was not a weapon that Grieve used often, for he never felt at home with it.

'Not at all. I was just doing what the lad asked me to do; putting him out of his misery.'

'You're not pretending that he asked you to kill him?'

'Surely. And why not? Jamie knew he had not long to go; six months at most, maybe less. He wished to die quickly and without pain, but he didna' have the courage to kill himself. That's why he came to me.'

'Why you?' In spite of himself, Grieve was beginning to be fascinated by what McPhee was saying. He had known people charged with murder or violent crimes give all kinds of excuses or explanations, but McPhee's was a new one.

'I had been a father to the lad ever since his own dad died. Anyone will tell you that. And there was no one else he could turn to, would do him a favour like that one.'

Without any prompting or encouragement McPhee gave his version of Jamie Gillespie's death. Seeing his friend in Edinburgh die of AIDS had made Jamie realise that he too was going to die and he had decided to prepare for it. After breaking his drug habit he had returned to Skye, determined to do what he could to help his family and to spare them as much grief and shame as he could. With the money he had saved while working in Edinburgh he had bought his mother a television and a washing machine, given his brother a hundred pounds, and bought himself a car which he would leave to Willie when he died. His intention after that had been to jump off Kilt Rock. That would be more bearable than a slow, lingering death and he believed that the people of Skye would see it as the courageous act of a young man who wished to spare his mother and brother further humiliation.

'The lad went up on the cliff more than once,' McPhee concluded, 'meaning to end it, but he couldna' bring himself to jump. So he came to me. I didn't have the stomach for it either, but how could I refuse him?'

As he listened to McPhee, Grieve began to feel uncomfortable. The story was preposterous and Grieve did not believe a word of it, but others might. By telling it confidently, no doubt after careful preparation and rehearsal, McPhee had taken the initiative of the interrogation from the police. Now the onus would be on them to prove he was lying and to do that they would have to show that he had a motive for killing Jamie Gillespie. At that moment Grieve had no idea what the motive might be.

'What about Gillespie's car?' he asked McPhee. 'Why did you take it away and hide it?'

'The car was a mistake, an oversight, you might say. Jamie and I hadna' thought about the car at all. He arranged to pick me up in Portree that afternoon and we drove up to Kilt Rock together. The idea was that we would leave the car by the roadside and you'd think he had gone there to kill himself. And that's what you would have thought, wouldn't you?'

'You forget that a witness saw you throw him off the cliff.'

'At that time of day? And in that light? No, if you'd have found the car in the road, you wouldna' have believed yon doctor. You'd have thought he imagined it.'

Grieve did not argue. What McPhee had said was too close to the truth. Even after Gillespie's body had been found he had been reluctant to believe that the doctor had seen him being thrown off the cliff.

'Then why did you take the car?'

'How else could I have got back to Sleat without being seen? As I told you, Jamie and I hadna' thought of that. If I'd walked or tried to hitch a lift it would have been a sure giveaway. Everyone knows me on Skye, Super.'

'Maybe you killed him just for the car.'

'Kill him for that old banger!' McPhee laughed, aware by this time that he had an advantage over the police. 'And I could never have driven it on Skye, could I?'

'Why not? With a spray job and new numberplates? Or you could have taken it over to the mainland and traded it for another car.'

'That's no very likely, is it, Super?'

'You'll be charged with the murder of Gillespie anyway,' Grieve said, clamping down his growing bad temper. 'And then we'll see if a jury believes this tale.'

McPhee's admission that he had killed Jamie Gillespie and his explanation for why he had done so spread over the island almost as quickly as the news that he had been lifted by the police. After dinner that evening Charles was discussing it with Mrs Tait.

'Will anyone believe McPhee's story?' he asked her.

'Why shouldn't it be the truth? Morag says Jamie told her that he had come home to die. He did what he could for his mother, bought her things to make her life easier and was ready then to have his own life brought to an end.'

'But I saw him struggling as McPhee went to throw him over the cliff!'

'Is that so strange? Even if he had asked Murdo to push him off, would he not be frightened at the last minute and fight against it, however brave he was?'

'I suppose so.' Charles was far from convinced. 'And would Murdo really have agreed to kill him, just as a favour?'

'He might well. He was genuinely fond of Jamie.' Mrs Tait hesitated, reluctant to say what was on her mind. 'And if Jamie had agreed to pay him, gave him a hundred pounds, say, then he certainly would have done it.'

Half an hour later, when they were no longer thinking or talking about McPhee or Jamie Gillespie but were discussing the practice and how long it would be before Donald Tait would be fit enough to start work again, Hector Monro arrived. He was carrying a folder under his arm and his manner was businesslike.

'Have you two heard about Murdo McPhee?' he asked them, and when Mrs Tait replied that they had he went on, 'That's why I'm here. We must do something to help the poor man.'

'What had you in mind, Hector?'

'I'm starting a defence fund for him, so that we can get him the very best legal advice.' Opening his folder, Hector took out a sheet of paper on which several names had been written. 'See. I've put down everyone who I believe would wish to contribute and I've phoned some of them already.'

'What kind of response are you having?'

'Excellent! I've put myself down for five hundred pounds and Carl Short is giving the same.'

'I'm afraid Donald and I couldn't rise to that.' Mrs Tait was always frank about money.

'Of course not! You have family commitments. Most people I've spoken to are giving twenty-five, fifty in some cases.'

'We'll certainly give fifty, but I'll need to ask Donald.'

'That's splendid!' Hector said enthusiastically, but one had the impression that he had been expecting at least a hundred pounds. 'We'll open the list to everyone; his friends and relations and workmates – everyone. They'll all wish to give something, I'm sure, even if it's no more than a pound or two. And the pub where he works in the summer has agreed to take up a collection for him.'

Charles realised that as a stranger to the island he was not going to be asked to contribute. He was glad because he would have felt obliged to refuse, not through meanness but because it would have been hypocrisy to help McPhee. The man's story was not to be believed, nor did he accept the interpretation that Mrs Tait and others were putting on Jamie Gillespie's reasons for returning to Skye. Jamie may well have come home, knowing he was going to die of AIDS before long, but there had been nothing in his behaviour either in Edinburgh or on Skye to suggest that he wanted a quick death and was too cowardly to kill himself. Charles also wished to know where Jamie had got hold of so much money, not only the money to buy the car, the television set and the washing machine, but the banknotes he had hidden beneath the floor. Hundreds of pounds, Morag Gillespie had said, perhaps thousands. What if McPhee had found out about the money, murdered Jamie and then stolen it, knowing that Morag would never tell the police?

He would have liked to have answers to these and other questions, but neither Mrs Tait nor Hector Monro would have been able to give them. The people of Skye, Kirsten had told him once, looked after their own and Mrs Tait and Monro would do just that. Charles knew he had no right to question their loyalty, even though he was convinced that in the case of McPhee it was misplaced.

'Murdo will go to prison, of course,' Mrs Tait said. 'For how long do you think?'

'Not too long,' Hector replied. 'He can plead that it was a mercy killing.'

'Hardly that, surely?'

'Why not? Everybody knows that there's no cure for AIDS and today the law is taking a more lenient view of euthanasia. Do you remember that case in Edinburgh a few months ago? That woman who helped her old mother to die was given a suspended sentence.'

'I hope you're right.'

Soon afterwards, when Monro had left to make more calls on possible donors to his fund, Charles asked Mrs Tait, 'Why is Hector doing all this for McPhee?'

'At heart he's a kind man,' Mrs Tait replied and then

173

she added with a smile, 'and it makes him feel important.'

She picked up a book and began reading. Although there was a television set in the drawing-room, Charles had noticed that she seldom watched any programmes. The reception was poor, she had told him, and the programmes not worth watching, but he believed that the real reason for her indifference was that Skye was her life and people and events outside the island held little interest for her. He could understand her attitude, for in the short time he had spent on Skye he had noticed the world in which until then he had lived gradually receding. A newspaper was delivered at the house every day and after the first few days he had begun to do no more than glance at the headlines, and the sensations they offered seemed curiously unreal and remote.

Picking up a copy of the British Medical Journal that lay on the table beside him, he tried to interest himself in the editorial article, which was a heavily biased and, Charles thought, unfair attack on the Government for not taking sufficient account of a report recently produced by the Royal College of Physicians. As he read, he once again felt how far away Skye was from the world and particularly from the world of academic medicine, but it was a world in which several thousand people had to live and it was their wellbeing that had to be the concern of Donald Tait and the other doctors on the island.

When the telephone suddenly rang Mrs Tait sprang up to answer it and she seemed disappointed that it was a call from a patient. She picked up her book again and, watching her as he spoke to the patient, Charles could see that she was not concentrating on what she was reading. He sensed that something was worrying her.

'Is anything the matter, Fiona? You seem restless.'

'No. Not really.'

'But there is something worrying you?'

'You'll think me foolish, but it's just that I haven't heard from Kirsten all day.'

'Have you phoned her?'

'Three times, but there was no reply.'

'Maybe her line is out of order.'

'No, I checked with the operator and it's not.' Charles wondered what he should say to reassure Mrs Tait and as he hesitated she continued, 'You'll be thinking I'm worrying needlessly and I may well be, but a day never goes by without Kirsten and I speaking to each other. If she had been going anywhere for the day she would have told me.'

'If you're worried, why don't you drive down to her cottage?'

'I may later, but Donald rings me every evening at about this time and I don't want to miss his call.'

'Would you like me to go?' Almost as soon as he made the offer, Charles found himself questioning it.

'It's an awful lot to ask.'

'Don't be silly! And a drive will do me good.' Charles held up the medical journal. 'This BMJ is slowly putting me to sleep.'

'All right, then; if you're sure.' Mrs Tait fished in the pocket of her cardigan. 'Here's a key to Kirsten's cottage. If she's not at home when you get there, let yourself in and call me.'

Driving along the road to Portree, Charles began to analyse his motives for volunteering so readily to go and see if Kirsten was all right. He did not believe that anything serious could have happened to her. If she had been taken ill or had had an accident Mrs Tait would have heard, and no doubt there was some simple explanation for why she had not been in touch with her mother that day. Why, then, was he going to her cottage? Was he, without realising it, hoping that he would find her at home and that once again she would ask him to take her to bed? He liked Kirsten, was at ease in her company and had found that they shared many views and tastes, but until a day or two ago he had not felt any physical attraction for her. Now, he knew from experience, things would be different. The brief intimacy they had shared in her cottage would have implanted an association of ideas and the desire he had felt for her then would re-emerge, no matter how he tried to suppress it, intruding in his thoughts,

175

often at inopportune moments and colouring his attitude towards her. He was not certain how he would react when he next saw her.

When he reached the cottage, saw no lights and that Kirsten's car was not standing outside, he realised that she could not be at home and was disappointed. Recalling that he had promised to phone Mrs Tait, he took the key that she had given him and went to open the front door. To his surprise, it was open and a few inches ajar. Pushing it further open, he called out Kirsten's name and hearing no reply called it out once more. The front door, as in many cottages, opened directly into the living-room and as he went in he switched on the light. There was nobody in the room and no fire in the grate. Nothing seemed amiss but as Charles looked around he heard a sound that might have been the sound of a door closing coming from the back of the cottage.

'Who's that?' he called out loudly and went through to the kitchen.

The back door was closed but not locked. Opening it, he looked out but could see no one. A short distance away from the back of the cottage stood an open shed in which, Charles knew, coal and peat were kept under cover, together with an old bicycle and a few pieces of wooden furniture, no longer used but not yet finally discarded. As he peered into its shadows he heard another noise, this time of someone stumbling, perhaps tripping over the cycle.

'Who's there?' he shouted.

'It's only me, Doctor. Willie.'

Charles waited and presently Willie Gillespie came out of the shed, stumbling again, this time over the piled-up coal. 'What are you doing here?' he asked him.

'I came to see Miss Kirsten, Doctor, but she's no at home, as you can see.'

'Have you been inside the cottage?'

'Yes. The front door was open,' Willie replied and then, remembering how he had escaped from the cottage when he heard Charles arrive, he added, 'and so was the back door.'

'Come with me.'

Charles wondered what he should do. He had no proprietary rights to the cottage and no authority for challenging Willie, but he could tell from the man's manner that he was lying. For a brief moment he wondered too whether Willie might have harmed Kirsten and whether her body might be lying among the peats in the shed. Then he dismissed the idea as absurd. If Willie had committed any crime he would not have hung around the cottage when he heard Charles' car pull up outside it but would have run off in panic.

Together they went back into the cottage and Charles locked the back door with the key that was in the lock and bolted it as well. Then he said to Willie, as sternly as he could, 'Now, why did you come here tonight?'

'As I told you, Doctor, to see Miss Kirsten. I wanted to tell her how sorry I was about Mairi, the poor wee creature.'

'But why did you come into the cottage? You must have realised Miss Kirsten wasn't here.'

'When I found the door was open, even though the lights were off I thought that maybe she'd had an accident, hurt herself in a fall or something.'

'Did you go upstairs?'

'Yes, Doc, just to make sure. But she was no there.'

Willie was wearing the worn sweater and ragged trousers that he usually wore. He looked as though he might have put on a little weight, but otherwise presented the same slothful, untidy figure. Charles felt sure that if he had intended paying a social call on Kirsten he would have dressed in more presentable clothes, but even though he was not inclined to believe his story he had no proof that it was a lie.

'You had better be off, then,' he told him, not attempting to hide his irritation.

Willie hurried away, clearly glad that he had been allowed to leave and that perhaps his story had been believed. Alone, Charles looked round the room carefully, trying to decide if anything was missing. He did not believe that Willie was a thief, but could think of no other reason why he should have broken into Kirsten's cottage. As far as he could tell nothing was missing and there were no signs of the hasty search one would associate with a burglary. The same was true upstairs in Kirsten's bedroom. He did not linger in the bedroom, feeling that by going in there on his own he was intruding on her privacy and taking a liberty which their short acquaintance did not warrant. In the bedroom that had been Mairi's he found some disorder, but nothing more than the untidiness one might expect in the room of an adolescent.

Returning downstairs, he telephoned Mrs Tait. She said at once, 'Charles, dear, you've had a wasted journey. I'm so sorry.'

'Why? What's happened?'

'Kirsten rang not long after you left here. She's been over on the mainland all day.'

'Did she say why?'

'No, but she's all right.'

Charles hesitated. 'Should I wait for her to return?'

'I wouldn't. She says it's likely she'll be late.'

Only after he had put down the phone and was planning to leave was Charles struck by another question. How had Willie travelled to Kirsten's cottage? He did not own a car and would not have come on foot all the way from Staffin or even from Portree. A friend might have driven him there but there had been no car standing in the road when Charles arrived. If he had come by bus, which seemed unlikely at that time of night, he would be waiting by the bus stop in the road outside or he might have set off walking towards Portree, hoping for a lift.

Leaving the cottage, Charles walked quickly up to the road. Willie was not standing at the bus stop, nor was there any sign of a bus, but as Charles was looking up the road a grubby white van drove past.

16

Early the following morning Charles was awoken by the telephone. The house had two telephones, one in the drawing-room and another in the surgery, and the instrument in the surgery could be taken upstairs and plugged into a socket in either Dr and Mrs Tait's bedroom or the room Charles was using.

'Charles? What are you doing for breakfast?' Kirsten's voice sounded uncharacteristically brisk.

'Eating whatever your mother cooks for me and enjoying it.'

'I'll cook for you today. My porridge is out of this world and I've some Arbroath smokies. How long does it take you to dress?'

'About twenty minutes, give or take a new razor blade.'

'Then I'll expect you before seven.'

'Seven! For Christ's sake! What time is it?'

'Just at the back of six.'

Charles picked up his watch from the bedside table and stared at it incredulously. The curtains were drawn in the room and he had not noticed that it was no more than barely day. Still drowsy, he wondered first whether Kirsten was playing a practical joke on him and then, dismissing the idea, if she were ill.

'Are you all right, Kirsten?'

'I'm fine. Why?'

'Attractive girls don't ring me at dawn; only patients.'

'Well, I'm fine.'

'Then what's this all about?'

'I'll tell you when I see you.' Kirsten may have sensed his doubt, for she said, 'You will come, won't you?' and then added, pleadingly it seemed to Charles, 'Please!'

The morning was still grey though clear enough when Charles, after a quick shower, left the house but as the road dropped down towards Portree he ran into a clammy sea mist almost thick enough to be called fog. Driving carefully through it, he wondered again why Kirsten should be wishing to see him at that hour of the morning. Her brisk, too cheerful tone on the telephone was out of character and her disappearance the previous day also needed explaining. He had not seen her since the evening when he had, briefly, shared her bed. Had she been avoiding him? On the other hand, she might be having some form of nervous crisis. Back in London he had often treated women patients whose bright smiles and aimless chatter could not conceal the anguish in their eyes; women who had, not for the first time, lost a baby, whose husbands had deserted them, even those who could not come to terms with the menopause. He had no means of knowing how Mairi's death may have affected Kirsten.

When he reached the cottage she was sitting in her car outside it waiting for him. As he pulled up she started the engine and opened the door on the passenger's side. 'Charles you're late,' she called out cheerfully. 'Jump in.'

He did as she had asked and as he fastened the seat belt asked her, 'What about the breakfast you promised me?'

'There'll be time enough for breakfast later. Was it not you who said that when God made time he made plenty of it?'

They drove along the road towards Dunvegan and, reaching Fairy Bridge, turned off on to the Waternish peninsula. As they drove, the sea mist began to clear and presently they could see below them to their left the shore of Loch Bay and the ocean beyond. Passing above Stein where the experiment to start a fishing industry on Skye had failed more than two hundred years previously, Kirsten followed the road as it turned inland, heading for Waternish Point, but before they reached it, as so often happened on Skye, they ran out of road.

They parked the car in a field near the ruins of Trumpan church, scene of a terrible battle, Charles had read, between the MacLeods and the Macdonalds. The Macdonalds had sailed into the bay one day, landed and set fire to the church, massacring its congregation. Only one woman escaped, badly wounded, and she had sent a child for help. The MacLeods arrived but, outnumbered in the battle that followed, were forced to raise the Fairy Flag. Supernatural reinforcements arrived and the Macdonalds were annihilated.

Leaving the car, Charles and Kirsten walked along the path above the cliffs that led to Waternish Point. The sea mist had completely vanished now and the morning was bright and clear with no more than a rustle of wind to disturb the calm of the sea. Across the South Minch the Outer Isles, Harris and North Uist, were still only hazy shadows but, as one watched, their contours grew sharper. Anywhere else the view would call for superlatives but on Skye, Charles was learning, views of an almost unbelievable beauty were commonplace.

They had scarcely spoken since they had left Kirsten's cottage, but Charles sensed that she had something to tell him. For some reason, though, she was waiting for him to give her an opening, a cue to begin.

'What happened to you yesterday?' he asked her. 'We were worried about you.'

'I know. It was thoughtless of me to go off without telling anyone.'

'Where did you go?'

'To the hills above Loch Garry,' she hesitated, as though it needed an effort to add, 'to the place where they found Mairi's – where they found Mairi.'

Charles knew there was nothing he could say to that. If Kirsten wished to explain why she had gone to Loch Garry she would, but in her own time. They walked for another few minutes in silence. Far out at sea a white yacht, leaning gracefully in the breeze, was heading towards the Outer Isles. Charles was filled with a sudden longing for them both to be on it, to escape from whatever problems that day might bring, for the freedom of a tiny boat in the vast emptiness of the ocean.

'I went on a sudden impulse,' Kirsten said at last. 'I don't really know why. Perhaps I hoped that my guilt would be exorcised.'

'What guilt?'

'For not taking better care of Mairi, for my share in the responsibility for her death.'

'Oh, for God's sake, Kirsten!' Charles could not check his impatience. 'How can you possibly feel any guilt? You gave that poor girl the only happiness she ever knew.'

'I know. I worked that out, but only later. All I could think of when I reached the place was that you and I had passed within a few yards of where she lay when we drove to Edinburgh, and again when we returned, and that Mairi must have been lying there dead, alone.'

Charles waited, knowing that she had more to tell him, much more. A priest in a confessional did not comment or question until the penitent's overflow of remorse had stopped.

'I wept at first,' Kirsten continued, 'crying, as I imagined, for pity, for poor little Mairi whose life had been brutally cut short, for what she had missed. Then slowly I began to realise that my pity was not for Mairi but for myself. All the time and trouble I had spent in looking after her, being a mother to her, patiently teaching her the things that other children learned instinctively; all that had been wasted. And the pleasure she had given me was at an end; yes, pleasure, at seeing her understanding grow, her skills develop; and the self-satisfaction of hearing people say how patient I was, how good and kind. All that was over now and my self-pity brimmed over.'

'You're being too hard on yourself.'

'No, I learned something about myself in those woods.' Kirsten looked at Charles. 'Do you know what I did then? I went down to Loch Garry. You've never been there, I suppose?'

She told him that she had left the woods in which Mairi had been found, crossed the main road and had gone down to Loch Garry, where she had parked her car and begun walking by the loch. After a time she had found a fallen tree by the water and had sat down to think.

'I looked back over the last few years of my life,' she told Charles, 'and realised how empty and meaningless they have been.'

'Hardly meaningless, or empty,' Charles protested. 'You started your craft centre and made a success of it; what you taught Mairi was little short of a miracle and you know very well how much your care and affection mean to your parents.'

'But what does all that amount to? It's so limited, so narrow. After Bruce was killed on the mountains I gave up nursing, retreated into a small, private world.'

'I can't see how you think that was selfish.'

'What have I done for Skye all these years? In the short time that you've been here, Charles, you've seen the worst of Skye and I don't mean only the violence, the murders of Jamie and Mairi. You've seen prejudice, ignorance and laziness. You've seen the harm that inbreeding can cause, the apathy of the people who live on the island, the way that visitors are exploited.'

'Maybe, but you're talking about only a small minority.'

'I agree, but what have I done about it? To my mind, living in a community is like belonging to a club. If you don't like the way the other members behave or how the club is run, you have two choices. You either resign or you set out to make the club better. In spite of Skye's failings, all its faults and the irritations that Gloria Short and other people find so exasperating, I love it. So I should be doing all I can to make life on the island better, richer.'

They had turned before reaching Waternish Point and were making their way back to the car. As they walked and on the drive to her cottage, Kirsten told Charles of what she planned to do. Later that day she would ask the head art teacher in Portree High School if he could find two pupils who would be leaving school that summer and who would like to work in her craft centre. She could afford to employ two and it would mean that she would have more time to train them in her own skills. For some years she had thought of starting evening classes in sculpture for adults and now she would put the plan into effect. With financial backing from the Highlands and Islands Development Board, she and her friends might be able to revive cottage industries, weaving, perhaps, and pottery.

'There's lots one could do in Staffin. That community centre could be used far more. Ceilidhs are fine but what about discussion groups? And when my father returns he could start a series of evening meetings, on diet and hygiene, for example.'

Privately, Charles could not help feeling that Kirsten was being carried away by what she saw as a mission. Competent and dedicated doctor though her father undoubtedly was, it was questionable whether at his age he would have the time or the inclination to become involved in a series of community health activities.

'Do you think your father ever regrets coming to spend his life on Skye?' he asked Kirsten.

'I'm sure he doesn't. You know what they say about Skye. It isn't an island, it's an intoxication, and my father is an addict.'

'Did he have any connection with the island before he first came here?'

'None.'

'Then what made him pick on Skye?' Charles had asked the question before but it had not been answered. He would also have liked to ask whether it had been Dr Tait's brush with the medical profession's ruling body over drugs that had made him decide to live and work on a remote Hebridean island.

Kirsten shrugged evasively. 'I don't know. I suppose he saw the opportunity and took it.'

When they reached her cottage she went into the kitchen to make their breakfast. As he waited, Charles looked around

184

him in the living-room, feeling that it had changed in some respect. The furniture had not been moved and the room was comfortably tidy as it always was, but even so he was sure that it had changed in some way. Then he noticed that the green marble sculpture of a young man's head was not on the table where it had stood. Because of its colour and its position on the table, its removal had made a surprising difference to the appearance of the room. As he noticed it, Charles suddenly remembered the previous evening, how he had found Willie Gillespie in the cottage, Willie's guilty manner, the bulge under his sweater. He could not recall noticing the sculpture when he and Willie had come back into the cottage, but the bulge had not seemed large enough to suggest that the sculpture might have been hidden beneath the sweater. He remembered then that he had not told Kirsten of the incident.

Over breakfast he told her. 'Your mother was worried about you yesterday so I came round to the cottage to see if everything was all right.'

'Yes, she told me she had sent you here when I called her. I'm sorry you had a wasted journey.'

'When I arrived I found Willie Gillespie here.'

'Willie? What did he want?'

'He made some excuse, but I believe he had broken into the cottage.' Charles described how he had found both the front and back doors open and Willie hiding in the shed at the back of the cottage. 'Has anything been taken from the cottage? Is anything missing?'

'Willie wouldn't come here to steal.'

'Where is that sculpture you had in the living-room? The head of a young man?'

Kirsten laughed, rather self-consciously. 'That isn't missing. First thing this morning I put it on display in the craft centre. It's for sale.' She looked at him directly as she added, 'That's part of my resolution for a different life; no living in the past.'

'That seems a little drastic.'

'It's a head of Bruce, you know.'

185

'I guessed as much.'

She began talking about Bruce, the young architect she had once planned to marry, and told Charles how the previous day at Loch Garry she had thought about their relationship, analysed it, recognising its weaknesses as well as its strengths. Had they married, her life would have followed an entirely different pattern and, even though the affection she felt for him had in no measure dwindled, she recognised now that it would not necessarily have been a better life. In the loneliness and grief that had followed his death, she had turned inwards, closing a large part of herself to other people, and in doing so had discovered resources and talents which she had never known she possessed. Now she wished to use those talents to the full and for others as well as for herself.

When she was making a second pot of tea for them he asked her again about Willie Gillespie's visit to the cottage the previous evening. 'Are you sure there is nothing missing from here?'

'Nothing that I've noticed.'

'Have you looked in the bedrooms?'

'I've not been into Mairi's room since I returned home last night. But there's nothing in there that anyone could possibly wish to steal.'

'Why don't you check?'

After pouring the tea she went upstairs to do as he suggested. When she came down again she looked thoughtful.

'Well?'

'The room does look as though it has been searched. Mairi always left it in a shambles and every morning I would go in and tidy. I remember doing that on the morning she disappeared, after I came home from putting her on the bus.'

'Is anything missing?'

'It sounds absurd, but I believe some of her drawings may have been taken. She was always drawing and I encouraged her. There would be half a dozen sheets torn from her sketch pad always lying around the room and occasionally

186

she would paste one or two of them on to the walls.'

'And you believe the drawings may have been taken?'

'There are none in the room at all, which is odd.' Kirsten shrugged. 'Anyway, they're worthless.'

By the time they had finished breakfast Charles realised that he must leave, for soon the first patients would be arriving at the Taits' house for morning surgery. He knew too that Mrs Tait would be wondering where he was, because he had not left a note for her and she would have long since finished her own breakfast. Kirsten went with him to his car.

'I never thanked you for the other night,' she said.

'Thanked me?'

'You know why. I don't have to spell it out.' She may have been blushing but in the bright morning sunlight Charles could not be sure. 'And I hope you didn't mind my dragging you out of bed at dawn today.'

'I'm glad you did. That view of the Outer Isles was out of this world. And so was the breakfast!'

'Sorry for unloading my thoughts and dreams on you.' She kissed him on the cheek. 'Yesterday was a watershed in my life. I had to tell you.'

17

The remainder of that day was so busy and disordered, jolted out of its routine pattern by a minor crisis and the backlog of work that this caused, that Charles had not time to think about what Kirsten had told him. Immediately after morning surgery he had been called urgently to the home of a patient where he had found a young lad running a high temperature with a fast pulse, complaining of a pain in his side and vomiting. Suspecting that the lad was suffering from appendicitis and not wishing to delay until an ambulance could be called, Charles had taken him, wrapped in a blanket and sitting on his mother's lap, to the hospital. At the hospital his diagnosis was confirmed and the boy had been taken immediately to the operating theatre.

From the hospital Charles had telephoned Mrs Tait and learned that more calls had been added to the day's list. Several patients had rung the house, asking for the doctor and complaining of symptoms that were ominously similar, a temperature above normal, nausea and diarrhoea. He wondered if it might be the start of one of those epidemics that sweep through a community, the effects of a virus, perhaps, not serious in a medical sense but bringing discomfort to the patients and a succession of long days to the doctor.

On his way back to Staffin Charles stopped off in Portree to buy toothpaste and after-shave lotion. He had parked his car in Somerled Square and was on his way to the chemists's shop when he saw Willie Gillespie coming towards him. Willie saw him, appeared startled, and looked quickly from side to side as though searching for a way of avoiding a meeting. When he realised that there was no means of escape he tried to bluff his way past with a smile and a cheerful wave.

'Willie, I want a word with you.' Charles put out a hand to stop him passing.

'Me, Doc?'

'Did you take anything from Miss Kirsten's cottage last night?'

'Take anything? I don't know what you mean, Doc.'

'Some of Mairi's drawings are missing from her bedroom.'

Fear flared in Willie's eyes. Like a bird trapped in a room he fluttered agitatedly, looking for an escape. 'I never went to her bedroom, Doc. I swear I never did. I don't know which her bedroom is. And I saw no drawings.' He paused and, seeing his protests were not having any effect, continued, 'What would I do with the drawings, anyway? They wouldna' be worth anything.'

'How would you know that if you never saw them?'

'If the girl did them they wouldna' be any good, would they? I mean, you met her, Doc.'

'If you did take them, and I believe you did, you had better take them back at once. If not you'll be in trouble with the police again.'

Now Willie's face was almost comical. He had more protests he wished to make but Charles did not wait to listen to them. More lies were all he could expect from Willie and there must be other, less tortuous ways of finding out why he had stolen the drawings.

After leaving Portree, Charles paid as many visits as he could, stopping only to telephone the hospital. He was told that the appendicectomy had been completely successful and that his patient was expected to make a rapid recovery. He felt the satisfaction he always felt when his diagnoses and the treatment he prescribed proved correct and this time the satisfaction was deeper because he had sensed that Mrs Henry, the boy's mother, had been afraid that her son was going to die.

Over lunch Mrs Tait had news for him and the telling of it made her indignant. 'Murdo McPhee has sold his story to a London newspaper for an enormous sum.'

'They're not going to print it now, surely?'

'No, not until after the trial.'

'How do you know this?'

'I bumped into Carl Short while I was shopping. Carl has friends in Fleet Street. Can you imagine what this will mean? Charles had not see Mrs Tait really angry before. 'Jamie, Morag and Willie and their private lives and all their secrets will be plastered over some tawdry rag. Nor will it stop there. We'll have seedy little journalists everywhere, prying and poking, trying to distort and smear life on Skye.'

'I suppose Murdo's story will be the same one that he told the police – that Jamie's death was a mercy killing.'

'You still don't believe that?'

'Not for one moment. For a start, I don't believe Jamie came home simply to die.'

'What other reason could he have had?'

'I'm not sure.'

Ever since he had come back from Edinburgh, Charles had been thinking of what he had been told by Jamie's friends. He had formed the impression that Jamie's behaviour during the days before he left for Skye had been too purposeful for a man who had given up life and was waiting only to die. At times Charles had tried sketching out an idea of what that purpose might have been, but it was no more than an outline of an idea and he needed more evidence before he could give it substance. So he decided not to mention the idea to Mrs Tait. In the meantime, he remembered a question he had been meaning to ask someone.

'Did you ever eat in the restaurant in Hector Monro's hotel? The one they say became so popular?'

'The one with the Italian chef? Only once. Donald doesn't care for nouvelle cuisine. As you can imagine, it's not his style.'

'The portions are too small?'

190

'And the colours too bright. If you want artistic arrangements go to an art gallery not a restaurant is what Donald says.'

'Can you remember the name of the Italian chef?'

Mrs Tait frowned. 'No, I can't recall it. I should be able to for it isn't all that long ago, but I've no memory for names any more. That's what happens when one grows old.'

After lunch Charles paid more calls, most of them on patients suffering from the same symptoms that he had encountered in the morning. He was convinced now that the epidemic was caused by a virus and was surprised that it should have spread so rapidly in a scattered community. On his way home, on an impulse, he dropped in on Jean Kennedy. He had seen little of the old lady during the past few days and, if the epidemic continued, he was not likely to have time for the luxury of a chat with a patient who was not really ill, at least not in the next day or two.

Thinking that she might reproach him for neglecting her, he began making excuses as soon as she let him into the house.

'I really have been very busy, Jeanie,' he explained.

'Not too busy to go courting up by Waternish at first light.'

'How in Heaven's name did you know that Kirsten and I were there?'

Jeanie did not bother to answer the question. 'You'll not have asked the lass to marry you, I suppose.'

'Stop teasing me, Jeanie!'

'You ken that you'll no find a better wife in London.'

'I'm sure you're right about that.'

'Then why are you havering, man?'

'I've no reason for believing that Kirsten wishes to marry and certainly not that she would ever wish to marry me.' Charles knew that his reply was inept evasiveness. He was not accustomed to such direct, unequivocal questioning.

'I know she would,' Jeanie said firmly and then she added, 'And she will.'

'Is it your famous second-sight that tells you that?' he asked, laughing.

'Aye, laugh if you will, but remember what Jeanie has said to you today.'

'Her mother was very worried about Kirsten yesterday,' Charles said, to change the subject. 'We didn't hear from her all day.'

'And where had she been?'

'To the mainland.'

'She'll be fretting over that poor bairn, Mairi.'

'Yes. She went to the place where Mairi was found.'

'She'll not have found the bairn's clothes.'

'As far as I know she didn't look for them. Why do you say that?'

'They'll have been burnt, or maybe weighed down with a stone and thrown into the loch,' Jeanie said, as though she were talking to herself.

Her eyes had the same distant, thoughtful expression that Charles remembered seeing in them when she had warned him that Mairi was going to cause Kirsten trouble. He knew it was absurd to feel uncomfortable, but he did and once more changed the subject, saying how impressed he had been that morning with the beauty of the Western Isles when he and Kirsten had looked at them from Waternish.

She may have sensed his discomfort, for when he rose to leave she looked at him mischievously. 'Now, don't go forgetting what I said about Miss Kirsty and you. Everyone on the island knows that Jeanie Kennedy has the gift.'

Charles realised she meant the gift of second-sight, of clairvoyance, of being able to peer into the future. He recalled how Mrs Tait had laughed at him when he had told her that Jeanie had seemed to know that Mairi was going to disappear and now he laughed at himself.

When the last patient had left the surgery that evening and Charles was putting away the medical records and other papers, he remembered the drawing that Mairi had pencilled for him while he had been examining her. The sketch was still in the drawer where he had put it, but beneath a sheaf of papers, or else he might have seen and remembered it earlier.

Taking it from the drawer, he studied it. The scene that Mairi had drawn, with a fishing boat at sea, a row of cottages and a hotel with a van standing outside, was commonplace, even banal, and might have been sketched from life in half a dozen places on Skye. More probably, though, she had not been trying to portray any particular part of the island but a composite scene, a combination of memory and imagination.

Mairi's drawings, although their draughtsmanship was surprisingly good for a girl with her disability, would be worthless as art and yet Willie Gillespie, or whoever had sent him to Kirsten's cottage, had thought them worth stealing. The most likely explanation, Charles reasoned, was that the drawings might give some clue to why she had been murdered. As he examined every detail of the scene she had drawn for him, he remembered what Jeanie Kennedy had said about the clothes Mairi had been wearing on the day she was killed. Jeanie had seemed certain that the clothes would not be found. Mairi had come to be examined by him because she was pregnant. Was it possible that she had known she was pregnant? Was there a link between her pregnancy, the drawing she had done for him and the disappearance of her clothes? An idea, shadowy and only partly formed, hovered elusively at the back of his mind. When it refused to take shape Charles felt irritated and frustrated.

The glass of whisky that Mrs Tait had ready poured for him in the drawing-room softened the irritation. As he was drinking it she handed him a brown paper bag which, she told him, had been brought to the house while he was in surgery.

'I believe it's a wee gift from Mrs Henry,' she said.

Inside the paper bag was a quarter bottle of whisky, but no note or message. 'Why is she giving me this?' Charles asked.

'Gratitude. The poor woman thought she was going to lose her boy and he's all she has.'

Charles knew that Mrs Henry, a bulky, dour woman had just the one child. She seldom saw her husband, a merchant seaman who liked his freedom, drinking and wenching and who only returned to Skye for brief visits when the mood took him and he was short of money.

'I can't possibly accept this,' he said, holding up the bottle.

'You can and you will,' Mrs Tait said firmly. 'I'm not having you offending our patients.'

'But I did nothing to deserve it!'

'Mrs Henry thinks you did. And when you thank her, none of your flowery London speeches. You'll only embarrass her.'

'Never fear.' Charles knew she liked him teasing her. 'I'm slipping quite easily into your uncouth island ways.'

'Good. I had the same trouble with Donald when he first came to Skye but he was a slow learner.'

'Tell me, how did your husband come to live and work on Skye? I've asked that question more than once but never been given an answer.'

He could see that Mrs Tait was amused and he sensed that had he not asked the question so directly she would have found a way of evading it. As it was she laughed as she replied, 'Donald came here to do a locum for my father, fell in love with the island and stayed for the rest of his life.'

'What's so shameful about that? Why have you never told me?'

'Kirsten didn't want us to.'

'Why, for Heaven's sake?'

'She thought it might embarrass you.' Mrs Tait laughed again. 'Donald married the doctor's daughter. Kirsten thought if you knew that then you might think we were expecting you to do the same.'

'And were you?' Charles asked the question flippantly.

'The possibility never entered my head,' Mrs Tait replied and she paused before adding, 'until quite recently.'

She was smiling but Charles sensed that her last remark had been honest. Did she know how near he and Kirsten had been to making love the other night? He was sure Kirsten would not have told her mother, but the bond between them was close and, like Jeanie Kennedy, with

194

observation and by intuition Mrs Tait might well be aware of her daughter's changing attitude to a man.

The salmon trout that Hilda had poached for their supper was delicious, so tender and moist that it needed no sauce, and served only with potatoes and a cucumber salad. When Charles commented on its excellence, Mrs Tait agreed.

'Donald and I love fish and here on Skye we can always eat it fresh. It has only one disadvantage. The smell lingers in the kitchen for hours, even if one opens the windows.'

'Have you thought of fitting air-conditioning?'

'The weather here is seldom hot enough to justify the expense.'

It was only when they were finishing supper that Mrs Tait remembered she had something to tell him. 'By the way, Amando was the name of Hector's chef; Amando Conti.'

'You remembered, did you?'

'No, Hector was on the phone and I asked him.'

'Why did he phone?'

'The excuse he gave was to tell me about the fund he's raising for Murdo McPhee. The money's pouring in, it seems.'

'You said that was his excuse for ringing. What did he really want?'

'To invite you round to his house this evening. He had guests for dinner last night and opened a bottle of rare vintage port. It has to be drunk, he says, so would you go round after supper and help him finish it?'

Charles wondered why he had been chosen to finish the vintage port, for Hector had struck him as a gregarious man and a generous host who would have plenty of friends. His surprise may have shown, for Mrs Tait said, 'Mind you, I believe the port is also only an excuse. Hector didn't get round to mentioning it until the very end of our conversation.'

'Then what do you think he really wants?'

'Reassurance. I believe he's nervous about going to the hospital. Won't that be tomorrow?'

195

'The day after tomorrow.'

Charles had arranged for Hector to visit the hospital, where he would be given an ECG, a blood count and other tests. He was confident that the man was not suffering from cancer of the stomach or any of the other complaints that he may secretly have believed he had, but a visit to the hospital would reassure him. Now, it seemed, he needed reassurance about what might happen at the hospital.

'He's an awful baby about his health,' Mrs Tait remarked.

'Then I'll go and drink his port and bolster his courage.'

'That would be a kindness. He suggested you should drop in at around nine-thirty.'

After supper Mrs Tait said she must drive down to Portree. She had agreed to serve on a committee of ladies that was organising a major charity event to be held that summer and the committee would be meeting that evening. Before she left she came into the drawing-room and Charles was surprised to see that she was carrying two shotguns, one under each arm, and a small box in her two hands.

'All right!' he cried, raising his arms. 'I'll go quietly.' Mrs Tait stared at him blankly so he went on, 'I've heard of shotgun marriages before but this is ridiculous!'

'Stop being a comedian! If you will, I want you when you go round to see Hector this evening to take these with you. They're Donald's guns and he is giving them to Hector.'

'That's very generous of him.' Charles remembered reading somewhere what the price of a pair of shotguns would be.

'He's giving up shooting, you see, and Hector has always admired the guns. They're a pair that my father had made for himself and later he gave them to Donald.'

'I'll take them, of course, but shouldn't there be a case for them?'

'There is, but I can't find it. Donald keeps the guns in a cupboard but he's so forgetful Heaven only knows where he's left the case. And you can take this box of cartridges, too.'

Charles would have liked to ask her why she was giving

away the guns that evening. Her husband would be coming home from hospital before long and he could give Hector the guns himself once he had found the case. Mrs Tait must have guessed what he was thinking, because she told him her reasons. Donald Tait did not shoot regularly but when he had made up his mind to, he would go out regardless of the weather. Once, doing that, he had contracted a nasty bout of pleurisy.

'So I have persuaded him that after this bypass surgery he must give up shooting for good.' Mrs Tait smiled, in the way of a benevolent schoolmistress who has subtle ways of imposing discipline, 'And I want Hector to have the guns before he returns.'

'And then temptation will be out of his reach?'

'Exactly!'

After she had left the room Charles examined the guns. Even though he knew nothing about firearms, he could tell that their craftsmanship was superb and, squinting down the barrel of one, he saw that they had been kept clean and oiled. Forgetful, Donald Tait might be, but he obviously took good care of the guns that Fiona's father had given him.

With time to spare before he should leave for Uig he picked up a book that lay on a coffee table beside his chair. It was an account of the scores of legends, many of them unpublished, which abound in every part of Skye, written by Otta Swire. The stories of superstitions, fairies, evil spirits, violence and treachery were fascinating and he only regretted that the book should have been illustrated with black and white rather than colour photographs, as they did not, for him at least, convey any sense of the real beauty of the island.

After a time he realised it was time for him to leave for Uig and he put the book down, reluctantly, feeling that he would learn more of the real Skye from it than over a glass of port with Hector Monro. Noticing that the two empty glasses from which Mrs Tait and he had drunk their whisky were still in the room, he picked them up, took them into the kitchen and rinsed them. Mrs Tait had been right when she complained about the smell of fish, for it still lingered in the kitchen and he wondered why it was that salmon, which could be so attractive to the taste, should be so offensive to the sense of smell.

The thought provoked a sudden startling idea. Then, as he pursued the idea, other thoughts, facts, Mairi's pregnancy, her drawings, the clothes she had been wearing on the day she disappeared, fell neatly into place. He knew then how Mairi had been murdered, not why as yet, but the circumstances of her killing.

Restraining his excitement, he went to the telephone, for he needed to explain his theory to someone and to have their confirmation that it must be the truth. There was no reply when he dialled Kirsten's number. She must be out, he told himself, perhaps talking to the art teacher at the High School about the plans she had for the future. With her new enthusiasm she would be impatient to get started.

He wondered whether he should call Superintendent Grieve. Testing theories, finding evidence to support them, was the responsibility of the police and he had no wish to play the amateur detective. On the other hand, Grieve, even if he could find out where he was, would probably not welcome a call at that time of night. So Charles decided he would do nothing. He could sleep on the idea, discuss it with Kirsten or better still with Mrs Tait when she returned home from her meeting. Action could wait until the morning. After all, there was no urgency.

18

As he drove north from Staffin and through its neighbouring townships, Charles was no longer thinking of Mairi's murder. There were still questions that remained to be answered – why she had been killed and whether there was a link between her murder and that of Jamie Gillespie – but he would leave the finding of the answers to the police. They had the resources and the time and the persistence to probe and bully, check and re-check until finally the truth emerged.

Instead he was thinking of Kirsten. His relationship with her was changing, slipping into intimacy and neither of them was resisting the change. Soon, he was certain, perhaps even later that evening unless one of them stepped back, they would be lovers. Recognising that he wanted to make love with her, he tried to analyse his motives. Was it curiosity or masculinity, the male's love of conquest? He was certain that it was not mere lust, but the thought that later she might again be lying naked next to him filled him with a quickening expectation.

And if they became lovers, what then? In little more than two weeks he would be leaving Skye and would that be an end to what had been no more than a casual affair? Was that what he wanted?

During and since his medical student days, Charles had known a good many women. He had lived with two of them, one for only six passionate and stormy weeks, the other for almost a year. With neither, nor with any other woman, had he ever thought seriously of marriage. Jeanie Kennedy was convinced that Kirsten and he would marry. This may have been no more than an old woman's fantasy, but other people must have observed the change in their relationship. Mrs Tait had joked about it, but had there been a hint of seriousness behind the joke?

Charles remembered Goodburn, the old mathematics master at his school, a man much given to laying down rules and precepts for life which he supported with quotations and very often misquotations from classical sources. 'When all roads lead to Rome,' he used to say, 'go there!' Were all roads, or at least all road signs, pointing him in the direction of marriage with Kirsten? Charles smiled at the thought.

He was jerked out of what might easily have become fantasising by car lights flashing behind him. The roads had been even emptier than usual that night and he had met no cars coming south. Enjoying the freedom of not having to use passing places, he had been driving faster than usual, which may have been the reason why he had not noticed the car that had come up behind him. To let it pass he swung into the first passing place he reached. The car, a Citroën, he thought, sped past and he could not make out who the driver was or whether it was a man or a woman.

Continuing round the north of Trotternish, he passed the stark ruin of Duntulm Castle, once the home of the Macdonalds. Almost all of the castle's many legends were steeped in savage cruelty, stories of prisoners, held in dungeons and fed on salt meat and fish until they died, mad through thirst; of a nurse who accidentally let an infant in her arms fall to its death on the rocks below the castle and, as a punishment, was set adrift at sea in a leaking boat; of bloodshed and treachery and the cries and groans of the ghosts who haunted it.

Glancing at the castle as he drove by, Charles remembered what Kirsten had said that morning about the laziness, ignorance and prejudice to be found on Skye. He was inclined to be surprised, not that the people of the island should have such failings but that, after centuries of deprivation

200

and exploitation by rapacious landowners, they should have remained in general kindly, courteous and compassionate.

Kirsten had been right when she said that everyone had an obligation to the community in which they lived. Because he worked in what was described as a caring profession he had assumed, without ever giving the matter much thought, that he was making his contribution to the community by practising medicine. What Kirsten had suggested meant going further than that. She felt that she should do something for Skye and its people, taking practical steps that would improve life on the island and, at the same time, help to negate the influences that were debasing it.

His views on Skye, like his relationship with Kirsten, were changing. At one time he had thought he could never be willing to endure its narrow, circumscribed life. Now he was beginning to understand its attractions. When they met in Edinburgh, Donald Tait had told him that people either hated Skye or fell in love with it. His infatuation may have been slow to start, but even so in the space of a short time he had become more and more involved in the island's life, sucked into a vortex of human relationships, of happiness and conflict, of kindness and malice.

He remembered the damp, depressing day of his arrival on the island with all its traumas, and his first surgery, after which Mrs Tait had driven him to make his first calls on patients, following the same road as he was taking now. She had pointed out the historical landmarks to him, Duntulm Castle, Flora Macdonald's grave, Bornaskitaig. The coast on that part of the island, she had told him, was dotted with lonely beaches and caves, a popular landing spot for the smugglers of the old days.

Smugglers! Smuggling! The words were a switch, electrifying his mind so that an idea that had lain in its recesses, inert and unnoticed, came startlingly to life. For the second time that evening he experienced the excitement of discovery, but held it on leash at first, checking as any doctor would, to see if every symptom confirmed his immediate diagnosis. Soon he had convinced himself that no other explanation would fit the facts and he knew now why Jamie Gillespie and Mairi McPhee had been murdered.

He also knew what he must do. Only a few miles away in Uig there was a single-man police station. He would drive there, rouse the constable, make him telephone Superintendent Grieve, wherever he might be. What had been happening and might still happen was too serious and too far reaching to wait until morning.

In his anxiety he must have accelerated and was driving fast, too fast along the narrow, twisting road. As he came to a left-hand curve he noticed what he thought was the shadowy outline of a sheep by the side of the road. Sheep frequently wandered on to the roads in Skye and drivers were warned to be on the alert for them. In this case the sheep, if it were one, was not moving, so Charles saw no reason to brake. The curve was tighter than he had expected, with the road dipping down sharply, and he took it faster than he should have done. It was only as he felt the back wheels of the car slip and was correcting the slide that he saw the sheep was not a sheep at all but a man kneeling by the road with a rifle to his shoulder. And as the car came up to him the man swung the rifle, following the car, and fired.

Instinctively, Charles wanted to duck, but he had no time to and saw in any case that the rifle was not aimed at him but at the car. He heard the report of the shot and almost immediately felt the car go out of control, lurching to the left, dipping sharply and then flipping over down a steep bank beside the road. The roof hit the ground but that did not check its fall and it bounced, rolling over once again. Leaning back in his seat, gripping the steering wheel and bracing his feet against the floor, Charles tried to stay rigid, unnecessarily, for his seat belt was holding him firmly.

The noise that the car made when it struck the ground was not as loud as one might have expected, no more than a hollow thump, and only on the second bounce was it accompanied by the sound of breaking glass. At last its mad somersault down the bank came to an end and it landed upright on all four wheels, lurched from side to side a couple of times and then was still. The engine had stalled and the only sounds were the creaking of metal and the tinkle of glass as the last fragments fell out of the shattered window on the passenger's side. The windscreen had splintered into a network of long cracks but was still whole, and so was the driver's window, which Charles had kept wound down as he was driving.

He was mildly surprised to find that he was still conscious and unhurt, except for a searing pain in his right leg. No bones appeared to be fractured and he decided it could be no more than severe bruising, probably resulting from a knock against the side of the car.

Unfastening his seat belt, he reached for the door handle. His first instinct was to get out of the car, for he knew there was always a risk of fire after a crash and he fancied that he could detect the smell of petrol. Then he checked himself. On the road above him there was a man with a rifle, whose object in firing at the car had obviously been to kill Charles. When he realised that his ambush had failed he might well use the rifle again.

Looking up the bank over which the car had plunged, he saw the man, standing on the verge of the road, his figure silhouetted against the night sky. Under one arm he held the rifle, with the other he was carrying a rectangular object with a handle. As Charles watched he began coming down the bank through the heather, clumsily, for the rectangular object, whatever it was, appeared to be heavy.

Charles was tempted to run. If he slipped out by the passenger's door, the car would be between him and the man with the rifle and he could make a dash for the safety of darkness in the hills beyond. Then he reasoned that a marksman good enough to hit the tyre on the wheel of a car passing at speed would have no difficulty in picking off a man, particularly one running through heather and with a badly bruised leg.

So he slumped forward over the car's steering wheel, feigning unconsciousness, but in such a position that he could see into the wing mirror fitted just outside the door.

From there he could watch the man, reflected in the mirror, as he came down the bank. When he reached the car, the man glanced inside, seemed reassured by what he saw and set the rifle down, leaning it against the bank behind him. The object he had been carrying was a large metal can and, placing this on the ground in front of him, he began unscrewing its cap. Only then did Charles realise it was a can of petrol and he knew at once what the man intended to do. In half a minute, a minute at the most, the can would be empty, the petrol poured over the car. A few more seconds would give the man enough time to back away and toss a match or a burning rag on to it.

He reached for the door handle. He must surprise the man, leap out and tackle him while he was still busy with the petrol can. Then he remembered the shotguns he was taking to Hector Monro and which he had laid across the back seat of the car. Reaching back, he found that they had fallen off the seat on to the floor. As quietly as he could, he picked up one of the guns, lifted it over from the back and laid it on his lap. The man outside, engrossed in what he was doing, did not notice. The cardboard box of cartridges had been lying on the front seat next to his and he had a moment of panic when he reached for them and found nothing. The box had fallen to the floor and split open, disgorging cartridges everywhere. Still bent over the steering wheel, he picked up two cartridges, broke open the gun on his lap and loaded it, remembering as he closed it to slip off the safety catch.

The man was behind the car now, sloshing petrol over the roof and rear window. Charles waited until he came back into his view and then thrust the shotgun through the open window.

'Put that can down and back away,' he said quietly but forcefully.

For a moment the man stood motionless, startled into rigidity, staring at the barrel of the gun and at Charles. Then he dropped the can, fell backwards, twisting to one side, and when he stood up again he was holding the rifle. Charles was stunned by the speed of his reactions, the reactions of a hunter, he thought, or of the hunted. Was the rifle loaded, he wondered, and then he heard the sound of the bolt being drawn back.

He pulled one trigger of the shotgun, squeezing it as Carl Short had told him he should and was astonished at his calmness. The noise was devastating. The man with the rifle disappeared, hurled back into the heather behind him. Then the report, echoing in the hills, died away and was replaced by an almost equally startling silence.

Putting down the shotgun, Charles got out of the car and walked the few paces to where the body of the man lay. Most of his stomach and the bottom half of his chest had been blown away, leaving nothing but blood and splintered bone. His face, though, was almost unmarked. Charles saw, without surprise, that it was Tom Grant.

19

The Citroën stood in a passing place a short distance along the road to Uig and Charles was glad when he found that the ignition key had been left in the lock. He would not have wished to hunt for it in the shattered body of Tom Grant. Returning to his own car, he switched off its ignition, even though the engine had stalled, just to make sure that there was no possibility of the petrol that Tom Grant had poured over it catching fire. Then he took the shotgun that he had not fired back to the Citroën, leaving the other gun lying on the driver's seat of his own car. His plan had changed now and he did not intend going to the police station in Uig. Instead he set out in the Citroën to find a phone box.

He found one by the roadside a mile or two nearer Uig and when he dialled Kirsten's number she answered almost at once, as though she had been waiting for a call.

'Charles! Where are you? I rang home twice just now but there was no reply.'

'I'm on my way to Uig,' Charles replied guardedly. 'Will you do something for me?'

'Of course. What?'

'Call the police. Speak to Superintendent Grieve, if you can. Tell him he'll find a crashed car and a dead man by the side of the road between Duntulm and Uig.'

Charles could sense Kirsten's shocked alarm, even though she was too controlled to show it. 'Are you all right?'

'I am, but Tom Grant is dead.'

'Was he killed in the car crash?'

'No, I shot him.' Reluctantly Charles was saying more than he intended to. He added, 'I had to. I had no other option.'

'Where are you now?'

'In a call box.'

'Shouldn't you wait by the car till the police arrive?'

Charles knew that she was right and that he should wait, but it would be half an hour at least before the police could arrive, probably more, and he was not willing to wait that long. Jamie Gillespie was dead, so was Mairi and, but for a stroke of good fortune, he would be dead as well. A cold, hard anger, stronger than logic or prudence, told him that he must act now, bring matters to a head, put an end to the cynical, ruthless tossing away of lives. He reasoned too that even though one plan to kill him had failed there would almost certainly be a second plan to back it up.

'Charles,' Kirsten hesitated, wanting to say more but unwilling to interfere. 'Be careful, won't you?'

As he drove towards Uig he realised that he was behaving irrationally. Why had he left the gun with which he had shot Grant behind in his car? Was it because of some muddled notion that the police would need it to confirm the story that he would eventually tell them, by checking it for fingerprints? And why had he brought the other shotgun with him, although he had left the cartridges lying where they were? Because he had promised Mrs Tait he would take the guns to Hector Monro?

Shock, fear and the nearness of death had disorientated his thinking. He must rationalise it, deciding for a start what he would do when he reached Uig. He tried to form a plan but thoughts of Kirsten kept intruding on his concentration. She had accepted what he had told her over the telephone unquestioningly, not asking for explanations nor offering advice. That must mean there was a rapport between them, a much closer rapport than he had realised. The idea intrigued him.

When he arrived in Uig and knocked on Hector Monro's

door it was opened to him by a middle-aged woman wearing a tweed coat and a hat. Although he had never been told her name he knew from previous visits to the house that she was the woman who went in daily to clean and cook Hector's meals. The hat suggested that she had finished her day's work and was on the point of leaving to go home.

'Oh, it's you, Doctor! Mr Monro's in his study.' She pointed towards a door which led off the hall, obviously not intending to show Charles in. 'That's me away, now. Goodnight, Doctor.'

She left the house by the front door, closing it behind her but not locking it for few people locked their doors in Uig. Charles heard her footsteps as she walked away down the gravel drive in front of the house. He hesitated, still uncertain of what he intended to do and of whether he should take the shotgun with him when he went in to see Hector, feeling it would seem ridiculous if he did. Then, deciding not to, he leant the gun up against the wall not far from the study door. He noticed that on a small table in the hall lay a number of unopened envelopes which looked like bills and unsolicited mail shots offering bargain holidays, time-share properties in Spain and cut-price car insurance. Even on Skye, it seemed, people could not escape the blandishments of the long-range salesman, but Hector, one would have thought, was not a man to be tempted by bargains.

Inside the study, Hector was sitting in front of a personal computer. The room was small but expensively furnished in a style totally alien to Skye, in the bright fabrics, glass and polished wood favoured by interior decorators, with a built-in television and video recorder and hi-fi equipment.

'Charles! Good of you to come.' If Hector was surprised by Charles's arrival he did not show it. 'Come on in and take a pew.' He switched off the computer, rather hurriedly, it seemed.

As he crossed the room towards the chair that Hector had pointed out, Charles limped, for his bruised leg had stiffened. He realised too that his slacks were stained with mud, and fragments of heather were sticking to the sleeves of his sweater, from when he had climbed up the bank from his car to the road.

'Hullo! What's wrong with your leg?' Hector asked. 'Did you have a fall?'

'Not exactly. My car rolled off the road.'

'Good God! Sit down, Charles! Sit down! You'll be needing a dram.'

Charles began protesting that he did not need a whisky, but Hector had already sprung up and crossed to a built-in cupboard below the bookshelves that lined one wall of the study. Taking a cut glass decanter and two glasses from the cupboard, he poured two outsize drams. Watching him, Charles thought his hand shook as he poured the whisky, but it may have been no more than a tremor.

'How did it happen?' He handed Charles his glass. 'The roads are dreadful here, of course, terrible! I'm surprised that we don't have more accidents.'

'This was no accident. One of my tyres was burst with a rifle shot as I was swinging round a bend in the road.'

'You can't be serious, Charles! Who would do a thing like that?'

'It was Tom Grant.' Hector was walking back to his chair on the other side of the desk and his back was to Charles, so Charles waited until he could see his face before he added, 'Tom's dead.'

'I don't understand. What are you saying?'

'I shot him.'

Hector's incredulous smile was a little forced. 'You're having me on, Charles. This is some kind of joke.'

'No. He tried to kill me, so I shot him.'

'I can't believe this! Why on earth should Tom have wished to kill you? I was not aware that you had even met the man.'

Charles decided not to answer Hector's question, at least not directly. 'It was Tom who murdered Mairi McPhee.'

'This is beyond me.' Hector shook his head. 'You're making the whole thing up!'

'On the morning when Mairi disappeared she went to

the Skeabost House Hotel, hid there and waited until Tom drove up in his van. While he was delivering fish at the hotel she climbed into the van.' Charles suddenly noticed that he was speaking slowly and carefully. He could only recall once having spoken in that fashion and that was when he had been lecturing to a group of student nurses. At the time it had struck him that he must be sounding absurdly pompous. He went on, 'Tom would not have known she was in the van until he next opened it. That would have been on the mainland, for he did not call at Carl Short's house that morning.'

'But why should the girl have got into the van?' Hector's expression was not incredulous now but watchful.

'Because in her own simple way she loved him. He was the first man with whom she had had sex.'

'Was she pregnant?' Hector was quick to see a reason why Grant should have killed Mairi.

'If she was, that was not Tom's reason for murdering her.'

Hector hesitated, as though he were afraid to ask the final question. 'Then why did he?'

'Because of what she must have seen in the van. Tom didn't carry only fish when he drove over to the mainland in his van.'

'What else, then?'

'Drugs. Drugs that he and his brother had helped smuggle into Skye. He would drop them off or pass them over to a courier at some prearranged point on the mainland and from there they would go into the network and on to the streets in Edinburgh, Glasgow and God knows where else.'

'You're imagining this,' Hector said scornfully. 'Where on earth would Tom get drugs?'

'Out at sea. He and his brother had a fishing boat, hadn't they? It would be simple for them to pick up a consignment of drugs which had been left for them at sea, attached to a buoy, perhaps, or tied to lobster pots.'

'And where would these drugs have come from?' Hector was not being scornful now and Charles realised that this was the question that really mattered to him, the answer to which would show how serious was the situation he faced.

'From wherever heroin and cocaine come from, I suppose, but they would have come through Italy.'

'Why Italy?'

'Because it was the Italian who worked in your hotel who set up the whole operation. What was his name? Amando Conti?' Charles took a sip of his whisky, waiting for any comment that Hector might make, but no comment came. 'He would be too young, I suppose, for you to have met him during the war. Was it his father you knew? Maybe you and he did a little business together on the black market.'

Hector's reaction was not what Charles expected. He appeared in no way disconcerted by the accusations that were being made, nor even surprised, but totally in control of his emotions.

'Is this just speculation?' he asked calmly, 'Or can you prove it?'

'I don't need to prove it, but the police should have no difficulty in doing so. Jamie Gillespie, working on his own, found out the truth or at least enough of it to blackmail you. That's why he had to be killed.'

Suddenly Hector was holding a pistol. Charles had not noticed him move or open a drawer of his desk, but the pistol was in his hand, ready to be fired. The pistol was not in itself menacing, for it looked too insignificant to be an instrument of death – not much more than a toy – and what made Charles uneasy was Hector's calm self-assurance. One knew at once that he was ready to kill, without compunction or remorse, to protect not only himself but the people with whom he was working.

'A pity about you, Charles,' he said. 'I liked you. When we first met I told myself that if Phyllis had been able to bear children you were the kind of son I would have liked to have: sincere, straightforward, considerate.'

Christ, Charles thought, the man means it! He's ready to kill me but he means it. He's mad! Fear, cold and pitiless, drove rods of iron into his stomach. He told himself to keep calm. Hector could be talked out of killing him, or if not talked out of it, tricked out of it.

'Put that gun away, Hector. That isn't going to save you.'

'You think not? Charles, what sort of idiot do you take me for? What sort of people do you think my friends are?'

A telephone stood on the desk to his left. Picking it up with one hand, he pressed the buttons he needed to call a number. Presently his call was answered and Charles heard a man's voice. All Hector said was, 'Things haven't worked out. We have an emergency. You know what to do.'

Putting the telephone down, he told Charles, 'That was Tom's brother. He'll be here in five minutes. We've had this plan worked out and ready for months. You see, I always knew it would end one day and I'd have to pull out and leave Skye. But someone else will take over, in another part of Scotland, perhaps. I don't know who and I don't know where. That's for others to decide.' Hector smiled. 'The people I work with look after their friends.'

'What are you going to do?' Charles knew he must keep the man talking.

'Tomorrow morning you and I will have disappeared. The little boat I keep in the water at the bottom of my garden will be found drifting out at sea. You will be dead, your body weighted down at the bottom of the ocean. I will be on Tom's brother's fishing boat, heading for a rendezvous with a ship which will take me on the first stage of my journey to the home I have ready in Italy, with a new identity, new papers, a new life. Everything has been arranged.'

'You're bluffing.'

'Get up, Charles. Slowly! Now turn round and start walking towards the door. Don't try any tricks. I'll be immediately behind and I'll shoot you if I have to.'

Hector was not bluffing. Charles knew that. He was going to march him somewhere and kill him, to another room in the house, probably, from where the sound of a pistol shot was less likely to be heard by neighbours and where any traces of blood could be easily removed. There was a small cloakroom leading off the hall. That would be

212

the place. The initial fear he had felt had passed and he was surprised that he was thinking calmly and logically. His only hope was to surprise Hector, to turn on him when he was momentarily off his guard. The best time would be as they were going through the doorway into the hall. He had left the door slightly ajar when he first came into the study and it opened inwards. When he reached it, he would grab the handle, swing it open and dive through the doorway, closing the door behind him, hoping it would give enough protection against a pistol bullet.

His plan was frustrated for Hector had expected something of the kind. 'Stop there!' he called out when Charles was still two or three paces from the doorway. Then he walked past Charles, still keeping the pistol trained on him, took the door handle himself and swung the door open. 'Carry on,' he said, waving Charles past him with the pistol.

Charles walked forward. It was as he crossed the threshold of the doorway that he saw Kirsten. She was in the hall, standing as close as she could against the wall to the left of the door to the study, holding the shotgun that Charles had brought with him. Immediately she saw Charles she raised her finger to her lips, signalling him to stay silent. Obeying her, Charles walked on, veering to the right and away from her across the hall.

Hector followed him and as soon as he came into Kirsten's view she said sharply, 'Drop the gun, Hector!' Hector stared at her, astounded, and she repeated, 'Drop it, I said!'

Still Hector hesitated. 'You wouldn't shoot.' His words were hollow, without any semblance of conviction.

'Don't gamble on it.' Kirsten raised the shotgun slightly until the muzzle was pointing at Hector's head and shoulders. 'And hurry! This gun has a hair trigger.'

For a few seconds more Hector hesitated. Then he let the pistol fall to the carpet. Charles, who had been watching, looking back over his shoulder, turned and stooped to reach for it but Kirsten called out to stop him.

'Stay where you are, Charles. Don't go near him.' Then she told Hector, 'Kick the pistol across the floor away from you.'

Hector did as she wanted and then Charles picked up the pistol, grateful for Kirsten's presence of mind. Had he bent down while he was close enough, Hector might have grabbed him, twisting him round and using him as a shield against the shotgun. He had barely grasped the pistol when they heard the sound of brakes as a car pulled up outside the house. My God, he thought, that will be Tom's brother. He turned to face the front door with the pistol at the ready.

The door was flung open, not by Tom Grant's brother, but by Superintendent Grieve, who was followed in by Detective Sergeant Mackenzie.

Grieve stared at the tableau in front of him. 'God Almighty!' was all he said.

20

'Why did the police go to Hector's place?' Charles asked Kirsten.

'When I told Superintendent Grieve what you asked me to tell him, that you'd shot Tom Grant, he wanted to know where you were.'

'But you didn't know I was going to challenge Hector.'

Kirsten smiled. 'It was not very hard to guess. You told me that you were on your way to Uig. Who else but Hector did you know there? Nobody. Besides, I had suspected for some time that Hector might be involved in some shady business.'

'Why?'

'How else did he get his money? He had that house in Uig built for him and do you know he used to go on a Mediterranean cruise every winter? His hotel can't have been worth all that much.'

'Did he actually go on cruises? I wonder. Perhaps he was going to Italy every year, building a house there as well, laying plans for the day when he would have to leave Skye.'

Kirsten and Charles were in Donald Tait's surgery the following day, waiting for Mrs Tait so they could all lunch together. It was the first time they had been alone since the dramatic events of the previous evening. After the arrival of the police at Hector Monro's house they had spent much of the night in Portree, for they, Monro and Tom Grant's brother had all been driven there by the police. There had been seemingly endless questions to be answered, statements to be made. It had been after two in the morning when they had left Portree, driven by the police, Kirsten to Hector Monro's house where she had left her car and Charles to Staffin, where he had found Mrs Tait, still up and waiting anxiously to hear what had happened. Monro and Grant's brother had been detained and by now would have been charged, though what the charges would be Charles did not know.

That morning Charles had held his surgery as usual and then visited patients in their homes, glad to find that the epidemic he had feared did not appear to have materialised. When he returned to the Taits' home he had found Kirsten waiting for him.

'In the last few months before she died,' Kirsten went on, 'Phyllis Monro was terribly unhappy. I thought then that Hector must be the cause of her unhappiness, although I didn't know why.'

'Do you think she had found out that he had become involved in smuggling drugs?'

'Looking back on it, yes. And it would have been agonising for her. Phyllis was very religious, but also very loyal to Hector. Can you imagine the conflict?'

'Poor woman!'

'When did you first suspect what Hector was up to?' Kirsten asked.

'Only when Tom Grant ambushed me. Hector knew I had been asking questions about Jamie Gillespie in Edinburgh. Yesterday he learned from your mother that I'd been trying to find out the name of the Italian chef at his hotel. He knew then that I must be getting near the truth.'

'And he was the only person who knew you would be driving to Uig last evening.'

'Yes, he invited me to go. He set me up. Originally I suspected that drugs were being brought into Skye from Edinburgh, then I suddenly realised that the reverse must be true.'

'But what made you think they were being smuggled in by sea?'

216

'It was a casual remark your mother made about smuggling in Skye in the old days. In the last century when smuggling was rife all over Britain, all the contraband was brought in by sea. Skye, with its long, uninhabited coast, would be perfect for smugglers. Hector's plan was clever but simple and there's no coastguard service to speak of on the island.'

Charles explained the line of reasoning he had followed. By chance Jamie Gillespie had seen Amando Conti in the hotel in Edinburgh where he was working and had seen that he was obviously wealthy. How would a chef become so wealthy? What was Amando doing in Edinburgh? How did anyone make a lot of money in Edinburgh? Jamie had started to ask questions among the drug pushers on the streets. Because he was known, he could have got answers to his questions that would have been denied to other people. He had guessed half the truth and, returning to Skye, discovered the other half.

'So he went and asked Hector for money to buy his silence,' Charles concluded.

'Blackmail?'

'Blackmail's an ugly word. For me it doesn't fit in with Jamie's character. He realised that his life and that of his friend Andy had been destroyed. He wasn't looking for revenge but for compensation and not for himself but for his mother. Jamie wanted to make up to her for all the unhappiness and hardship she had suffered and he didn't see why the agents of his destruction, the drug pedlars, should not pay.'

'It cost him his life.'

'He probably knew it might but he was going to die of AIDS anyway. In a way I admire Jamie for what he did.'

'You're getting as bad as my parents,' Kirsten said, laughing. 'Their patients can do no wrong.'

'Hector was stupid. The lad can't have asked for much. Ten thousand pounds? Twenty, at the most. Every packet of drugs he was smuggling in would have been worth twenty times as much. Why didn't he string along with Jamie? He must have known the lad would soon be dead.'

'Perhaps Hector didn't make the decisions.'

'You're probably right. The whole operation would have been run by other people in the background; people in Italy, no doubt, perhaps the Mafia – who knows?'

'How do you suppose Hector became involved in the affair? How did it start?'

'We'll probably never know. My guess is that he met Amando Conti's father during the war. The Italians were looking for a way to smuggle drugs into Scotland, and Skye would be the ideal place to do it; remote and partly at least cut off from the mainland. The Italians knew Hector, knew that he was greedy and would be easily manipulated. So Conti was sent to Skye to put a proposition to Hector and, if he agreed, to set the operation up.'

Kirsten was sitting in the same armchair in which she had sat when Charles told her that Mairi was pregnant. He remembered how then she had flopped into the chair and how dejected she had seemed. Now she was not dejected, only tired. Lines of fatigue and of the strain of the previous evening showed in her face. Charles supposed that if he had handled matters differently and had gone directly to the police after shooting Tom Grant she would have been spared the danger and the stress to which she had been exposed.

'Then it was Hector who told Tom Grant to kill you,' she said.

'Yes. Tom was working for Hector. Hector would be told when a consignment of drugs was about to be delivered and would tell Tom where and how it was to be collected. Tom did the rest.'

'I always thought Hector didn't like Tom. They hardly ever spoke.'

'That must have been part of the cover. Hector would find ways of getting messages to him.'

Kirsten sighed. 'I might have guessed it was Tom who had seduced Mairi and she was upset after the ceilidh that night because he had ignored her.'

'I don't see how you would have noticed that.'

'And on the morning when she disappeared, she put on her winter coat because she knew it would be cold in his van.'

'Don't start thinking of what might have been,' Charles told her. 'No living in the past, remember!'

Getting up from the armchair, Kirsten came round the desk to where he was sitting and, standing behind him, put her hands on his shoulders and kissed him lightly on the cheek.

'You were crazy to go and confront Hector like that last evening.'

'I know that now. It was just as well that you arrived when you did. Why did you come, anyway?'

'Because I sensed somehow that you might do something bold and reckless.'

'And it was just as well Hector didn't realise that the shotgun wasn't loaded.'

'Not loaded!' Kirsten said indignantly. 'What do you think I am? A helpless woman? I made sure it was loaded before I threatened him with it.'

'But where did you get the cartridges?'

'From the cupboard in the hall where I knew Hector kept his guns.'

Charles realised that he had never even thanked Kirsten for arriving so opportunely at Hector's house the previous evening and was ashamed of his thoughtlessness. Turning in his chair, he pulled her face gently down to his and kissed her on the lips. Before he could say what was on his mind Mrs Tait looked round the door. She seemed neither surprised nor embarrassed.

'That chair is beginning to suit you,' she told Charles.

'Do you think so? I'm almost wishing it were mine, permanently, I mean.'

'Well, Donald is older than you probably imagine.' And then, afraid perhaps that she had been too bold, Mrs Tait added brusquely, 'And now if you two could cut out the unbridled passion we'd have time for a drink before lunch.'

The three of them went into the drawing room and Charles began pouring the whisky. That morning he had thought of buying a bottle of champagne and opening it before lunch as a little celebration, but somehow champagne had become associated with Hector Monro and Hector was something Mrs Tait would wish to forget. When he was passing round the glasses the telephone rang. Mrs Tait answered it and he saw anguish crease her face as she listened to what she was being told. She made no comment until the caller had finished and then said simply, 'Thank you for letting me know,' and put down the phone.

'Hector's dead.'

'Was it his heart?' Charles asked, wondering at once whether he had failed in his diagnosis.

'No. They found him in his cell with his throat cut.'

'How on earth?' Kirsten demanded. 'The police take weapons away from prisoners, don't they? Even braces and shoelaces?'

'They have no idea how he got the razor. They don't even seem to be sure that he killed himself.'

Mrs Tait reached in the pocket of her cardigan for a handkerchief, which was as close as she would come to tears. In spite of what he had done, she would grieve for Hector, the memory of their long friendship focusing on his virtues and clouding his failings. Charles could understand her feelings but he did not share them. Hector Monro, like Jamie Gillespie and Mairi and Tom Grant, had been a victim of faceless men a thousand miles away, the friends who, he confidently had believed, would look after him, but he was also a victim of his own greed. Through greed he had brought the cancer of corruption and violence to Skye. Now the cancer had been cut away and Charles felt the relief that any doctor feels at seeing a patient restored to health and the inner satisfaction of knowing that he had played a part in the healing.

'Poor Hector!' Mrs Tait said sadly.

'You shouldn't feel sorry for him.' Not for the first time Kirsten put into words what Charles was thinking. 'He would have destroyed Skye.'

'In his way Hector did a lot for the island. Now his memory will be hated, while you, Charles, you'll be a hero.'

'And quite right too!' Kirsten smiled at Charles. 'Happy the physician! The world proclaimeth his successes.'

'Do you remember the rest of that saying?' Charles recognised her paraphrasing of a quotation from Francis Quarles which had always been a favourite of his. 'The world proclaims the successes of the physician and his mistakes are covered by the earth. But for you, Kirsten, my mistake – and I – would have been buried by now. You saved my life.'

'Then don't make a habit of looking for trouble. I may not always be around.'

Charles resisted the temptation to tell her that he hoped she always would be around. This was not the time for declarations. Anything he said now might sound too facile, an impulsive response to the emotion and euphoria of the moment. And yet, looking into Kirsten's eyes and seeing unspoken promises and an affection as deep as his own, he felt he must give some token, however slight, of his commitment. He knew now where all roads led.

'Exactly how old is your father?' he asked her.